Lucy Treloar was born in Malaysia and educated in England, Sweden and Melbourne. She is the author of *Salt Creek*, which won the Dobbie Literary Award and was shortlisted for the Miles Franklin Literary Award and the Walter Scott Prize. *Wolfe Island*, Lucy's second novel, won the Barbara Jefferis Award and was shortlisted for the Prime Minister's Literary Award and the Christina Stead Prize. She is a previous winner of the Commonwealth Short Story Prize (Pacific region).

Lucy's essays and short fiction have appeared in publications including *The Saturday Paper*, *Meanjin*, *The Age*, *Overland* and *Best Australian Stories*. She is an occasional teacher of creative writing.

A graduate of the University of Melbourne and RMIT, Lucy lives in inner Melbourne with her family. *Days of Innocence and Wonder* is her third novel.

Also by Lucy Treloar

Salt Creek
Wolfe Island

LUCY TRELOAR
DAYS OF INNOCENCE AND WONDER

PICADOR
Pan Macmillan Australia

The author is grateful for the support of an Australia Council for the Arts Grant,
a Creative Victoria Grant and a City of Melbourne COVID-19 Arts Grant

Pan Macmillan acknowledges the Traditional Custodians of Country throughout Australia
and their connections to lands, waters and communities. We pay our respect to Elders past
and present and extend that respect to all Aboriginal and Torres Strait Islander peoples
today. We honour more than sixty thousand years of storytelling, art and culture.

The characters in this book are fictitious and any resemblance
to real persons, living or dead, is purely coincidental.

First published 2023 in Picador by Pan Macmillan Australia Pty Ltd
1 Market Street, Sydney, New South Wales, Australia, 2000
Copyright © Lucy Treloar 2023

The moral right of the author to be identified as the author of this work has been asserted.

All rights reserved. No part of this book may be reproduced or transmitted
by any person or entity (including Google, Amazon or similar organisations),
in any form or by any means, electronic or mechanical, including
photocopying, recording, scanning or by any information storage and retrieval
system, without prior permission in writing from the publisher.

 A catalogue record for this book is available from the National Library of Australia

Typeset in 11.9/16 pt Adobe Garamond Pro by Post Pre-press Group
Printed by IVE

The author and the publisher have made every effort to contact copyright
holders for material used in this book. Any person or organisation
that may have been overlooked should contact the publisher.

 The paper in this book is FSC® certified. FSC® promotes environmentally responsible, socially beneficial and economically viable management of the world's forests.

For the children, always missed, always loved

Author's note

I ACKNOWLEDGE THE Traditional Owners of the Ngadjuri, Kulin and Kaurna Nations, on whose lands I wrote *Days of Innocence and Wonder*. I recognise their ongoing connection to and care for Country, its lands and waters. Sovereignty of these lands has never been ceded. I pay my respects to their Elders, past, present and future.

Wirowie is based on the small town Terowie on Ngadjuri land in South Australia's Mid North. It appears to the outsider much as I have described it here, though the people are all imagined. All other place names are actual.

The name Tundra is pronounced with a soft T, almost a D, and the 'u' as in 'full', in accordance with Ngadjuri pronunciation.

Ngadjuri Country

It was like a garden of Eden when we first saw it.

'pioneer' description of the area around
the lost town of Amyton on the Willowie Plain

NOTES

*The past is not a dream; it's awake as can be.
We live with it. We live in it.*
     Till

On the matter of my identity I am not sure what to say.
     Me

Brunswick, midwinter 2004

THE MAN WALKED up the path to the kindergarten and talked to the two small girls playing together on the other side of the fence, and when he left he took one of them away. He turned and looked back at the girl who stayed behind and winked and called out to her. The words carried well through the still air. When she didn't move, he strode off – the outside-the-fence girl skipping, actually skipping at his side, her red coat bobbing against the worn grass. She looked back, this red-coat girl, and waved and faced forward again. The one left behind could still see her, still see her, her coat being so bright beneath the gathered trees. Then she was gone.

People said she ran at life, as if it made what happened her fault. And why say 'what happened' when 'what he did' was the truth. People say this all the time, as if events are just moving around waiting to strike people, random as lightning, when it is people, people, people.

There were two of them and then there was one. Do you see what I am saying? They had plans. Then the plans didn't matter. They were not transferable. They could not survive. The moment one of them stepped through the fence the girls were separate and the one outside was skipping ahead into darkness. And the one left behind, who had stayed inside the fence, had no idea how to live in this world.

Chapter 1

Brunswick, December 2021

Four days after Christmas, Till packed her bag and told her parents she would be heading out the next day and they said, 'Oh, really? Where?' and she said 'Just out', which they took to mean out to see a friend or something like that when she meant Out West, west and north and after that she didn't know and could not say. Some strange things had happened – she could not bring herself to describe them – and old habits of silence overcame her.

'Come on, Birdy,' she said, and her greyhound Birdy came loping up the hall.

'Surely you're not taking Birdy,' her mother, Zoe, said. 'Leave her here.'

Birdy came.

The world looked off kilter in the early light, the street wide and empty and strung on either side by the long ropes of electricity, swaying as if suspended from the sky. It was still dark to the south and north, dark to the west, and in the east, red and orange and lilac flung upwards from the horizon. A single light, no more than a speck, shone as far away as the railway line, indigo night still hovering above. Nothing else. She stood in the middle of the road. Birdy waited at the door.

Then the light by some freakishness of angle and the creeping sun caught on the lines and ran so they seemed lit like heated filaments, and a skein of light shining through clouds found a swarm of tiny insects drifting like bonfire sparks around the flowering wattle. Yet people say there's no magic in the world.

Till drove down the wide road as if freed from chains, Birdy curled at her side at first, then in the back where she sat sphinx-like, her little chin resting on the window frame, regarding the world. Till sang one or two of her lesser songs, the ones she liked, humming a little before settling into the grind of it. Even that was a pleasure though. She was leaving it all behind.

She and Birdy had been out walking on a cool spring day. It could have been any day. It was nothing special. There was a man in front of them with a hat on the back of his head, his thin clothes moving around him in the blustery wind, his unbuttoned jacket flying back, everything about him washed out, greyish and almost dank, as if he was dissolving into air or appearing from storm or rising from water. Immediately, she noticed his walk. It reminded her of someone from a long time ago and she didn't want to think that it was more than that. She remembered that person only a little, but the feeling was enough.

The long-ago man had a sloping walk with deep biting steps and an exaggerated spring that to Till now suggests someone unencumbered by regret and lifted up by small pleasures and anticipations. She has never forgotten it. She couldn't describe it when she was five, and no one asked such a question. In her memory, his age is indeterminate. He is always much older than her, of her parents' age or a little younger or a little older. He has no-coloured hair and no-coloured skin and no-coloured eyes. To describe him is to lose him. She never notices his features. It is the way he moves. I'm just out walking in the sun, his walk seems to say, enjoying my time and my freedom as is my right. But his head weaves this way and that as Till has noticed hunting dogs do, snaking along, scouting for predators or prey.

Birdy did this when they walked together. It was the way she moved in the world. But she tried not to draw any connection between the two, because Birdy's heart was as pure as her instinct. Her nature was to hunt small animals and to be gentle with people, especially those she trusted and loved. She was always true to her nature. What might be ahead or in hiding somewhere about? What might be hunted? A cat, a bird, a possum, a rabbit? What might be smelled? A crust of bread, a pocket of dog treats, a dog of old acquaintance? The two sides of Birdy's nature travelled together effortlessly. If she ever bit a person, Till knew she would be ashamed, even if it was an accident. It would be an act against her own nature.

Seeing this man walk now, Till turned silently and backtracked and found shelter deep in a thicket of trees and shrubs where she hid looking out at the bright colours of people passing by, hardly breathing, shaking, until she became frightened in a new way by the realisation that she was in someone's small encampment – these times of homelessness – and fled again, this time for home.

This was more than a month before she left. She would have fled at once but for the travel restrictions that had not quite been abandoned. Strange to look back on them. It was the beginning of her leaving. It was when she decided, I mean. There was another thing that happened before Till's flight and exile. I will say more about that, I suppose. I will have to. She felt too foolish to talk about what she'd seen. Spoken words would make it real, and people would say, *It's in your mind, Till. No need to worry.* Till kept quiet. It had happened before. She avoided the park, stayed at home or drove in her car or walked in the nearby lanes, and as soon as she could she left. She had been driving ever since, more or less. She was safe in her car, even if she was on her own. The roads were clear for mile after mile, no one behind. It would take something bad, a reckless person, to stop her.

Here she was thinking the old familiar things. She was mostly in the world of her childhood at such times. The sun had struck through the window and she had lain in its warmth on the back seat, her parents in front, the light flickering on the car ceiling above as they passed trees and clouds, birds flew overhead, and the sun overtook them. It seemed as if the world encircled them and they were at the eye of it, as if it were there for them. She felt untouchable. Who coming across these plains towards them would stop her parents driving their big car? How would they do such a thing? How would they dare? No, she was safe. And her parents were safe too. They all were. Always, being in a car did this. It was peace to her.

Nothing had happened to Till, but something happened all the same.

Chapter 2

January 2022

AT THE TIME Till began her journey to the town that became her home, she didn't know exactly where she was headed, much less how long it would take. The point was the journey – it was only in cars that Till felt truly safe – so she kept driving. It wasn't such a complicated story. She was being stalked, so she ran. She drove for weeks, drifting around the routes of old road trips they'd taken for Zoe's research, west and north into South Australia, travelling deeper and curving through yellow expanse.

She had only scattered memories afterwards. They rose like the road's occasional mirages – palm trees and slender people walking, a train rushing towards her fast as flood, children in hats and bonnets, a whip thrashing the air and bullocks raising their slobbering noses to sob, and withered livestock slumped to desiccated ground. Perhaps she dreamed some of it while she was napping on roadsides, Birdy twitching at her side in dreams of her own.

I could tell you some things that happened, and maybe I will. Each was its own mystery that she passed through; each removed her a little from her own. Early in her journey, she helped a woman drag her husband from a car crash and waited with her while he died. Later, she slowed through a long cloud of white butterflies, and a day or two later picked up a jittery young hitchhiker who was running from his life. And she drove into dense smoke that continued for kilometre after kilometre on the Ngarkat road to Pinnaroo, not knowing if licking flames lay before her.

When Birdy began sobbing and lurching about, Till turned and said, 'It's okay' – lying like adults couldn't help doing, to reassure themselves too – and nearly ran off the road. 'Woops, Birdy, sorry about that.' Birdy's head swam into view in the mirror and she bumped Till's cheek with her wet nose. Till pressed that furry cheek against her own. 'We're okay, Bird. I've got you.' (I would have said that it was Birdy who had Till, but never mind.)

A small calm voice in her head – Annunciata's – said, *What is going on with you, Till? What are you feeling? Why take that risk?* Till's answers were the same as always. She had her guilt to consider and her life to live. If Annunciata were there she would have told Till that was why she left Melbourne, so the danger was behind her, but she was still herself. She couldn't help that. She should have turned back, but she drove through the fathomless smoke for a long time, until it started thinning, then further, until looking in her mirrors it was a backdrop and then just a low smudge, which by lunchtime had disappeared, as if she'd driven through a gateway into another universe where it was a brilliantly sunny day.

The thought of motels made her feel visible, trackable. (She had not quite left her fears behind.) Anyone might stop in and ask whether a young woman and her greyhound had passed through. I'm not saying she was right, I'm saying this was her thinking. There was just one she stopped at on the edge of Peterborough when she was desperate for a shower. (Otherwise she made do with water heated on the little camp stove she bought somewhere or other.) An old man wheezed up to the door with his fox terrier and she felt sorry for him. The motel was FOR SAL, and she could see why.

She learned to sleep in the car. Other people did. Why shouldn't she? Sometimes there were small gatherings of other women, and they slept in their cars in the shelter of a tree canopy, a clearing, the back of a service station, the edge of a town park. Some of them knew each other from towns hundreds of kilometres away. There was always farm work, people said – citrus along the Murray or further afield in New South Wales, potatoes in Victoria, grapes everywhere, stone fruit, berries, cherries – another world. They dreamed of safety, roofs, respect, hot water, dignity, but this was what they could afford.

Isobel, an older woman in jeans and a hoodie, had appeared in a couple of towns, the second time sitting on a log while stirring baked beans over a camping stove just out of Kapunda. A few other women were pulling in, reading the signs of comfort and the safety of company. Isobel waved and patted a spot on the log for Till, and greeted Birdy, and in between kept talking, sometimes getting up to poke around in the back of her car. She said, 'The road's no place for a young girl like you. You should be home. Do you have a home?'

'I have family.' Till said this almost proudly. She did not want to talk about why she'd left.

'Oh pet, we all have family,' Isobel said with an edge of reproof. 'It's family don't always have us.'

A police car rolled by and the women tracked its passage. Police could be trouble. Groups of strangers make townspeople uneasy; they might take matters into their own hands. Sometimes people came by with donations of supplies. It was not clear whether this meant *Please stay, we have more*, or *Now we have fed you it is time to move on.*

One night there was a bonfire at the edge of a farm a little way off, bright in the black, with its light flickering into gathered trees. They watched the flames in the darkness, and in the watching they seemed to linger so she could observe each flame, each spark rising. She lifted her nose like an animal. It was just a fire, burning off old rubbish, but it seemed for a moment like a warning and gave her a strange feeling. She left early after a poor night's sleep and kept driving, still heading nowhere.

Her phone buzzed in her back pocket.

Please send us a text. Love Mum and Dad (as if they'd sensed her unease)

I'm fine Tx

She returned the phone to her pocket.

The land turned dry. Scattered signs saying Goyder's Line (1865) began to appear, and the name of the road, Worlds End Highway. Like the parched land around here, somehow it suited her feelings. There had been road trips this way. Photos showed her baring her tiny teeth in front of a Goyder's Line sign, so it must have happened.

Zoe, an historian at a Melbourne university, had a map of this old surveyor's line on her study wall. It appeared as a giant wave sweeping across the state, an echo of the coastline, an irregular heartbeat, or a tsunami of Imperial pink. Its message was for farmers, or pastoralists as they were often called. Crops could be planted inside the line – that's where money was to be made. Outside the line was only suitable for grazing. The map assumed that all the land was for taking. Till had read Zoe's work on abandoned farms, oral records from the region and changing rainfall patterns in the 1800s being replicated now. Hard times were here again. Of course, none of these hard times were anything like those inflicted on First Nations people through murder, disease and dispossession, but they preferred not to think of that. (It was the squatters who did all that, not the pastoralists, who arrived a little later, the old families said.)

It was as if the First Nations people just melted away, people said. But that is another story. It is *the* story, is what I mean, but it is not Till's story, which is not a single filament on a single butterfly's wing in a cloud of butterflies stretching for miles compared to the long richness of the original world. It reminded Till of a mirror at her great-grandmother's, which was foxed with age and small, and poorly lit except late in the afternoon when the sun hit it. It gave the illusion of revealing everything important about a person, and was inherently deceptive as all mirrors are in their way. Tilt the angle and anyone or anything might appear or disappear. It's what the colonisers did: altered the angle, held themselves in a kind light. I suppose we all do that.

It was never where they were going that mattered, it was the road trip itself, being in the car. Sometimes Till could believe it would always be this way; they would always be driving, her mother would be looking about with wondering gaze. 'See that?' she asked sometimes, but Till never did, and her father didn't either, though sometimes he'd say, 'Oh yeah'. But he liked being with them, his 'girls'. Not a person she didn't know could talk to her in a fast-moving car; not a one could approach without her parents being by her side. No one knew where they were; no one could find them.

The land grew harsher. Ruined houses lay everywhere, empty-mouthed and hollow-eyed, sometimes fenced off and distant. One presented such a dreamlike appearance in the dense light of late afternoon that it was a shock to see her black dog and orange car and the long grey road when she turned.

Till came upon a scotch thistle and the tracks of small creatures in a creek bed. The light all around was so thick it seemed solid as water, swaying above the ground, trembling within bowls of trees, pouring along dry creek beds. 'Peppermint gum, acacia, saltbush, weed, weed,' Till murmured, words she knew from her mother's work. 'Saltbush plain, clay pan, denuded landscape, treed landscape, stressed river system.' She and Birdy had passed a dead wattlebird each day in a Brunswick lane, its wings spread against the ground as if still in flight, observing its slow transformation from near-life to matter. The words were like that.

Here, every day, she walked a roadside ossuary of bleached lizard carcasses and kangaroo bones, and smaller bones, stark white, like snippings of lace among the pincushion flowers. It seemed as if everything she saw came back to this: E's bones, how bleached they might now be – as clean and white and picked as this?

Days of Innocence and Wonder

No one was there to save Till or decide where to go next. Was it the beginning of the journey or almost done? If she were to tell someone that the land was yellow and of a severe horizontality, and the sky was blue, they would not understand that its beauty was sometimes tiring and her eyes needed to rest. She pulled off the road and had a nap. Then she could go on again. But she was tired of circling and making decisions and finding somewhere new each night – tired of trying to sense danger and safety.

It was an accident, finding Wirowie, like all the other places. The sign on the highway proclaimed the name, as if the town was self-evident. There was nothing there. The country being so empty made it seem like a prank, and the turnoff nothing but a road cut straight into more nothing. Still she took it. In an hour or two, blue shadows would take over from orange light and settle over everything; they might as well stop and make camp. She might have turned back, but clustered buildings came into view, small houses of asbestos siding clutching the ground like limpets to a reef, outbuildings with their doorways askew, and a huge yard filled with cars and utes and trucks.

They stopped and walked the wire fence line, Birdy sniffing and moving her ears, Till watching and listening for snakes. A little of the day's warmth had caught in the earth and lifted around them, bringing some clean grassy scent. The ancient cars were butted up like stonework and fabulously lit by the late sun. It turned their ice cream colours – duck egg blue, sherbet pink, dove grey, lilac rust – luminous and otherworldly. Their curious curved bonnets and sculptural prows made them seem more creature (an eagle, a tapir, a rhinoceros) than machine.

They faced the road as if waiting to see what was coming or what show might be about to begin.

A stalk of grass caught in her sandal and she paused to pull it out. Insects sounded all around and from somewhere far away a rooster stretched its throat and called across his world.

The main street was a ghost town, a film set with everyone gone, everyone dead, everyone forgotten, soon to arrive or recently departed, and everything left behind waiting, as unreal as that. Utterly still. Leaves and shadows might have been carved. The sky was cavernous blue. Turn off the road in any direction and asphalt made way for red earth and loose stone. Till pulled in outside the *Wirowie Gazette* office (1875) and let down her window. Warm air poured around her. She and Birdy stepped into the mystery and began walking. This part of town seemed to emerge from the plain like a fragile geological formation: the shopfronts with their delicate arched windows, the raised walkways, the deep shade of the porches, the light-filled street cleaving the town in two, and Till walking through it as if it were her kingdom. The air was so heavy it absorbed sound. Insects moved slowly.

When the long station building of caramel-coloured stone came into view around a corner it presented an archaeological appearance, like some ruined temple complex wavering from the plains of grass. It felt like a personal discovery, and because of that, hers. She and Birdy approached gingerly. Stonework crumbled from it in places. Wooden fretwork drooped and fell from the platform veranda and curtains of sagging chain wire fencing encircled it all. The platform was fissured and rutted as old road. Grasses sprang up in profusion from its cracks, all gone to seed and dried silver white.

The ghosts of travel – hope, possibility, escape, change – seemed to haunt the station. The train would be here any minute. They would stand, move towards the river of iron, step onto it and be swept away. It would never come but it didn't seem to matter. Till and Birdy sat with their backs to the station house wall. The afternoon's stored heat leached out and kept them warm while they ate – a cheese sandwich, a punnet of small tomatoes and dog food. Birdy seemed resigned to the absence of meat, declining a tomato but accepting cheese in its stead with an expression of suffering disappointment. 'Sorry, Bird,' Till said.

This place was nowhere. It was hardly even tethered to the earth. It might float away. There was nothing really to see but tracks, the central platform covered in wildflowers, and three enormous palm trees on the other side. Down past the old water crane, the afternoon sun lit up two vast grey silos and their shadows plunged across the tracks towards the new part of town.

Till moved the car to the end of the station building near the water tank, and slept there as hidden as she could be, listening all the while for strange noises. There was just the wind. In the morning she knocked the side of the water tank bottom to top – close to full, but who knew how clean. She turned the tap and ran it into a small saucepan. It looked okay. She'd set it to boil for a few minutes and cool and see what it was like later. For now, she got water and food for Birdy from the car boot and an oat biscuit for herself, and lit her little stove to heat the last of the water she had with her for coffee.

It was just past dawn. The faintest haze hung in the air despite it being so dry, and the sun rushed across the grasses and red dirt, and the sky seemed to rise from the horizon like a flung sheet – blue silk, faded at the selvedge, billowing free. Cockatoos in the palm trees and the peppermint gums beyond began acrobatting around and screaming, huge white things crashing and falling from their shelter, so carefree that Till paused, envious. Birdy wandered up the platform, and Till had the feeling that it might be the fiftieth time she had watched this – her black dog in the silver grass – and there was something painful in that, since they would be on their way soon.

'Birdy,' Till called, and Birdy turned and loped back. Till dragged a section of the wire fencing apart and turned the handle on the waiting room door, pushing then shouldering it, a wrenching gritty sound, and it made way. Inside, sandy mortar and crumbled stone had fallen from walls and windows. The building was dissolving, catastrophically in places, except for the pressed metal ceiling high above, still intact but for some rust. It smelled mostly of outside and a little of damp stone, though not unpleasantly.

'Hello?' Till whispered, startling no one, but Birdy snuffled in the corners of the long room without caution and disappeared through a doorway. Sun streamed through the transom window and through fissures and holes in walls, lighting up piles of rock fall and dust motes, a large woodstove in blue and cream enamel set into a wall cavity tiled in primrose yellow and white, and ancient benches from the platform, Till presumed from the graffiti – 'Liz and Bear 4 Eva' and so forth. What stationmaster aesthete had chosen this perfect combination? 'Hats off to you, sir,' Till said, and left it reluctantly.

The next room was the ticket office, Till guessed from the curiously proportioned window, and beyond that was a storeroom with shelves, and a wide connecting corridor with a deep basin. She turned the tap. A terrible groaning in the pipes began and a trickle then a gush of brackish looking water emerged. It did not clear. Still, it was running water. Wall brackets were all that remained of a water heater. Another small room containing a majestic porcelain toilet, and a tin lean-to with an enormous shower hung over a sloping grate in the floor. Till stood looking at it all.

You know the way memories rise? Like methane from the deep sea floor – unstoppable as that. (Like billions of other people, probably, Till had acquired a body of random information during lockdown.) It can be a sickening feeling.

'But will we all die one day?' she asked her mother once. Zoe had stared at her with such bleakness that Till knew for the first time that she could not protect this person who was supposed to protect her. Zoe's pity was not only for Till, but for herself. How do you sleep and walk and smile, knowing it? The love of parents, of another body, a beloved child (Till presumed) were only distractions.

'Sweetie,' Zoe said, 'it won't always feel this way.'

Till didn't believe it. She was twenty-three. She had made a deal with death or herself that she would kill someone before she let them kill her. That was her final word on the matter.

The fiction that childhood was a time of innocence was intolerable to Till. It was adults who were the innocents in this belief. Children knew. Something crept over people as they emerged from childhood, like cataracts, blinding them to the truth, which was that the world could be horrifying. Sometimes a child might break through and reveal to an adult the terror that could circumscribe their lives. Adults didn't want to be reminded. *You'll grow out of it*, they said. She shouldn't generalise, but she had seen her parents' faces; she knew they remembered.

No, don't think about it. Put it off.

Chapter 3

Wirowie 2022

On the second night, Till had dinner with a policeman in a Peterborough pub. He was a laughing sort of guy, who spied her through the gloom and acted as if she was the centre of his world, which she might have been for a while. She couldn't remember how long it was since she'd felt another's touch. It would be months. Sometimes Till leant towards a new man despite her fears. I don't feel what she does. It's some brew of muscle and scent, a manner. I wish she could hear me. *It will end in tears.* She drank a little and got chatty and even enjoyed the flirtation. It had no particular meaning to her. It was more like running a few scales on a piano. She didn't notice his hard edge or watchful gaze, as if he was assessing his own impact the whole time, his patter, his taut body, his strut.

He offered to see her home and seemed surprised when she told him where she was staying and not to bother.

'Wirowie, god.'

'Yep,' she said. 'The station.' Having said it seemed to make it true. Why shouldn't she stay there again? Driving back down the highway made it feel like going home. It was a good feeling.

*

Till dragged the security fencing back next morning, swept out the waiting room with an old tin dustpan and a hearth brush she found by the stove, stacked the fallen stonework into neat piles, then boiled water from the water tank again and set it to cool while they went exploring. It might have been her place. It was strange to stop driving each day – unsettling. Her travels, places, people, the things they said, became a story she told herself at night to soothe herself to sleep.

Each day she moved more from her car inside. It was more convenient that way. A low table of scrounged house timbers resting on piled stones worked well for her stove and kitchen things, and if her attempt at getting the woodstove alight failed when thick smoke filled the room, there was an open fire that kept any night chill at bay. She scavenged for firewood in fallen homes. There was more than one unspent wood heap around. When had people abandoned hope of this town? At night she pulled the wire fencing closed around them and padlocked it and in the morning pulled it back as if drawing a curtain. Birdy went out for a wander. She sniffed her way along, intent and sinuous through the pale grass, all the way to the end, turning round and coming back down the narrow path she and Till were making bit by bit each day. Pathways don't lie. The realisation arrived slowly, as if Till's vision had cleared. They were staying.

Their path led through the platform's grasses to its end, down the stairs, through the railway line meadow. This was her route, invisible to the old town to the west and the new town to the east, to the side roads that led to the double line of ruined and abandoned shops on Main Street. She walked past thick doorsteps worn down at centre, peering inside at empty shelves or fallen ceilings or collapsed walls. The facades, windows and doors survived; time and weather had mostly had their way with the rest. It might once have been like Orroroo, a town further north, though it was more elegant and smaller. The Hidden Waters Emporium was overhung by an almond and a peppercorn tree, its weatherboard lean-to dissolved almost to translucency in the dry air. The almond tree overhanging its fence was covered in soft green nut casings. Once E's mother had set Till and E outside with a little bowl of almonds in their shells and their own small proper hammers (Till's had a blue rubber handle; how she loved that hammer), and they banged the nuts, mostly squashing them, until they started to get the knack of it. Then they ate them.

The shops might give you something of the flavour of the town. The Wirowie Institute (1879), *The Wirowie Enterprise North Eastern Advertiser* printing office (1884), *The North Eastern Times* Wirowie News office (1881), Thomas Taylor's Blacksmith Wheelwright Machinist (1884), TV Sales & Repairs, a tea shop, a haberdashery, The Lubritorium, Rosetta's Travel Requisites, Finch's Real Estate, a shuttered pub with a return veranda and fancy iron lacework, shops with random window displays (a teapot, a tray of mugs, a dress, secondhand shoes, things like that) as if someone felt an empty window was too lonely and these old things they had lying about would do – the end stages of civic pride.

How would a person know if they were living in the end times? Till felt as if she might be. She was looking around for something to change her mind.

Some nights later the policeman from Peterborough came wandering up the platform, not too fast, taking his time to look around. Till watched him from the water tank. He kept on, called out, 'Hey,' and waved two bottles of drink. She finished filling the bottle with water and walked towards him.

'It's changed since I was last here,' he said. A smell of alcohol wafted from him.

'When was that?'

He looked about, across the line. A big moon was rising over the palm trees. 'A while ago now.'

They sat on the platform for a couple of drinks and went inside for more. If anyone asked me I'd say Till wasn't thinking of her safety, though she would be willing to act if necessary. She'd trained for that. It was just that sometimes she seemed to drown herself in risk, or forget about it. I'd seen similar in her before. By then, part of her wanted to forget being watchful and cautious, and to sink into feeling, the softness of skin, the muscle beneath. They went to the bedroom. He kicked the bedroom door shut leaving Birdy in the waiting room. Till looked around – trying (failing) to see it through a stranger's eyes – at the camp bed, the broom propped in the doorway, the neatly stacked stone, the kerosene lamp turned low, casting a faint light over it all and, soon, the man sprawled on his back. It had seemed a pleasant scene earlier. Her mind was already turning to afterwards. How to get him to leave. She could never go to sleep with a stranger. Perhaps she could start a conversation about whether he had ever before had sex in the ticket office of an abandoned and crumbling railway station in an almost-ghost town in the mid north of South Australia. (It was the first such occasion for her, locationally speaking.) He would probably say no, but there might be other things to talk about, or he might laugh, or have a strange story of his own. In this way she could get through the night and sleep tomorrow.

'So you really live here? Like this?' he said, almost with contempt. It seemed as if she had become something different to him because of this ruin that was her shelter.

'I sort of do. We can call it a night. I don't mind.' She spoke in a careless way, like he was the kind of guy who people, including her, would not think anything much of at all.

But he pulled her down and soon it was too late. They stripped and even before he flipped her over she began to have misgivings. He looked at her breasts in an assessing way, was he happy with them or not. He was not exactly with her, but at some small remove – the back seat of the cinema – playing a movie reel in his head of a hot guy and an expectant cock and a woman who delighted in being told that she liked being hit, and in the hitting itself. He used the word 'spank' as if that made it fun. Till was embarrassed for him. Mostly she was angry though. He hit hard. That part did not end well. While he was on the ground crawling away from her, groaning then roaring with rage, holding his nose, which was trailing crimson blood everywhere, what a mess, she stood away and opened the door. Birdy came in. She was panting from the warm fire and was happy to see Till. All her teeth showed.

'Stop her. Don't let her near me.' He spat blood.

'You're frightened of dogs?' Till said. 'Oh my god. She won't hurt anyone except a small animal. Or you if you hurt me again. I don't think she'd like that.' Adrenaline had cleared her head a little. She picked up her phone and took a few pictures of him. 'If casual violence is your thing you might check with someone first or it's assault, not a good time.'

'You broke by dose.' Snotty blood kept appearing.

'Self-protection.' Till threw a box of tissues towards him.

He fell back on the bed. 'Just having some fun. Think you're better than me.'

'I didn't before. Do now.'

He looked at Birdy, side-eye. He had that much sense. Till didn't want Birdy to bite him, not exactly, she didn't want him permanently maimed. She had enough on her conscience. He curled on the bed, his hand to his nose.

'Time to get going,' Till said.

'I won't do it again.'

'True.'

'We were just . . . you know—'

'You think we were fucking?' she asked. 'My god. You were assaulting me. What's your name again?'

'What?'

'I'm Till, you're—?'

'Rod.'

'Rod. Really? We mustn't have introduced ourselves. Get going, Rod.'

'I can't drive like this.'

'You think I care?' She hated him for what was happening. 'I'm very strong,' Till said. 'I'm a good fighter. I could probably kill you. Not that I would,' then softer, 'you hear me?'

'Huh?' He blinked slowly and his gaze steadied, his pupils in and out. 'Wait, what?'

'You heard.' She donned her dusty clothes and twisted her dark hair up and swathed herself in more darkness – her leather jacket, though it was warm outside (but it was her armour and it would be cooler by dawn), her black scarf, her black jeans.

He felt around for something to cover himself – a T-shirt – watching her, fumbling around for more clothes, exposed now that she had dressed. Till looked at him, assessing herself as much as him – what had she been thinking, that sort of thing. *Idiot.* That was alcohol for you. And now that she had hurt his feelings his expression was childlike as well as enraged. That wasn't good. Men with hurt feelings could be volatile.

She bundled the rest of his clothes. 'Get up.'

'What?' He got up and made a pathetic half-lunge at her and she took him by the arm fast, and when he struggled, twisted it up high behind his back and shoved him through the waiting room and he couldn't resist because she had made sure already, long before, that she was strong and knew how to pull an arm behind a person's back until it was under enough stress and how to maintain propulsion to keep control. She couldn't wait to be rid of him.

'Open the door,' she said.

He opened the door with his free hand and she shoved him out, threw the clothes after him, paying no attention to his muffled yells – 'Crazy bitch' and so forth.

She stood in the doorway facing the night, her black dog beside her, watching him. 'Pick up your shoes too now.' He swayed on his feet. 'Move.' He moved faster then, pulling on his jeans, hopping about, then shuffling down the platform with his laces trailing.

Over the train tracks the fronds of the palm trees were shifting about, darker than the sky and making a soothing sound. He was only a bad choice, and she was finished with him.

'What if I come back?' he called.

She turned her head. 'I don't advise it.'

'You are fucking gone in the head.' He was shouting now.

'I've got reasons.' But she said it softly.

Till went back inside for a quilt, padlocked the security

fences and left the platform in the other direction. It seemed safer not to hang around. She might have had some trouble if he was sober. Now that her bravado and rage were dwindling she was shaking. She wanted to tell someone – mostly Annunciata – that she'd handled the situation. (I will tell you more about Annunciata, I suppose.) Why was it that she hated herself then, and blamed herself too? She shouldn't have let him in. Her edge was somehow blunted after the years shut away. It might have been that.

She walked the soft edges of the road, which put her in mind of footprints and cop shows and evidentiary matters. A person would be able to track her path if they had a mind to, but the probability seemed distant and they had no reason to. She should think ahead more. It was just that sometimes when she'd had a couple of drinks and felt a bit loose inside, she was prepared to try someone new.

Birdy was like an extra shadow walking at her side, darker than the darkness, silent, calm, alert despite it being time for sleep. They wove a quiet line around the bulging cones of light beneath the town's few streetlights, along the empty street. Further on as shops dwindled and front gardens grew deeper, other life forms shifted about – small creatures, roosting birds perhaps or ground-dwelling things: lizards, snakes, mice. Birdy's neat ears pricked and fell like antennae. Not a person could ambush them. Birdy could see for miles, and she heard and smelled better than Till. There was peace in that knowledge.

She wouldn't normally be out on her own in dark night, but she was tired and so was Birdy and when she had gone far enough as she judged it, meaning the low glow of sparse streetlights had fallen away and the asphalt of the road had narrowed and made way for rutted dirt, she departed the track to one side, pushing a path through the grasses, feeling them brushing against her legs, to where it was mostly clear of tussocks and such. She crouched and cleared a patch of ground, skimming her hand across its surface until it was free of stones, and shook the quilt out as if setting a picnic and they lay down. Till drew the edges of the quilt over and about them. Birdy gave a small sigh as a person might say, *At last*.

Often when trying to sleep Till's mind was filled with times when she had exerted her strength against men during her years of Krav Maga sessions, or imagined encounters with men to come, in which she acquitted herself well. It helped to manage her fears. The thought of her strength and deftness, the swiftness of her thinking – darting a few seconds forward and looking back, assessing a person, their way of responding to other things and how that might translate to their physicality – and the thought of her knowledge and experience of weight and joints, assessing herself and the times she fell short in her responses – misjudging, recovering – soothed her. Say someone came up from behind and grabbed, she could snap her head back and smash their face, pull their arm and twist, scrape their shin hard while they were focused on their arm, that sort of thing. Yes, if something happened she could look after herself, and she could look after Birdy if it came to that. But this night Till watched the stars and all their wild patterns and felt the cool air on her face and in all that space, with not a lock and not a window to shut and nothing at all to keep the world out, she went to sleep. Who would find her in the middle of that?

Sometime in the night the stars began to flee and the earth to hurtle through space. Memories rose of this night and others, and when Till tried digging her hands into the soil there was nothing but dust and loose stone, nothing a person could grip to. There, some stalks of grass at her fingertips. Some dry pieces pulled free. She reached, spreading her fingers around the whole clump of it, dry and living, until she had it contained in her grasp, testing the roots' hold in the soil, and in this way she did not fly into space. Eventually the stars slowed, and the night was still and Birdy was untroubled, merely twitching lightly in her dreams of hunting. Till buried her face against Birdy and curled her hands in and they became invisible. It was easier outdoors. She couldn't be cornered and no one could spoil Birdy's kind and gentle heart. Who knew that darkness could be shelter.

I suppose you're thinking, Oh, she's not well – in her mind I mean – but why would she be? Would you? She might not have believed herself well all the time; she might have been well some or most of the time; I believe it's not always easy for a person to know. But despite all that, despite what I have said here, I maintain that she's the sanest person I have ever known.

It is time.

Chapter 4

Brunswick 2004

THEY WERE PLAYING outside at kindergarten when the man stopped to talk. It wasn't their fault. It was not Till's fault – I want you to know that. Please remember that.

She was five years old when her best friend, whose name she never said – E, that is all – was stolen away from kindergarten, from inside or outside, she wasn't sure, no one was. Well, she couldn't say and in any case, couldn't really remember and didn't want to. She avoided reading about it. She left the room if people brought it up. People speculated that she, E, might have slipped out with another family like she was one of theirs, or she might have come out with Till and Zoe or George, whoever was collecting Till that day (though she hadn't, Till knew for sure since Zoe or George had arrived after E left) and run away, or maybe a person took her and somehow came inside to do that. As I said, Till couldn't recall.

This is what I hate. Once you start remembering, more of it comes. Those old news reports make it sound as if events moved in an orderly way when it had felt chaotic, inconceivable and weird, and was mostly a blur to Till. She kept thinking E would find her way back, she would be at kinder the next day or the day after, she was hiding, she was playing a funny game.

Till only knew what I have said here because of things other people said and things she tried not to read but read anyway more than once, that she had no memory of in any case. Had two of the kinder teachers run through the streets, wailing as they searched, as one report said? Had a mother had hysterics at the kinder teachers and anyone who tried to reason with her? Was that E's mother? She would ask Zoe about it one day.

This was not true. She would not ask Zoe about it ever, but she told herself these soft mistruths. They allowed her to proceed in life. The mistruths were sheets of barely formed ice that she slid her flattened body across, her weight spread so evenly, her eyes ahead on a verdant shore, which itself was a lie. There was no verdant shore. There was only one moment to be traversed, and another, and another.

Everyone was asking Till about a man. What did they want her to say? Her throat stopped, her voice wouldn't work.

Till and E did know a man who stopped sometimes at the wire and spoke to them. He liked their names, he said, especially E's. That made Till jealous and she hated herself for that, because he was so dumb, so why did she care? But she couldn't help it. It made her show off. She did a handstand. He hardly noticed. He mostly talked to E. That might have been because she talked back. E was a chatterbox and a live-wire people said.

Once, Till asked her mother where E was living now – with her grandma or in the bush in a cubby maybe? Her mother said, 'No one wants to upset you, sweetheart, but I'm not going to start telling you lies. You know what I'm saying?' She stroked Till's cheek, and her mouth trembled – Till's mother's, I mean. In a way Till did know what she was saying. She knew enough not to ask again. She didn't talk about and no one at home used E's name. It was better that way.

Even after Till became Till, having changed her name, people knew who she was, especially when she was little and looked like the photographs, and if they did not always smile and say hello in an exaggerated way to show how much they cared without saying, *Oh my god, you poor thing, how awful, is there any news that I could pass on to everyone I know?* which is what they sometimes, though not always meant, they still noticed and were curious. She liked the quiet people who just smiled, as if letting her know that they were looking out for her.

That's how she knew that what happened had changed them, and how Till kept reminding them of their fear. She didn't want to do that. They couldn't help their curiosity. Here's something Till learned: never to remind people, something that became easier as people moved and her appearance changed. She would not say E's name anyway, or her own for that matter, but she tried not to think it either, as if it might show on her face and mark her as the other girl. Let the name die for a while and recover its innocence, let it be rediscovered in a hundred years time and let people wonder then why it fell into disuse, why people turned against it. It died before it could grow stale and become a curio or an old lady's name – Edna, Beryl, Gladys.

Memories mostly didn't connect to each other as far as Till could see. They were floating in separate boxes in her mind: the time the guinea pig died, the time she had a kaleidoscope, the time she ran out of the school, the time they went for a long drive in the sun, the time her friend went for a walk and didn't come back. They had nothing to do with each other. They didn't tell a story. Till's life was in pieces, as I have said; as far as she knew, everyone's was. No one had ever said otherwise, though she sensed that there was a difference. But if they were, why were other people so untroubled? She apologised for missing appointments and dates and forgetting dinners and so on. Her parents said she was scatty. Everyone needs a word, which is another kind of container. She was in the scatty people container. Much later when she became a singer, people learned to ring her to make sure she'd remembered gigs and promotions and interviews with journalists and so forth. It was awkward to miss those. 'Calendar apps work really well,' her manager told her, 'but you have to use them.'

I have to tell you this too, so you can see. (I'm sorry, Till.) It was not entirely true that Till could not remember. It was only what she said, though it was true in a way since she could not remember the man's face. She didn't like to look at him, but didn't know how to say it. His head was higher than hers and E's, she could see his belt buckle, his fingernails were long, he had zippy shoes. His pants were grey.

It was Till and E's special place. They made small brooms with small pine branches and swept out under the bushes to make their secret world nice. They had a collection of containers, cups and little tin saucepans that they used for cooking and scientific experiments: the mystery of why red petals did not make a beautiful red liquid and how it might be achieved – that sort of thing. It was some alchemy they hadn't divined yet.

He stopped on his way past and said stupid things. They were the destination, Till realised one day, even then, from the way he acted surprised. He said they had pretty names as I have already mentioned; he asked what game they were playing in that quiet bushy area round the back. An old scout shed overhung by an ash tree was a step or two beyond the fence, and he stood in this space. It was shadow to people walking past. The man had seen the space though. He had an eye for such things. He teased them about their activities – 'Perfume again?' 'Shops again?', and he winked at these words in an embarrassing way. 'Play', as he called it, using the word strangely. 'What play is that?' he asked, as if the concept itself was incomprehensible, as if he had never experienced such a thing himself. The Till of now, not her child self, wondered what sort of child he might have been, and about his childhood, though she tried not to. She, five-year-old-not-yet-Till, thought he was dumb the way he interrupted.

Till had felt sorry for him in a small way even though he disgusted her. Mostly, she wished he'd go away. 'Don't say anything,' she said quiet and fierce to E as he approached once, 'don't talk to him, he's so annoying', but E said he was funny or sometimes she said he was silly. No one liked silliness at Till's place, but the way E said it was like an endearment. It was the first time she heard and understood the slipperiness of words; she did not think that when she said he was annoying to E she had meant terrifying. But if she had used those words it would have meant knowing that they were in danger, and people turn from that knowledge even if it is true. In fact they had been in mortal danger, which was worse, and without knowing these words, Till had felt what they meant in the same way you feel a knife blade close to your flesh. It seemed possible to Till much later, thinking of this misunderstanding, that she and E might later pull apart. Childhood loyalty and grief and anger at what happened to E made her hope not. She was E's friend, and it was not likely that E would now find another. She would not betray the friendship in death.

Wirowie

A long thread of light was burning on the edge of the plain when Till came to herself and light began its drift. Light meant she might be seen and remembered: a stranger with a blanket and a noticeable dog and no car to be seen. She lifted her head and looked around, slowly and with care. There was no movement. The landscape appeared so flat that an elevation of a metre was a hill and gave a person a godlike view – as if they could see the whole world, not only the run down to the silos and the station beyond, its stonework starting to fall about without exactly dissolving. She could feel the bruises on her back, her legs, her backside.

A light mist of drying dew hovered from the ground, everything cool and with a scent of grass drying. They walked down the road edge along tree line and fence into town, past a horse in a paddock stripped to red dirt, on the other side of the road from an allotment that was decorated, if that is the right word, with rusted old bicycles, all sizes, strung up along the wire fencing. Behind them, shorn sheep roamed through a queer congregation of metal sculptures. She hurried past them in this light – their shadows were so long – only slowing when she saw her car by the station water tank. The station was behind Main Street, and she'd seen nothing looking down its length, and the station road – Railway Street West – was quiet, so could he have seen her? Still, they approached three times – from Main Street down a short side street past a war memorial, from the north, and obliquely from the train line a little to the south. They drew closer. Till threw small stones onto the roof, sending them rattling down the tin. That would get him moving, if he was there. But there was nothing but the cool sweetness of morning, humming with potential as all days are.

Till could have got in the car and driven off. She didn't think of that. Something about the station still felt like coming home. She knew it a little, she could picture herself in it, or here. It was broken but could be fixed. After last night she had defended herself and it both. She went inside and locked up again and stripped so she could wash. She stroked her own body and felt the small bones of her face, her own softness. No, she loved her bodily self and did not wish to betray it. Afterwards, she held her phone over her shoulder, around the sides, and took enough photos to get a sense of the damage: a couple of handprints, bruises – three large – fingermarks on her arms. She took more photos of the blood on the floor before she cleaned it.

Outside again, Till refilled Birdy's water dish and gave her some food and ate an apple in a patch of sun on the station platform, swinging her legs over the edge while Birdy snuffled up and down, then settled. It seemed as if Birdy had decided this was home days ago, returning to the patch of sun she found each day, lying there, moving when the sun moved like a black sunflower. A rooster crowed. Till knew the sound, the very rooster, and waited for the answer from the north end of town – the rooster with the extra syllable in its call. There – there it was. This is how she knew she belonged.

About the things Till had seen in Melbourne – she told herself she was wrong. She put the man in one those compartments of her mind and pushed the thoughts and fears down, the way she'd been trying to for years.

To describe the policeman and others like him as a thrill would be to acknowledge a sickness in herself. What did the almost pleasure of danger mean, if it was more than a distraction. People might imagine it a death wish – Till's psychiatrist Annunciata had talked about this; her eyes had told Till her thinking – but that wasn't true. Till didn't want to die. But there was also her mind to consider and her black fear. There was that. She wanted to turn and look into it and know it and she was prepared to kill it if that could be done. If that meant killing a person though . . . A person might lose one burden only to pick up another. But if it were the right person she thought she could do it because there was the matter of vengeance to consider and the imperfection of justice. And there was the other thing about touching another person, which she missed. Sometimes she was lonely.

A proper broom, a dustpan and brush, a mop and bucket, sponges – they were the first things – not that this decay didn't have some attraction of its own, but its poetics were not for living in. She went out and bought these, just to make a start. Another few years and the whole thing would come down. The only sign of electricity was some beautiful old switches, but Till was used to charging her phone in the car, and her camping lamp lit the waiting room well enough. Water was a juggle. She mistrusted the tap water, could not bring herself to shower in cold water, and bought water casks in Peterborough or Orroroo. The tank water was for washing clothes and herself and for cooking. She was almost getting used to it. The tap's squeak was familiar now, not an alarm, an air-raid siren, a shark bell that would bring the whole town, such as it was, running.

Once, when she got back to the station after her run, there was a note threaded through the wire in front of the door. *Lead in tap water. DO NOT DRINK. Okay for washing and showering.* So people had noticed her. That felt strange.

She explored more seriously over the next week. There was rot in the window frames, subsidence and collapse in the south-west wall, three cracked or broken window lintels, fallen fretwork, cracking in platform, timber floor heavily worn, paint flaking on interior walls, electricity, plumbing, tank water, ownership? She poked at loose stones. One fell on her foot the very day a YouTube video had advised 'taking due care', since large stones could break legs, and then where would you be. She could take a hint. She searched through a couple of Wirowie ruins for sturdy planks to use as wall braces, bought work boots in Peterborough, and stopped at the motel she'd once stayed at to arrange having a shower there every day or two in return for some small payment. 'Too easy,' the owner, Doug, said, utterly unsurprised. Who knew what he'd seen in his time.

Till had been setting money aside for years without ever telling herself why. (She'd done well with the music for a few years.) If you ask me, she wanted to be ready for whatever it was a person might need to be ready for. There was no knowing what it might be. How would a person predict her current circumstances: flight, exile, a need for shelter? Well, she was glad of the money now.

She went shopping at the service station–hardware shop in Orroroo, Oldham's, where she had filled the petrol tank a few times. She consulted her list and wandered and gathered things and piled them on the counter. Sometimes the woman who worked there – Tundra Morscheck – and Mr Oldham called out with advice from the counter or came and helped.

'I better be getting back to the station,' Till eventually said.

'You're awfully young to have your own station,' Mr Oldham said.

'Am I?'

'Around here? I don't recall any on the market . . . Sheep?'

'No, no no. Trains. Well, not anymore. I live in a railway station. It's not mine exactly. In Wirowie.'

'The station in Wirowie? My goodness. People do seem to get fond of it. My son . . .' He cleared his throat. 'He liked it a lot. I haven't been there for a while. Moved up here a few years ago.'

'Really? No one else was doing anything with it, so . . . People don't mind. I don't think they do. Do you think they would?' She stopped short. She'd prefer not to know if he thought they'd hate it.

Mr Oldham looked at her not unkindly. Interested. 'I wouldn't know. I suppose not. I wouldn't mind if I still lived down there.' He seemed to be waiting in case there might be more.

Finally, Till said, 'I'm fixing it up.'

'Oh yes? On your own? Anyone helping you out?'

'If things get too heavy, I can always ask. It's not too bad so far. The stone sort of crumbles. It's the worst.' She thrust out a leg and rocked her heel against the ground. 'I had to get boots to save the toes.' The thought made her laugh lightly for some reason. It seemed so normal.

The woman wiped her hair off her face, perhaps to see Till more clearly. 'Next time you're in,' she said.

It seemed like she might say something else, but she was quiet, and in the end Till just said 'Yeah', and it seemed okay. There would be a next time. They had agreed on that.

Only one shop in the whole of Wirowie was ever open that she'd seen. The handpainted sign in the window said *Antiques, Collectibles and Bric-a-Brac – Make an Offer!* She pushed the door. The floor was like the station waiting room's: deeply worn, unvarnished, the boards soft and pale. Inside, the shelves were thickly clustered with hundreds of figurines: shepherdesses, women and girls with ringlets and bonnets, shepherds with brown curls wearing jaunty clothes and sheep dogs with plumed tails waving, small boys blowing horns raised high to the pressed metal ceiling. She knew how these things felt in your hand – her great-grandmother's tremulous voice was there for a moment: 'Careful now, sweetie; en't she a pretty thing' – knobbly, smooth, cool. Her great-grandmother's dresser shelves held a few of her own mother (Till's great-great-grandmother) MaryAnn's treasures, mostly shepherdesses and young ladies. They peered into the distance from the old dresser shelves like ships' figureheads carving through heavy seas. Up here it would be nothing but wheatfields in a good year, a haze of red earth in a bad one. They held their bonnets to their heads and their curls blew back.

MaryAnn might have stared from a window, the shepherdess in hand, stroking her china curls and wondering if the world might offer a little more to a young woman like her than she had here. After some more such evenings, perhaps she had resolved to act, wrapped the figurine in a clean handkerchief, put it in her reticule as if signing a contract of intent, and stepped on a train for Adelaide to start again. Till had done the opposite, but perhaps it wasn't so different. And here they all were, these dainty china creatures, abandoned after a last failed crop, the closing of the railway, the dismantling of a house, flight from ruin, a change in taste. What bowerbirds we all are, and how fickle.

A leather skinned man, in fine old clothes of a cut from a generation or two ago, worn and beautiful as the floor, perched in the furthest, darkest reaches of the shop behind the counter, hovering rather as if preparing for flight while Till looked about. He cleared his throat and that was all.

Till called out 'Hey' and he lifted a hand.

'All for sale,' he said. 'Sing out if you need some help.'

She picked a shepherdess and a little brown working dog and paid for them. He wrapped them in a sheet of old newspaper, butcher-style, and tied it fastidiously with white twine.

'You staying then?' he asked. He was looking at her more directly now.

'Excuse me?'

'Been seeing you around.'

'Really? I suppose I am.'

Two people from houses on side streets – one in the new town, as she thought of it, one at the far western road of the old town – had raised their hands and called out 'Morning' in the last week, and she felt as if she'd been caught trespassing, but agreed it was morning and raised her own hand and went on, trying not to scuttle. She felt furtive so she probably looked it. She wasn't alone in that. There was a small, rancorous hillbilly group that kept to itself on the north-west corner of town – no harm in that. She'd only passed them once, and avoided them since. People knew who their tribes were even in a town this size. Till was squatting. She didn't know how she felt about that. She expected the subject of trespass to come up, but the man said nothing more except his name, which was Ken.

'Come around and have a look,' she said. 'I have tea. And biscuits.'

'Oh yeah?' he said. 'I might well. That would be the station? You're living there? I heard you were.'

'You did? I think I've seen four people here – you're the fifth.'

'That'd do it. Don't even need that many.' He spoke in a dry way and when Till laughed he did too. 'I haven't been to the station in years.'

'Really?'

'Trains are always late.' He laughed. He nearly got Till, but she caught herself in time.

'You'll like what I've done to the waiting room.'

She put the figurines on the mantelpiece at the station. Perhaps when MaryAnn had held her figurines as a tiny old lady they took her to a street or town or station like this, or plains of grass and a stone house or worn down mountains or mounds of saltbush burning and dust flying into the sky or plain misery or the day she left. Sometimes the meaning leaked out of things. On her own, Till rested her forehead against the cool window of the waiting room until she had taken in her likeness to everyone else, her own ordinary humanness.

'You've got yourself a job here, all right,' Ken said when he dropped around. 'You two.' He tapped the figurines in a matey way as if greeting old friends. He took in the walls, shook his head and sort of breathed through his clenched teeth. 'I didn't realise.'

'I think it's doable though, don't you?' Till brushed some sandy residue from a patch of repairs in a houseproud way, wanting it to present at its best. She didn't want to let down the station, or the town.

'Oh, yes, certainly is, I'm sure.'

'I've got these books and there's videos online. I'm making progress. See?' She pointed at a big patch to the right of the woodstove that she'd been working on.

'I do, I do. Winter'll be here before you know it, yep. Might need the electric put on.'

'I was wondering about that.'

He went closer to the worst wall, the one facing south, and poked a little with a finger as if he'd seen something. 'Tell you who you need? Stew. He'll know. Yep. He's your man.'

'Stew. Where would I find him?'

'That's the tricky bit. Not Stew, his wife Bev. She's not happy.'

'About?'

'Well, you and the station, I've heard. She's got things going on. It's not personal.'

It sounded personal.

'She can't throw you out. It's none of her business. I don't think the owner would mind. Not when you're making improvements.'

'I was wondering about looking into buying it maybe.'

'Oh yes?'

He came wandering around with her and he seemed to like what she'd done. She'd stripped and painted the wooden trim outside and put it back up. He gave a little nod of appreciation. Then they had tea and Anzac biscuits, which he pronounced delicious.

*

Till saw time rushing past in this town: buildings rising, bustling, thronging with people, emptying, failing, falling, and now here she was. She could see how it went. A roof collapse was a disaster. The railway closing was a disaster. Not a car had passed in all the time she'd been there. She could have napped in the middle of Main Street.

Dry grass, fallen tin, piled stone, dry water tanks, half-dead trees. A lizard, no, a snake, eased itself in the sun at the base of worn pickets, and the leaves rustled. 'Oh Birdy,' she said, holding her collar, and crossed the road and started back the other way. There was a handpainted sign over there that gave her a strange feeling. She hadn't yet crossed to it – stood in its presence, she meant.

It was opposite the arid zone botanic gardens, the children's playground installed following a fundraiser in 1982 and opened by local councillor A.S. Finch, near the First World War Memorial, next door to the blacksmith museum installation staffed by blonde-wigged shop dummies modelled on the actress Julie Christie, circa 1970 by the look. It was roughly painted on an old shed doorway, large enough to be read easily from the other side of the street:

BEAR
WAS FOUND HERE
ON 5–3–2016
HAVING BEEN
KILLED

The words were white, the wooden door black, and the weathered shed the colour of dried blood, none of the colours applied with density, so the writing seemed ghostly, like a drowning person straining towards light from the deep. It put her in mind of a creature she'd seen on a laneway fence in Brunswick.

Everything (apart from the information or testimony or warning; the sign had a little of all these things) about the town was older than Till, from before she was born and things began to go wrong. There was some power in the decay.

A text message arrived from George: *Sweetheart, dear Till, please tell us you are alive*

I am, yes I am . . .

Chapter 5

Brunswick 2019–2020

They named the time Black Summer later, even though it started in spring. Till broke up with her boyfriend the week the fires got going. (She wanted to take a break from singing, but he wanted his girlfriend to be the singer. She reflected better on him that way.) The dead birds and leaves and ash raining down, and the stench of incineration and the skies obscured, and the vision of the country become inferno and the animals become fuel swept thoughts of the boyfriend away. Soon she felt nothing for him, though she cried for the billions of creatures that died. She was not unusual in that. By summer her street had turned into a smoke filled canal with vehicles gliding through it like strange sea creatures. A dust storm of disintegrating farmland rained down two days in a row, turning houses, parks and roads into sepia landscapes. Everything wept tears of mud. Bushfire benefits were the last gigs she sang at for a year. She paused more than once during the final one to cough brown gunk from the depths of her lungs.

Pretty soon afterwards the arrival of the disease people had been fearing obliterated what remained of her life. You might not want to be reminded of this time, as I have heard people say, but I don't know how to ignore something that changed the way we all lived. It was like a firecracker fizzing about on the ground. It made us all jump.

Soon the fires began to seem like a story from a generation ago. Taken together, it was a time that made people uneasy. There was a flurry of movement as people decided where to ride it out. At such moments you want those around you to care whether you live or die. Till's landlord sold her house, and when she and her friends couldn't find anywhere new, Till moved home, back into her upstairs room overlooking the street. The four doors between the street and her room – screen door, front door, hall door, bedroom door – were reassuring, and there were bells on her bedroom door and windows 'just in case', as George liked to say.

Life shut down – no gigs, only a little music online, the world turned silent – and sometimes it seemed there was nothing to do but half-sleep through each day. What was the point in writing a song if she might die before anyone heard it? If she didn't write the song, she thought less about mortality; it was easier that way. She watched every episode of a survival series, including a Scandinavian one, in which they philosophised about the meaning of life and family and wept while inspecting their empty fishing nets. They were lonely and there were mosquitos. The US one was more triumphal. Till judged herself for finding it more entertaining and began reading Daniel Defoe's *A Journal of the Plague Year* as a corrective of some sort, though to what she could not say.

People had hardly changed in the last three hundred and sixty years. Some flouted quarantine orders and the other regulations like there was no tomorrow; they fibbed about being sick. While out on her daily walks, Till drafted letters to Daniel Defoe across the centuries. *Dear Mr Defoe, I write from the other side of the world and hundreds of years into the future with the news that people are much the same as they ever were in times of disease. They are still running around seeing friends, infecting other people and lying when they get caught.* Till found her one-sided correspondence with Mr Defoe soothing. 'So much for progress, Bird,' she said. Birdy opened an eye then went back to sleep.

People turned domestic, as if they were children playing a new game, which Till referred to privately as Apocalypse House. They signed up for online classes: yoga, drawing, singing, dancing, breadmaking. The whole world was making sourdough, or said they were, and since everyone was an expert now, they'd say tight crumb, nice crust, could have risen for longer, what flour do you use and so on in a chatty way, which people like to do, and perhaps also to say that they knew about this too. Obviously, people needed to know about breadmaking if the world was falling apart. You probably remember all this, and don't want to be reminded, which I understand, but I don't want to forget its weirdness. It was a time that effortlessly combined rage, tedium and dread, each feeling exacerbating rather than ameliorating the others.

Till ran before dawn, did weights in the garden, and pull-ups on a bar threaded through the grapevine until her arms trembled. Then she started on her punching bag. It was important to retain muscle and strength.

On Zoom meetings, Zoe and George said, people talked about the skill set they could offer a survivalist community if society collapsed.

Till flourished her toast. 'You can do bread, Mum. You're all set.'

'Everyone can.' Zoe had tired of breadmaking, and now Till bought it at an expensive artisanal bread shop in East Brunswick every three days. Standing in the bread queue was her big social outing.

Till said, 'Daniel Defoe says it's not making the bread that's the problem, it's the equipment. If you've got grain, you've got to grind it, and how do you cook it without a tin or an oven or a special hearthstone to bake on?'

Zoe recalled *The Long Winter*, a touchstone book of her childhood about a pioneer family and the winter of 1880–1881 when their town in South Dakota came close to starving. 'They ground wheat in a coffee grinder,' she said. 'They took turns, and at the end of the day there was enough for a small loaf of coarse bread. I could take the coffee grinder.' This was a hefty yellow enamel contraption, displayed on a kitchen shelf with a small yellow china bowl and a blue and white plate. Then George said he liked a nice wholemeal, and in this way survival became a wholesome culinary event.

'I suppose we'd take a generator and a camp oven and everything else,' Till said. 'You can probably order them online.' She could feel the romance leaking out of her plan; soon it would all be gone.

Years before when her parents were making an effort – or perhaps, it occurred to her now, just trying to do something fun and normal – they went camping by a river somewhere. Late in the evening a truck pulled up, opened its back doors, turned on a throbbing generator and began playing an action movie on a huge screen inside. A radiant block of light fell across the clustered family on their camp seats and the other people pausing in the background at this miraculous distraction until it diminished somewhere in the shadowy trees in the huge darkness under the stars, which were somewhat less bright now with the competition from the movie, and Till went to sleep in perfect peace to the sounds of gunfire, explosives and screams. She had been dreading bedtime – the thought of the gossamer-walled tent that even a very blunt fingernail might penetrate. Her childhood would have been easier, she felt, if she'd had a movie playing in her bedroom each night.

None of their plans seemed in keeping with the survival venture, but she doubted it would come to that. 'You could grow vegetables, Mum,' she said.

Zoe brightened. George reminded them that he had been very handy with a hammer in his time.

It was sad how useless they all were. 'The thing is,' Till said, 'you have to leave the city and set up the community before anyone gets sick. It's too late then, Daniel Defoe says. And then you have to cut off all contact, including with suppliers and workers. That means no tradies, no Bunnings. It will be the time when the guys – people, I mean – who are handy with hammers come into their own. That's you, Dad. Birdy can hunt rabbits and I'll sing to everyone around the campfire. I'll tell them stories of my perilous past. People always need entertainers.'

Zoe gave her such a look. 'Yes,' she said, 'yes they do,' and Till knew the incident-ette of earlier in the week had not been forgotten.

Each week, Zoe and her friend Adrienne Salvaris from further down the road did the shopping for elderly neighbours to save them from exposure to infection. They walked up the street to the supermarket where they worked their way through the small lists curled in their pockets (500 ml f.c. milk, 1 pkt Sctch Fings, sticky tp., smll sprd. but., 3 crts and so forth; it broke Till's heart to read them). Then they pilfered a shopping trolley and ran it home along the footpath. They could have used a car. No one would have cared. Till had seen them from the park. Birdy pranced at the sight and Maud the kelpie (still spry, though elderly now) ran to help them herd the trolley, yelping and snapping at its wheels. What a sideshow. Zoe and Adrienne were both cooped up. That was part of it. The truth was they liked to string the whole thing out.

Till and Birdy had come across them on Adrienne's front porch, a cane chair each, while they wiped down the groceries with sanitiser. They were laughing hard, flinging their heads back. Who did that these days? Adrienne was in her thirties and she was beautiful, with black Medusa hair that she wore in a huge clip. She smacked the arm of her chair, overcome. It gave Till a lift.

'Shopping days,' Adrienne almost shrieked. 'You're not taking shopping days from me, Zo. I live for them. When else am I going to get any me time? How sad is that?' She wiped her eyes. She and her partner Stella had three small children and none of them was cut out for home schooling.

Till leaned against the pickets. 'Sweetie,' her mother said, 'and Birdy. Hey Birdy.'

Birdy pricked her ears and pressed her nose to the palings, peering through with her small dark eyes.

'Sing us a song,' Adrienne said to Till.

'Oh, I don't think so.'

'Ah, I miss a live show. Go on, lovely.' But Till didn't go on, she froze right up. She hadn't sung for months – some bushfire fundraiser. What would you sing on someone's front porch, and what if people stopped to watch? It took time to become her performing self. She couldn't just do it, like that.

'Never mind,' Adrienne said but she didn't smile, just returned to wiping the jars and packets of noodles and tins and biscuits, the bags of crts, the apls, the bns and so on, but soberly.

'I couldn't live with myself if, you know . . .' Zoe said, to no one in particular, waving a packet around, trying to restore something, or conceal something that had departed. 'Imagine.' It was a point of pride with them that they kept the street in toilet paper.

'You need someone with some scrap in there,' Adrienne said. 'And let me tell you, has your mother got scrap.'

'I bet,' Till said.

'Be grateful,' Adrienne said. 'You're a lucky girl.'

'Yes.' Till nodded. 'I am a lucky lucky girl.' Adrienne looked at her, a lawyerly look, as if she'd noticed something Till hadn't meant her to.

'Okay,' Zoe said. 'I suppose that's it.' She bustled then, to distract. She was loyal in that way. Right now she was trying to ease things for Adrienne. She leaned forward to put the last of the things back in the bags, before dusting down her front and turning her face to the sun as if in satisfaction and pleasure.

But Till knew the signs. Sadness and some anger had arrived (why couldn't Till just be normal?) and Till wished she hadn't stopped. They'd looked carefree and she wanted to warm herself against that, but she had spoiled it and she knew that regret would cling for a while, along with the sadness. That sort of thing could not be rushed.

Small things expanded and occupied her mind, like the walk to the bread shop through the silent and empty streets, the terraces rising like the walls of abandoned canyons. A somnolence had settled over the city. It was like a long hibernation, like slow grand music, like that. They all had to listen to it. She liked to check out people's masks and sometimes their hats – someone in a black fedora one day. People queued in silence. They would not speak but they were not alone. On a still day a little warmth spread from them, and their warmth touched one another's warmth and in this way they felt less alone. She would never forget it.

Till spent her outside time walking in the parks. George was working from home. (He was a notable Arabist and in some demand as a negotiator, even in these online days.) Zoe began painting a mural on their back fence in between working. Till came out and watched. Zoe painted (flowers and trees and animals – whatever took her fancy) while she listened to music or press conferences, turning off at politicians she hated. The Salesman, she called one, and labelled the others: 'Crook, fraudster, minion, sycophant.' Maud roamed up and down, herding pigeons or pouncing on mice and rats slowed by poison. They crept along fence lines dazed and oblivious to danger. Further down, Adrienne was creating gardens against fences, leaving just enough room for cars to squeeze past, though who didn't park on the street these days, who cared.

Till and Birdy walked the lanes when the parks were busy – a strange, separate world, arcadian, weeds grown tall, butterflies drifting, fruit trees hanging over fences. Till made notes of things she saw: pigeons guarding each other while they took turns to bathe in puddles after rain, birds warning each other about Till and Birdy, dead rats, choko vines, a persimmon tree fought over by rival gangs of starlings and Indian mynas, fallen fruit, a dead dove, a stool against a fence, a milk crate containing old treasures, a drug dealer and his desperate client.

It was spring or a warm spell in autumn the first time she noticed this particular thing, in the first or fifth or second or third lockdown. The sun was shining, and perhaps there were leaves on trees, not the ground. That would mean late summer. (It wasn't all bad, that time, if you kept the picture very small.) Someone had painted a sad-faced staring-eyed creature on a metal fence, like Moominland's Groke, a creature of loneliness and darkness that kills the ground beneath her. Nothing will grow where she has paused. Was the Groke melancholy or malevolent? Maybe both. Till couldn't decide.

When I say that the sign about Bear made Till think of that image of the Groke in the almost exactly instantaneous simultaneous present–past, what I mean is that it seemed not graffiti, not picture, but message.

It was this, time blurring, even while it was happening, that she found hardest. And looking back how would she recall sequences? Would it matter when she had done something or thought something else? How were you supposed to remember when the world and all its markers had become untethered from life? Only a few months later people could hardly remember a thing they'd done in those years. Perhaps it would be like this: a picture there and gone, but waiting to reappear.

What I mean is life broke apart and I stopped noticing things and all the ways they connected. I should have paid attention.

Chapter 6

DROPPING IN AT Oldham's service station to pick things up and chat, was a cornerstone of Till's life just then. It helped hold her world together. She was building a life, not just a home. She didn't realise that. Mr Oldham's shy unfailing courtesy yielded to nothing. Sometimes he asked, 'Will that be all?' but not as if he was trying to increase his profits. Or he said, 'Would you like your docket?' (*Docket*, that old-fashioned word. Till loved it.)

The Shop, as Mr Oldham and Tundra called it, perfectly combined utility with aesthetics. Sometimes Till wandered up and down the aisles that stretched to the left of the counter just for the pleasure of it. She couldn't put names to most things. Just chewing gum on the counter, black rings in various sizes (what for?), tyres for . . . different things, oil, kerosene, turpentine (she loved the smell of turpentine, but she would look after her brain and not buy any), various tapes (duct, electrical, sticky), a section for screwdrivers and pliers and hammers and such. Also wire in different gauges.

Pigeonhole shelving, in a wood darkened with age and stained with the many things it had stored, was the majestic backdrop to the counter area. Compartments were filled with small useful things: rubber bands and a box of new navy blue pencils with red ends that said Oldham's Garage Second St Orroroo SA 5431, and some pencils in gold or silver that said Wagener's Motor Wreckers Parkside Adelaide SA 5063, tiny pots of paint – fire-engine red, sunflower yellow, sky blue, emerald green and so on – billiard chalk, wood files, folding rulers. She liked the smell of it most of all. It smelled of the useful things of the ages. Even thinking about these things was calming. They were the opposite of memory. It was not a trivial or superficial place.

'You all right?' Mr Oldham asked her once, early on.

'Yes,' Till said, the first couple of times. 'I like looking.'

Till consulted the expanding notes from her research into stonework repairs and building and restoration, and gathered tools – trowels, saws and chisels, brushes, hammers and levels, mallets, cement, and lengths of stout timber. There was always something she'd forgotten. Sometimes she only wanted one thing. She was not entirely sure what she was doing.

Mr Oldham said, 'You don't have to buy something every time. We like a chat. Bring your dog in next time.'

'Oh, I like a dog.' Tundra looked out to Till's car and Birdy panting out of the passenger seat window. 'Not too many of her sort around. We've got old Maggie here.' She nudged something at her foot. 'She's a good one.'

'I didn't know you had a dog,' Till said. She leaned over the counter where a little red kelpie lay on a mat. She flopped her tail in greeting and panted. 'What a sweetheart.'

'Well.'

That was how she realised a little of what they might think of her (that she was a sad case, too diffident?) and that they'd noticed Birdy waiting patiently in the car with her head leaning out. Summer was heating up, so that was good. Birdy came in and flopped on the cool concrete floor and waited for Till, and on a cool day Birdy and Maggie watched from the mat behind the counter in canine solidarity. Some dogs get on and some don't. In this way, they are not unlike people.

Children walked steadily along the road from town to highway each morning as if pulled by a piece of string. The school year must have started. There weren't many of them: five or six, in clean neat shorts, brightly coloured T-shirts and runners, and white deep-brimmed hats hanging on their backs by a cord. Each carried a backpack. One of the girls had long pale hair pulled back in a ponytail. One of the boys had dark curly hair. His best friend was a boy with orange fairy floss hair that almost fizzed in the light. Their shoulders bumped together in a friendly way, keeping each other's bearings in the world: *I'm here; you're not alone; s'okay.* They didn't even have to glance at each other to know. They just knew, walking along looking straight ahead, knowing that their friend was at their side. One day they played a game of stepping on each other's shoes and laughed and shoved whether or not they succeeded. Another day the biggest girl had a new netball that everyone envied. It bounced perfectly. She took the ball very seriously. All the others watched.

Till didn't look out for them, just noticed them walking around the time she was having a cup of tea on the platform, or from the ticket office window beneath the half-pulled blind, and craned her head to catch the last of them and noticed when they were gone. She hadn't seen them on the town playground on the empty main street, or in the botanic gardens on Main Street. There was a young woman with a pram and a toddler, and the five children, and that was all in the entire town as far as she knew. The children walked on their own.

A little dark-haired girl wore a red dress one day and that morning, Till crossed the tracks and went up West Street along the road parallel with the one the children walked from town to highway, and in that way, as they passed the front yards of houses and she passed the backs of the same houses, she was able to glimpse them through gardens and down the sides of houses, past sheds and hoarse dogs and the caryard, until her street ended at a corner, which she had either to turn onto or retreat from or stop at. She walked down a few metres. The children were heading for the highway and that made her run. What if they kept walking onto the road and a car or truck was passing and smashed them all? What if a car stopped and someone took them away and left people wondering forever? She stopped, her heart beating fast. She rubbed Birdy's head and Birdy swayed from her touch. It was a lot of children together. There was safety in that. Still, she ran to the corner of the road they were walking, Birdy gliding alongside, looking in the direction they'd faded towards.

There they were, drifting along like a dream in the morning light. And a small yellow bus came along – SCHOOL BUS written on its side – and slowed and stopped only a minute or so after the children had arrived at the highway – the timing was quite precise – and they climbed aboard and were gone. Till watched until the bus disappeared. They were safe but her heart pounded just the same.

All of Till's life then was parallel with the other lives around her. It was just sideways glimpses and wondering about what she saw, and it was parallel with her memories too.

*

Till developed a sort of routine – something even other people might recognise as a routine, I mean. About once a week she spoke with her parents. She told them what she could bear to tell them, and that wouldn't upset or worry them. She said she was staying in Wirowie 'for a while'. 'A while' could mean anything. She knew Zoe felt the humming vagueness in those words.

After a few weeks, she asked, 'What exactly does that mean, sweetheart?'

'Just what I said. I like it,' Till said. 'It's got a good feeling.' She knew it wouldn't satisfy.

'That's the way,' George said, which meant only that he was trying to be positive.

They told Till about Melbourne opening up and masks – whether people bothered with them or not, or if eating out was safe. It seemed strange to Till now, but she was politely interested.

Each morning after breakfast, she and Birdy ran Wirowie's perimeter: low houses of asbestos and brick mostly to the east of the station, with gardens that were hanging on, oleanders and couch lawns, hybrid tea roses and massive palm trees topped with fighting cockatoos, like they were the town's emblem. They ran all the way to the wrecked caryard and turned north and kept on for a kilometre or so, just running steadily. There was no rush. Everything was late summer dry, the sun well up by then, but she liked that. Birdy pounced at grasshoppers and rustling sounds. Till found a stick and began thumping the ground to send vibrations with some vague understanding that it might alert snakes to get out of their path. Once, she grabbed Birdy before she snatched a fat blue-tongue sunning itself, holding her collar and running her along until they were past. It was just a side road, with only a couple of houses and big empty yards of red dirt.

Sometimes she saw an oldish man sitting on his porch with a cup of tea. The first time he had gaped at the sight of them. She was surprised to see him too. Well, there was nothing wrong in what she was doing and too late to pretend she wasn't there. She raised a hand – 'Morning, mister' – and, startled, he had raised a hand in return. He was used to it now, just called out, 'Morning, young lady.'

She turned west, crossed Main Street and kept on. There was a low, scrubby rise and a street running along its base with houses facing the rise, which was lined at its base with a wire fence. She followed it south and part way along came to a large worn sign – SHOOTING RANGE – beside an immaculate lacework iron gate painted white with a latch, closed, and another sign:

PLEASE CLOSE GATE
WHEN SHOOTING
is in PROGRESS

The gate was closed. It was quiet. There was no one around that Till could see or hear, no shots being fired. She thought of the man and imagined him fleeing up the hill, stumbling, gunshot, and faltering – maybe pain. Till was not sure she could shoot him, but she did want him dead.

Once, when she was five, Till told her mother that a man said hello through the kindergarten fence. Zoe said, 'Did he? That was a funny thing to do,' and that was all. Close to twenty years later Till didn't know the words to describe what the man was like when he spoke, and how his attention had felt bad. Her mother didn't think anything of it. Not her fault – Till knew that now, and Annunciata had agreed that this was so. People don't pay attention to everything; they get distracted. Sometimes parents can't protect their child, or, not perceiving the danger, don't. They're just not expecting it, and also they don't want to live in a world in which they should be so careful. But she blamed her anyway as she blamed herself for not screaming the kindergarten down. Sometimes a friend doesn't know how to save a friend. The words didn't come out, much less a scream. They don't listen to the meaning behind the words. Her father didn't either. What else could Till have said? She had said the words she could find and nothing changed.

Till once had a teacher who squeezed children's arms or belittled them when their shoelaces came undone and no one said anything. Children were struck with straps of leather and rulers of different lengths and widths at Zoe's school. George would not speak about school at all.

If a person wanted you dead, then you might end up dead. Nothing you could do about it if they were truly determined. Chance might save you, but there was still the time after that when more chances and luck might be needed. This was what Till thought about heading back to the station. It seemed a distant possibility here. She liked the station, since arrival and departure were built into it. It held her there and set her free. Even if the town was as rotten as ships' timbers, the hulking silos held it steady and stopped it floating away.

*

Days of Innocence and Wonder

On a blazing day Till sat under the station veranda, Birdy at her side. The glare beyond the veranda was ferocious. The wind buffeted along, thrashing the grasses and palm trees. Fronds crashed to the ground from time to time. It was too hot for outside work, too hot for anything. Till had always loved this weather. Hot wind against her skin.

Ken ambled around the corner and up the platform, slowly. Birdy moved her tail and lifted her head and flopped back.

'Ken. Out on a day like this,' Till said.

He sank to the bench and pushed his hat back and wiped his face thoroughly with a large checked handkerchief. Till went and got him a glass of cold water – the luxury of a fridge. It hadn't been so hard to arrange electricity, after all. She wasn't used to it yet and she felt like she was offering him riches. They chatted about this and that – mostly the weather and when rain might be expected – but Ken seemed to be waiting to say something, even if he wasn't sure about saying it. He cleared his throat, cleared it again, and sipped his water, and finally spoke.

'I have to tell you something. Doesn't feel right not to.' He gave a quick, shy glance at Till, then stared at his beautifully polished boots. He was dapper in his way, in his soft white shirt and belted pants.

Till had such a feeling of dread.

'You know you mentioned maybe wanting to buy the station?' Ken said.

'Yes.'

'Well . . . I'm the owner. I should have told you. I realise that now. I'm sorry.'

It was like being winded. It was all going to end. Till knew it. 'Why didn't you say?'

'A young girl like you. A nice dog. I didn't think you'd be any trouble. I wouldn't have to say anything. It's not like you could wreck the joint. I try not to think about it too much. Makes me feel guilty, like I've let it down. It's just there, you know?' He saw her face and patted her arm quickly. 'Oh, don't you worry. I won't have you getting upset now. I'm not going to throw you out. My god. Why would I? You're doing all the hard work. It's looking good already. It's going to look great. I only bought it to stop the council knocking it down. People are fond of it around here. It's a bit of town history – wouldn't be the same without it.'

'It's beautiful,' Till said.

'What am I going to do with a station? And I only fenced it off because they were threatening to fine me. Public safety. Lord, some people just love rules. As if I care who goes exploring.'

'Hall monitors,' Till said, recovering slowly.

'Idiots,' Ken corrected. 'Excuse me. Councillors.'

'So . . .?' Till asked.

'As to buying, which I only mention because I'm not a young man. Wait long enough and you could have it for nothing through adverse possession. I looked into it. That's one option.'

'Doesn't seem very fair since you bought it.' She thought for a bit. Ken waited. 'And what if we had a fight and you threw me out?' Till said. 'I don't like the police around here. They would definitely not be on my side.'

'Police have never been my friends either. Anyway, you don't look like a fighter.'

'I am sometimes.' She couldn't help laughing, and he laughed too. She'd only met him a few times and already the thought of fighting with Ken was ridiculous.

'I'm thinking about how much you might worry. Are you a worrier?'

'Oh,' Till said. That terrible thing that happened to her sometimes, happened. Tears sprang into her eyes. She couldn't stop the rush of feeling. 'Yes. I am a worrier. I can't help it.'

'Had a feeling.' Ken nodded gravely and he did not smile or in any way act as if he thought her ridiculous. 'So. Are you looking to buy?'

'It depends,' Till said.

'On how much you can afford? I'm serious now. Don't go saying too much. You've got repairs, plumbing I'm guessing, and so on. I bought it, oh, years ago – not sure exactly when. Cheap in those days. There's stamp duty, but that shouldn't be too much. I have enough money. I don't need any more. But if it means something to you to pay, I understand that. You'd be doing something for me too though – something for you to consider. You'd be taking a weight off my mind, I don't mind telling you. I can see you're serious about it. You'll see it through. Thing is, everyone likes it but no one's got time for it.'

'Ken,' Till said. She blinked. 'It's too much.'

'Now, now.' He patted her arm again. 'One other thing. I've never told people I bought it. I'd prefer it kept that way. Less complicated.'

Chapter 7

THERE IS SOMETHING I should tell you – about Till and clothes, which might not seem important, but clothes always matter and always say something, especially if you don't dress like your family. Till wore black every day, only varying her sleeve length by the season.

When she moved out of home into an old terrace on Faraday Street, Zoe sometimes stopped in to see her. She, Zoe, spent sizeable sums of money to look like an aging bikie, in designer jeans and a cashmere tee and a cropped leather jacket with subtly stitched padding about elbows and shoulders and sides – all ready to protect her from any accident that might befall if she tripped while strolling off for a catchup over coffee – superb red curls, high cheekbones, that no-colour lipstick. That was the inner north for you. 'Down from the mean streets of Brunswick, Mum?' Till asked. It was that, or in summer perhaps something sculptural and Japanese in the bias cut and the soft drape, the uneven hem, the ravaged seams, the boiled finish, the dainty pleats. Artisanal ruin is expensive; people forget that.

Zoe's friends from the south and east more closely resembled bag ladies in their crumpled organic linens, peach cottons, raw silks, embroidered blends – the coarseness or less often the closeness of the weave signifying wealth if you knew the way to read it. Travel east across the gentle slopes of inner Melbourne into the strange low hills and winding roads of Hawthorn or Kew or even to their clinging outposts, say Surrey Hills, and on a warm day you would see white-linen-clad milkmaids drifting the footpaths like thistledown, while the activewear people mostly sat drinking coffee, an 'oodle at their sides before driving home in their European AWDs. The bikies (not the actual bikies) had working dogs, mostly kelpies, to show their ironical attachment to the real Australia. The cumulative effect was of a sumptuous coarseness, and collectively, if they congregated for a barbecue or end of year drinks, of some tribal summit, which it was in a way. It was possible to be an outsider even in your own city.

My point is this: clothes meant one thing to Zoe, which Till mostly succeeded in not judging, another thing to Till. (George dressed with quiet refinement, but with less interest than Zoe.)

'Oh, look, Till,' Zoe called from her office, one lockdown day or another. 'Look what I found.'

It was a photo of Till, taken from a scattered heap on her desk, and she held it out as if asking, *Do you remember when you were this person? Do you hear her calling you back?* And also, quieter, *I wish you were still this girl*, which she might not have known she was saying. But since she didn't say any of the words there was no need for Till to answer. And Till might have been wrong in her interpretation, or only partly right. Zoe might feel it without knowing; she might not think it at all. Till took the picture from her mother and looked at this stranger, this dear wee girl, as her grandmother used to call her. It was from early times, and she seemed unmarked and unguarded in the way she looked out at the world, as if from the tiny secure house that was herself, her wispy dark hair floating about her face, her bright red jumper. She wasn't laughing for anyone. She was being herself and no one was making her be otherwise. It was the last such picture.

The man had liked her jumper. He called her the Cherry Ripe girl. It was the way he said it. You don't wear a colour after something like that.

E liked brightly coloured clothes with spots and flowers, or perhaps her mother did. She had been a laughing woman. But Till thought it was E too. She was lively is what Till meant, and she loved attention. It was different for Till, they were different, and still they were friends, and they had made up their minds to getting married when they were grownups. There was no one else they would ever love more. They had decided together while making perfume out of mashed flower petals and water. It was a simple betrothal ceremony: they anointed each other with a dab of perfume and laughed. Till told her parents they were getting married one day and they told her about the law, which made them sad, but they said no one could stop them loving each other and living together if they wanted.

E had a red coat and it was on account of this, Till's memory of E in her bright coat in dark winter, and the thought of what the man had said, that made Till hide her jumper so no one could make her wear it again. A few weeks later her mother or father bought her a bright coat of her own, thinking to distract or cheer her up, Till supposed. Probably she had asked for one once because she liked E's. She screamed when her mother made her wear it. She, Zoe, said, 'Don't be so ridiculous, S—'

and said Till's name as it was then, which already she could not bear to hear. She screamed and Zoe shouted. The coat was too bright in the dank winter air; everyone would see her; it was like she was becoming E. Maybe it was why he'd noticed her. In the end they had to give it away. They stopped using Till's name because of the screaming. When she started school she wouldn't answer to it, though she had stopped screaming about it by then. Children like other children to have a name. It's hard to play games without one. It might have been around then that she first met Annunciata.

Till's clothes bent dark after this, even in summer, and although this was common in Melbourne, it was less common in children, and Zoe went on buying her pretty clothes and hoping Till would wear them. Even after Till's years of training, and feeling as if she could look after herself, she still wore black. It is hard to change the clothes you feel at ease in once habits have set; they become part of you.

Now, in the study, Zoe reached up to cup Till's face. 'I wish you'd wear something more cheerful, sweetheart. I'm sure you'd feel better for it.'

'I think you mean you would feel better,' Till said. She wasn't going to change. Black was the truth. She couldn't believe the photographs. She had worn pink jeans and red and white stripes. Flower hats, patterned leggings, a special top with a pompom trim that still made her mother sigh when she came across it in some cupboard. All these photos of her brightly dressed were in a box in the attic where they wouldn't startle. Very rarely one or other of them, Till or Zoe, would drift through them when they were looking for something else, even perhaps occasionally George, though how would they know. Whatever griefs he felt were private.

In the end Zoe gave Till a flowered handkerchief and Till kept it in her bag for years, and if she was frightened about a performance she would tuck it in an inside pocket. Till did not exactly picture anyone onstage with her keeping her safe, but she felt as she had once or twice before: as if she was sitting at someone's side on the front porch step, shoulders touching and pushing off each other, separating like magnets pulled, as if each was for the other a kind of shore, the idea of which made them safe. No one could stop that. But as to who it was, she didn't know.

Sometimes she wondered whether she and E would have kept on being friends, and if they would have gone to the same schools. Obviously what happened wasn't their fault. Till knew that and Zoe knew that. All the same, neither of them could help thinking that if one or the other of them had done something different things might have unfolded another way. Then Till and E might have split up in Year One over those small plastic ponies with nylon manes and tails or Tiny Teddies or one or other of them showing off too much in the other's view about those shoes with wheeled heels or heels that sparkled insanely on impact.

The car had wavered along like a hallucination, the window open, the hot air filling her mouth, drying her tongue until it was an unfamiliar leather-ish thing and she couldn't have said a word if she'd tried. Sometimes, less often, they drove at night and the shadows cast by moonlight flickered in the car, a mystery, and she heard her parents murmuring or silence and she thought there could be nothing better in this world. The car and the heat, the red roads flying away on either side, the distantly scattered postboxes, did not feel bereft, but pure as her own contentment.

There were a lot of road trips, tidal movements west for holidays, east for home, north-west for Zoe's research. The photographs in one album show a dark wisp (her own self) with wide eyes, so still and fixed of expression as to be almost doll-like. She wears a dark navy T-shirt. Zoe and George grin unnaturally on either side. Oh yes, they are having a wonderful time. Till didn't know if she remembered it or not. Maybe she never would. She was a stranger to herself.

When the people came to talk to Till after what happened, she couldn't tell them anything. She could hardly see him in her mind. He was grey, even his shoes, and indistinct. He had zippy shoes, she told them. He had – she touched her teeth. 'He had teeth?' someone asked. She nodded. 'What about his teeth?' The people were sitting on the little chairs and they looked so silly. They leaned towards her. It was rude to stare, everyone knew that. Till didn't tell them. Zoe and George were holding onto her. No one could take her. She waited for their chairs to break, but they didn't. Zoe said, 'You're such a good noticer, sweetheart. Anything you can think of.' Till had a feeling about his teeth, that was all. She didn't have any words for them. She didn't even have the words to say she couldn't explain them. She said, 'I don't know.'

Sometimes she felt as if her language developed so she could describe those teeth. They grew in her memory, jostling from his mouth, his bite wavering as if he might have been gnawing at thick wire to escape a paddock or grinding his teeth in fury at dead of night. What she meant to say to the people, what she would have said if she could, if she had the words that came to her fifteen or twenty years later, was that they were teeth of evil intent. She thought those teeth would be capable of biting something still living, that they would not flinch at movement, would grip harder. If teeth could be said to be the window of a person's soul, which Till knew they couldn't with greater clarity each year (since good teeth were a matter of luck, or wealth, or a healthy diet and good hygiene, or a family that valued dental care, or membership of a comprehensive health insurance scheme with dental extras), his soul was rotten, fissured and savage. His teeth, as I have said, grew larger in her memory, and when her mind flashed across them, as it still occasionally did after all these years, it was as if he was nothing but teeth.

They had never caught the man who took E. There had been two cases before some years apart, but none after. Every few years, media and the police speculated about reasons and appealed for help, to jog memories, George said. Overcome by remorse he had taken his own life; he had moved interstate or overseas; he was living in an isolated part of the country to remove himself from temptation; somewhere in the world he was in prison; or he had died in an accident or of natural causes. But there was not a sign or a word.

Till liked a song with a plaintive counterpoint, a deep undertow. E liked bright songs that made them dance. 'Let's go!' she'd scream when it was time to go outside, and they would go outside even if it was cold, first putting on their coats. E's was red. Years later when Till came across the word sassy, which was a word not really used in Australia, Till thought of E and her coat. Till tried to be something like that for E's sake – apart from the clothes – so that there was some of her, or something like her, in the world. Sometimes it was as if she and E were the same person. They did everything together; they had travelled the same paths for so long.

Afterwards, people said that Till, as she later became known, was only five and she would forget or adjust. Five years isn't so long in one way, but it is long when it's your whole life. A dream is like a ghost. Till didn't know the weight of a ghost until later. They get heavier. E's small hands, familiar, chill and not unfriendly, clung about her neck. (She knew they were not really there, but she felt them just the same.) No one could understand, and if she wanted to tell someone, how would she say it? Till's throat began closing at the thought. No, best just to go on.

Chapter 8

TILL AND KEN worked out a price for the station that they could both live with – much less than market value, but still more than Ken wanted – and ownership was transferred. Ken seemed relieved about it, in fact almost giddy when they signed the papers. He bought a bottle of champagne to celebrate and they drank it from mugs on the platform.

Till told George and Zoe.

'I see,' Zoe said. 'And what about your singing?' (As if Till was throwing over a stable career path.)

'I'm taking a break from it. I want to do this. I like it here. If I need to, I can catch a plane. We've got the internet. It's not Outer Mongolia.'

'Oh well,' George said doubtfully. 'If you feel it's right . . .' This was as close as he would ever get to criticism.

The conversation made Till feel feckless. She didn't exactly need a job yet – it wasn't an emergency – but her savings wouldn't last forever, and if she didn't have a job, life wasn't much different from lockdown, except that doing renovations was different from roaming streets and lanes and the internet. She went looking.

There was no work in Orroroo. In Peterborough, the

pharmacist in the peppermint green uniform – 'Sheila' her name tag said, which Till considered retro even for a rural area – looked at Till's black clothes and before Sheila had said a thing, Till could see she'd made an equal and opposite judgement about her. She was not a good fit.

The man at the pub just down the road said sure there was work for people willing to do the work. He rubbed his nose rather delicately on its side. Till took his deadpan gaze to mean that he had his doubts about her on that score, but was too polite to say so outright.

She would only diminish herself by begging or standing straighter or looking defiant. She said, 'I don't mind work, but I do have a dog. If you don't mind the dog, I don't mind the work.'

'A dog. You want the dog in here while you work?'

'It's not about want or not want. That is my condition for working here. I'm all she's got. I can't leave her.'

'It's my place. I set the rules.'

'Sure,' Till said. 'I understand.' She left. A breeze wafted up the street, and dust, a few dry leaves eddying on the ground making their sound, shifting trees above, high high blue sky, all dazzling after the stale air and darkness inside. Birdy had settled herself on the porch, paws hanging daintily over the edge. 'Hey Bird,' Till said, touching her with a gentle foot. Birdy lifted her head and began panting, showing her beautiful white teeth.

'This her?' It was the man from the pub.

Till nodded. 'Come on, Bird.'

'Bird?'

'Birdy. It's okay – I don't mind. I'll find something.'

'Job's yours. Start tomorrow.'

'What?'

'My mother had greyhounds.'

'How about that, Birdy?' Till said. 'You're my lucky girl.'

There was a small stage covered in thin red stair carpet to the side of the bar where Birdy curled on a small blanket while Till worked – three afternoons and evenings a week. At first Till took her for a stroll up the street during her dinner break; after a while one or two regulars who'd befriended her took over, one of them the wheezing motel keeper, Doug, whose motel she still showered at. Sometimes Birdy sat at their sides and they stroked her absently as they talked. 'Bird, Till,' they'd greet them on arrival, then 'Pat' to the owner. Pat said Birdy was good for business.

Rod swaggered in one night. He didn't see Till, or he ignored her. She didn't care which. She watched him repeat his performance on another young woman, who laughed and flicked her hair and was flattered by his attention. (Till had not been flattered, but she had enjoyed herself for a while.) When the woman went to the bathroom, Till followed. She showed her the photos of her bruises and mentioned the back door exit if she was interested. The woman decided she was. Till made up an A4-sized notice with a close-up of her bruises and a message – *Watch out for the policeman* – and put one on the back of each toilet cubicle.

A week later Rod turned up at the station to tell her to take the signs down. 'Think you're funny,' he said. Someone had told him.

'It wasn't a joke. Bad for business?' she asked. Casually, she took a picture of him and emailed it to herself.

'What was that for?'

'You seem the type to hold a grudge. If I'm wrong, no harm done. If I'm right, I've got a record you were here.'

He made a grab for the phone. 'Give me that.'

Till stepped back. 'Too late. I already sent it. Add it to the other pictures – all the bruises, your broken nose. I'll stick them on the police station door if I have to.'

It was Pat not Till who took the signs down. 'I'm sympathetic, but it's not worth the grief. Small town. Can't afford to piss off the police, love.' It didn't matter. She didn't see Rod there again. He might have felt some shame, though that was hard to imagine.

Still, she looked out for Rod in Wirowie – not wanting more of the same treatment, if that is what you're thinking – and on the roads, but there was no more trouble. It made her wonder whether he was less tough than he pretended or more disconcerted by her photographs than she thought.

Tundra was like still water. She had a little cap of dark hair, and laugh lines in her cheeks and about her eyes – visible when she was talking – but when it seemed no one was looking and she wasn't presenting herself for anyone, her expression settled into sadness, as if it was a deep pond she rested beside and drew something from that sustained her. Till waved at her from the door of the shop on Tuesday morning. Tundra was straightening one or two things down one of the aisles. She wore a sleeveless white shirt with scattered pink flowers and denim shorts that reached her knees, which seemed to be the fashion in town at that time, and a clean, ironed, pale-blue apron bordered with white rickrack braid tied about her waist. It had a big pocket in which she kept useful things, Till had observed – anything she needed or ever could need in this setting, and things Till had often needed herself: elastic bands, a hankie ironed into a perfect square, a pen and notebook, a pencil which she licked the end of before writing when she was checking stock. Sometimes she mistook the pen for the pencil and licked the inked end and looked about to see if anyone had seen and made a face if they had.

'You want Roy? He's just ducked out. He'll be back in a tick. Or can I help?'

'Just some chewie on the way past.' And when Tundra smiled in a way that seemed to be laughing at her a little, Till said, 'I *love* his shirts.' And she said it in a cute way, to disguise her affection. Immediately she knew Tundra would not like it, and she was right. Her face stilled. Till shook her head and was on the point of trying again, when Tundra spoke in a low steady voice, not angry, but clear and certain.

'You think I'm someone who fusses about my man's appearance, making sure no one can look down on us, on me? You think I'm an old-fashioned housewife, got something to prove? Fresh shirt, dinner on the table every night, lamb chops, potatoes and peas?'

'No,' Till burst out, thinking at least that question was answered. They were attached to each other. It was the way they didn't chat all the time but had an understanding and way of moving around each other and getting each other coffee or tea or found a pen for the other the moment they patted a pocket. She couldn't help noticing.

'Well, good.' Her hands rested comfortably on the counter. She was a measured person. She was sure of her place, and she wasn't flustered or angry, but she wanted to be clear. 'You don't know Roy. He is someone in this town, all around here. Ask anyone and they'll know him. Roy Oldham. You stay long enough you'll find out who. You can take my word on that. He surprises a lot of people. No need to make the same mistake others have.'

'I'm sorry,' Till said. 'I didn't mean how it sounded, however that was. About the shirts I meant . . . I mean they tell you something about him.'

'Oh yes, I suppose they do, that's true,' Tundra said and nodded slowly, as if now Till had surprised her. 'What do they say to you, if I might ask?'

'That you, that you' – she couldn't use the word love, though that is what she meant – 'you care about him.'

The woman lifted her eyes and rested her gaze on the fluorescent light above. Her mouth moved up at the corners in almost a smile.

'I mean he wears that shirt like armour, you know? It is the crease in the sleeves, like a reminder to people.' (What was she saying?) 'He is not on his own. He has you.' Till took some breaths. 'What he believes in is in that shirt. Looking right matters. You respect yourself, you respect everyone, and people give you attention and respect. His shirt reminds people you have his back. And I think' – and now she considered Tundra more closely – 'he is the same for you. People know you have him. Is it a warning too? That sounds weird. Sorry.'

Tundra rubbed her cheek a little and nodded. 'You've been paying attention.'

'I have to watch people,' Till said. 'It keeps me safe. Mostly.' They paused then, not exactly sizing each other up, since they had already done that. 'He is a person you would not like to disappoint.'

'Yes.' A heaviness came over Tundra then, drenching her face in sadness. 'That can happen. Not always easy for people. It's hard if a person's going through a weak patch. You know.'

Till didn't know, but nodded in agreement anyway, and said, 'But also, you are the fierce one. You are one to watch for too.'

'Oh, pet, I won't be coming for you.' She reached out and clasped Till's forearms and gave them an affectionate squeeze. 'No reason. You've got no harm in you, have you? None that I can see. He can be fierce too. Sometimes people forget that, or they haven't seen it yet.'

Till stopped herself crying with some rapid blinking – an old trick. 'No harm to you or Mr Oldham. I hope you don't mind that I visit.'

'Not at all.' She leaned closer and said confidentially, 'I might as well let you know Roy's taken a shine to you. He's keeping half an eye on you already. Don't tell him I said that.'

'I won't.'

'Okay.' Tundra inclined her head again. 'Roy worries about you, a girl on her own, "a nice little thing", he says, so you know.'

'I have Birdy. I'm not quite alone. But thank you.'

On the way home – what a thought that she had a home; perhaps it was the conversation that made it feel that way right now – she played over their words as if they were beautiful beads, familiar already but interesting anyway. Till liked that Tundra hadn't said things to cover silence or ask what Till watched for in people. Perhaps she had learned on her own that everyone was frightened of something. This was a theory of Till's. (She had some others, not relevant just then.) She didn't know if that was true. It was an awkward thing to ask every person she met. She had asked a few people and mostly they said spiders or drowning or broad beans (that was Zoe), usual things, but she couldn't imagine not being fearful. It would be a good feeling she presumed, if you were aware of it or had experience of true fear. She really couldn't imagine it. Even thinking about it reminded her of the things that terrified her.

She felt lighter for her conversation. It was as if she'd tethered herself to a piece of ground, and now she could look around, see what might be next, what she might like to do. She knew people. She might explore a bit more space in this world. If anyone asked her something about her morning, she could say she'd been down at Oldham's picking up a few things and they would know what she meant and look at her differently. They would feel that delicate line she had cast. What I mean is that Till began to feel as if she belonged a little.

She knew her way around the grid of streets of Wirowie: four running north-south, six running east-west, some lined with honey locusts which cast a scattered shade. She drove the length of Main Street's cavernous abandonment, and came to the general store, which had a sign out the front saying, 'New Coffee Machine!' And the door was open, which in a town like this felt like an event. The thought of a good coffee. Till and Birdy walked back and peered through the window, past community notices – *Vintage dragster approx. 1975, Floral Couch – Free! (Pick Up Only Third Avenue)* and a phone number, and others in a similar vein – then through the open door. A young woman with a lot of red hair wearing a yellow silk damask gown with a sweetheart neckline sat behind the counter. Till refused to remark on the woman's eccentricity, as she presumed it was – some blaring visual demand for attention. She had a proud, bitter, hurt air and, judging by her scowl, a filthy temper.

Till almost smiled, but that might be the end. She didn't know what end, only she didn't want it to arrive. 'I wondered about a coffee,' she said. 'A latte. Could I have a soy latte please?'

'A soy latte.' The woman might as well have said fool, interloper, nitwit.

'Yes, please.' Till glanced at the shining silver machine.

'No coffee. Machine's out of order.' She didn't say sorry about that or look in the slightest bit embarrassed.

'Oh. So the sign?'

'Kind of a joke around here.'

'Of course.'

'Hey, I didn't ask you to come in.'

Till looked around. She wanted to have come in for something, to have made that woman treat her like a person. Her hostility was inexplicable, and almost impressive. Long double-sided shelves ran down the middle of the shop floor and more shelves lined one wall, and deep bay windows stretched on either side of the inset door. In all of the shop, scattered in forlorn groups, orphaned in some way, there were three loaves of sliced white bread, an almost empty box of two-minute noodles, four family-size bottles of Coke and a few bottles of water in the fridge. Birdy snooped around, sniffing delicately.

The woman watched. 'Dogs are supposed to stay outside.'

'Oh, really?' Till said.

'Really. Hey, dog,' she called. Birdy ignored her.

'Her name's Birdy.'

'After the annoying singer?'

'After her whole name: Baronrath Midnight Blackbird. Birdy. Failed racer.'

She raised her eyebrows. 'Of course. Hey, Birdy,' she called in a sweet voice, and Birdy came over skittishly and rested her chin on the woman's lap. 'You know you shouldn't be in here,' but pretty soon she was crooning over her velvet ears, all the usual things.

Till took a bottle of water to the counter.

The woman said, 'I suppose you think I'm one of those quaint country town types pining for the city, like my name's, I don't know, Priscilla or Darlene.'

'I really don't mind what your name is.'

'Lucky me. It's Marian.'

'Till. I just came in for a bottle of water.'

'Coffee.'

'Right,' Till said. She paid with money she had withdrawn in Orroroo. Cash had become unfamiliar to Till and disgusting; she handled it with her fingertips.

She and Marian had a conversation in mime.

Till: deadpan, hands Marian a twenty dollar note.

Marian: delivers look: *You have got to be kidding, my god, how thoughtless can you be,* or perhaps, *city bitch.*

Till: impassive, waits.

Marian: rings it up on the cash register, drawer flings open, thrusts the twenty in, releases spring catch, pulls change from meagre reserves, slams drawer shut, delivers change.

'People like you,' Marian said.

'Like me?'

'I suppose you're from Melbourne or want to be. Everyone thinks you are.' And at Till's confusion added, 'Black clothes, city dog. Car rego. Pretty obvious. Word gets around about women like you.' She spoke in a bitter, contemptuous sort of way, as if she'd missed a chance in life or had regrets.

Till let her eyes move across the woman's dress. The woman looked like she might hurdle the counter and strike Till. The dress slithered. She wore it well, as well as it would be possible to in a small shop selling hardly a thing in a town with hardly a person.

Marian pulled at her shoulder straps and smoothed the dress over her hips. 'I lost a bet,' she said. 'What's your excuse? What's with all the black? 2020s goth revival for the end times? Someone die?'

'Oh,' Till said. She put a hand to the counter. 'A while ago. I can't wear colours.'

'Oh god. Shit.'

Till touched her forehead, which was cool and clammy, and it was as if her mother had put her hand there, right there, and it was a comfort, and she felt stronger.

'I'm sorry.'

'No, no,' Till said. She swatted her hand about in the air as if the thought of E was no more than a troublesome fly. 'Nothing,' she said vaguely. 'You didn't know.'

'Come sit down for a minute, come on.' So Till did sit down on a wooden stool Marian dragged out. 'Sorry I was such a bitch.'

'Nothing goes unnoticed around here, is that what you're saying?'

'Not exactly. We've all seen you around, don't worry about that. I mean, what are you doing here? No one moves here. What's going on with you and the station? A bit weird.'

'Yep, madness. I had to leave Melbourne, and I came here. And that's it really.'

'That's not it, is it though. No one comes here.'

'It kind of is in a way. I found it by accident and I liked

it. I like the roosters – and the cockatoos. I love this street.' She waved vaguely towards the windows and the emptiness beyond. A tumbleweed would not have surprised. Somehow the heat had gone out of their talk, as if they were friends coming to rights. 'Well,' Till said. 'Thanks.' She removed the lid from the water bottle, raised it in a sort of toast, 'Cheers.'

'Have you met Bev?'

'No.'

'You're about to.'

'You,' Bev said, coming in the door. She was a middle-aged woman, very square in her body and deep in her chest and with thin, very tanned legs. She was like a big Buff Orpington strutting around, scratching at doorways, pecking at people to make them jump. Till immediately placed her into one of her mother's categories of womanhood: top chook, which I will tell you about in a minute. She glared at Till, who honestly was ready to go home and contemplate her future.

'Hello,' Till said. 'I'm Till,' just trying to be pleasant.

'I know who you are. I know where you live. Who did you ask if that was okay? You needn't think it'll last. Missy.' Her words came out on a low even rhythm, and the final word was like a blow.

She ignored Till after that, bought some milk and left.

'Yeah,' Marian said. 'She can be tricky.'

Chapter 9

Brunswick 2020–2021

WHEN THE LEAVES had fallen, and where fence palings had broken or pulled away from posts as the timber warped and writhed free, Till peered further into people's back gardens all along the lanes. The place she thought had a lemon and a quince also had a fig, an olive, and an apple. Another place had a cherry tree behind the persimmon – something to remember for summer. But perhaps the owners of the garden would want them in a way they had not wanted the persimmons. She wondered if a time of hardship might come, and what might make people share their fruit. What might she do to get it? Would she climb fences in darkness while Birdy waited in the lane? She knew she would if she were desperate, even though she had never been desperate about food. Maybe she could run a guerrilla fruit supply system. She ate a persimmon once in a while through May and June, and a mandarin each day, until all the low-hanging fruit was gone, and took home lemons and oranges for her parents.

This was what her life had come to – the things she thought about these days. Was it any wonder she sometimes walked along and calmly said to no one or Birdy, 'Fucking hell, what is going on with the world?', which was not a usual thing for her.

And when Birdy looked at her as if wondering how to contribute to conversation, Till said, 'Thoughts, Birdy? Existential crisis at your end, by chance?' Birdy just walked on nobly, fossicked for lilly pillies and waited for Till's mood to blow over.

Sometimes in the winter of the first year – the second and longest lockdown: one hundred and twelve days – Till went into her mother's study for a change of scene. Everyone was drifting even if they were pretending to work. Often, Zoe was at her computer watching a sliver of the world play some shaving of the past, some different mind's eye: Tove Jansson dancing like a hobgoblin on a shadowed hill, that sort of thing. After some minutes, she roused herself and turned. 'Oh sweetheart, you're here. You're here.' Till didn't know what to say.

A chance descent down some internet rabbit hole that began with a tweet had led Till to black and white pictures of the last wild thylacine of Tasmania, shot and dying. They haunted her. Two photographs showed a young man in a hat of unfamiliar style worn at a jaunty backwards angle, just after he shot the creature in its shoulder. The photos are almost identical; the man, Wilf Batty, as he was called, is smiling in one, not the other, and the dog's posture has changed. Wilf Batty is holding his gun upright, kneeling beside the thylacine and grinning with satisfaction. He is triumphant. The caption says *Wilf Batty with last wild Thylacine*. In another posting of the same image the caption reads *Wilf Batty, the man who ended a species when he shot the last wild Thylacine in Tasmania 1930*. Till would like to delete that picture from the world so she wouldn't be able to remind herself of the detail, the many details. But she knew she would never forget them, photograph or no.

Wilf Batty cradles his dog, stopping it approaching the thylacine, which is leaning against the fence with a thin piece of rope holding it in place. Blood stains its left shoulder; its eyes are closed; there is a grimace on its face. She hopes it is dead, but she knows it isn't. The dog looks distressed too, leaning towards the last wild thylacine in one picture as if it wishes to give comfort, to sniff it with sensitive nose, to touch it with delicate tongue, to apologise for the man's uncivilised behaviour. The man holds him back quite tenderly, as if saying, *It's okay, buddy. I'm just going to torment this Tassie tiger a while longer, the last wild one ever, think of that.* Maybe the dog is hinting to his owner that he should do something. So there is no comfort for the thylacine anywhere, unless perhaps in the feel of the dead timber against its head, not even from the dog, whatever the dog might wish.

Another photo taken a short time before, she supposes, shows the thylacine half-lying on dirt amid building rubble or on some wasteland, waiting to die. Till pictures Wilf Batty catching sight of the perfect, lonely, hungry creature gliding along a fence line and grabbing his gun and shooting it. The background of the photo is filled with ravaged land: acre upon acre of tree stumps, the remains of the thylacine's home, the home of the things it would have eaten, so it was forced to come in close to this farm and its livestock, to chance its life for more life, to take back a little from all that had been stolen.

The thylacine holds its head forward and curving down, gasping for breath, or to ease the pain. It is almost done. It is waiting out these last pieces of life. Wilf Batty waits with it. He has vanquished this old foe, the stuff of legend already. What a king of this world he is, caught between the documentation of his shame and the documentation of his victory. He doesn't know that.

Zoe said, 'There is some madness in people. When they have destroyed almost everything, they have to keep going, just make sure they haven't spared a single thing. Kill it all so there's no reminder. Shame, cruelty and greed. It's a lust. They're so . . . thorough, you know. Wipe it all away so nothing can remind them. Cut down the trees, empty the sea.'

'People.'

'They say it's all in the past.'

'What? What's all in the past?' A dreadful rushing heat poured up Till's chest and up her neck and hit her cheeks. She shut her eyes and held her breath until she felt faint.

'Oh sweetheart,' her mother said, not seeing her state. That was the problem with stillness. 'I don't mean anything in particular. That we know better, all that. I mean just that computers and photographs and paintings mean the past is always here. We can see what other people saw.'

'It's different from where we are though. That thylacine was just a pest and a challenge then. It's time that's made us understand. But it was wrong, even then.'

Till left the room then. I mean, what was she supposed to say? Some things just were monstrous. Nothing, not time nor circumstance could excuse them. He watched the creature die in pain. He had the time to get a camera and record it. He was smiling. She would like to kill Wilf Batty. She would like that very much. And while he was dying she would explain to him the meaning of his suffering.

It was perhaps no wonder that one day during a lockdown – autumn, I think, a beautiful day – Till got in the car and drove west, to the end of the street, the outer limits of her suburb, the permitted five kilometre radius, Melbourne itself and finally the state border.

It seemed as if plenty of people had a way of persuading themselves that their small transgressions were of no great significance, or only what everyone else was doing anyway, or that the rules didn't matter or didn't apply to them or were stupid for any number of reasons, or that they had not broken them at all on the basis of some loophole or technicality. It seemed as if they thought they were exceptional in some way.

Till did not. She knew she was transgressing and she went ahead with it.

It might have been because of the thylacine, because of the photograph that had become fixed in her mind, because of the way it made her think about other people, men, teeth. Or it might have been the sadness of a father and son she had seen in the park, or just because she had been locked down for so long, but she wasn't on her own in that.

She did not care if she was caught and it might have been her unconcern at every passing car, including police cars, that left her unchallenged. How would anyone know she was doing the wrong thing? It was lovely but strange to just keep on, the traffic so sparse, everything quiet, and the birdsong when she finally stopped so clear, the magpies' call and response, call and response, listening to each other over great distances now in curiosity and wonderment, and the roads emptying the closer she got to the border until she could have driven down the middle of the highway for mile upon mile. It was as if the world had emptied, but in the most orderly pleasant way, as if people had walked joyously towards death or some other oblivion offstage, and it was all weird, as everything was now, but beautiful too. She had forgotten the feeling she has in a car. She is untouchable. It is almost euphoric.

She made up a story about going to stay with her grandmother to look after her at the beach and told it to the policeman at the border permit checkpoint. (Was that what they were called? Language rose up for that time and was already falling away.) He wrote her address in Melbourne, and her grandmother's address in South Australia. He made a joke about her 'Mexico plates' and watching out, how everyone would be looking out for them. The way he said it, it seemed like he meant the whole state. The police would be checking on her every single day, knocking on her door to make sure she was home and asking questions to make sure she never left during her quarantine, she shouldn't worry about that. Being flirtatious in a cop sort of way. 'Ha ha,' she said and kept going.

She had nothing but a container of water and some liver treats for Birdy, and a bag of carrots for the road. The carrots were a secret. She shouldn't even have had them because of the border restrictions. She would have eaten them all by the time she got to her grandmother's, but they were weighing on her mind along with other misgivings. If she stayed at her grandmother's, her grandmother would have to be in quarantine for two weeks too, meaning she would miss her refugee activism group and her book group and her other activities.

Till turned around and came back to Melbourne. She had driven more than a thousand kilometres, which, since the furthest she had driven for months was two kilometres to the bread shop on a rainy day, was something. She went to bed. Looking back later, it seemed like a sort of test flight: could she do it, and where would she go?

In the morning she looked up the picture of the man who shot the last wild thylacine. It was his teeth that she wanted to check. Was he smiling enough to show them in the way she saw them in her mind? Till could not bear these pictures, but she made herself look as a punishment for her failings. There was some mystery in them. The man was a monster, but also not a monster. The two facts were irreconcilable for Till and perhaps also for the man's dog. She tried to make them fit together so many times and always failed. What was the name of the dog, that good dog? She wanted to know that, and she wanted to tell Wilf Batty what she thought of him. It didn't matter how carefully Till looked at the pictures. She would never understand them.

It was about him, not the thylacine.

Chapter 10

Zoe's categories of womanhood included: the queen, the princess, good egg, sweetheart, heart of gold, hall monitor, netball type, head girl, sad sack, mean girl, outsider, life of the party, know-all. Some others. People were mostly mixtures of things. For instance, Bev was a top chook with a little hall monitor mixed in. This was not a desirable blend. Some types were seldom mentioned, though the categories were well understood and continued to exist. Zoe had trouble with queens; her sister Zuleika, mostly called Leiky, hated mean girls who pretended to be good eggs: 'The deceit!' For Till it was any hall monitor/netball type. They made her feel so low, even though she had a bit of mean girl in her if she was stressed. Best not to lie to herself. That made her feel low too.

Till had listened to many discussions between Zoe and Leiky about categorisations and people they knew: the differences between top chook and queen (top chooks had to keep asserting themselves; queens assumed their power); netball types were more contemptuous than mean girls; tragedy queens were performers, while sad sacks were introverts. That sort of thing. She had her own views on the matter, but Zoe's allegiance shifted to her sister when they were together and they fell into their old bickering laughing in-joke habits, and Till, on the outside, had to be careful.

Till once asked whether there were categories for men. Zoe and Leiky broke off their discussion and gave Till almost identical withering looks.

'First of all,' Leiky said, 'who cares. They can work it out for themselves. Second of all, not as interesting. I say that as someone attached to a pretentious sweetheart.'

'True,' Zoe said.

Sometimes they were like the same person split in two, except that one of them, Till's mother, tried to conceal that person from Till. Leiky was exhilarating, and frightening too, and not always likeable. (Till could almost hear Leiky saying, *As if I care*.)

'While you,' Leiky said to her sister, running her gaze over her, 'are married to . . . hmmm . . .'

'Kind of a workaholic sweetheart.'

'Yeah, probably the closest.'

'What am I then?' Till burst out.

'Sad princess, don't you think, Zo?' Leiky spoke so fast that Till knew she had wondered that very thing, had probably discussed it with her pretentious sweetheart Sebastian, christened Wayne, something Till only knew because she'd heard Zoe talking to George one night when she'd had a couple of drinks and was feeling waspish.

'Wayne . . .' she'd said with a whinnying drawn-out end, 'doesn't realise that Wayne would be so uncool that it would actually be cool by now, like a man named after a cat or a dog.' Maybe Waynes called their dogs Sebastian these days.

'Woops, sorry, Zo, said too much, I'll be going.' Leiky stood quickly, pulled her floaty kimono-wrap thing about her, swept up her exceptionally beautiful battered bag, and blew them both kisses. 'You two,' she said, 'if you knew how alike you look in this minute, all your feathers puffed up. Don't think I didn't see what you were thinking, princess,' and she tossed her head. 'Pretentious, moi?' And she fluttered her fingers above her head as she swept away.

'Who even tosses their head?' Till said.

'Or flutters her fingers. She's ridiculous,' Zoe said wistfully. 'It's because of her name. *Zuleika*.' Her voice became affected.

'*Zoe*,' Till said, in the same voice.

'*Till*,' Zoe said in a mocking way.

They stared at each other and their wild gazes flung aside. Till blushed. Zoe stared fixedly at nothing at all.

Where was it from, that stupid name? Well, she knew. What had she done to her parents? Her mother had been ashamed of her. Oh god – how to stop this.

'She is completely ridiculous,' Till said, stepping over her own name and her mother's mockery. On the spot, she invented a new type for Leiky: aging babe – life of the party. Slight affection rekindled in her at the thought. She wouldn't forgive Leiky for what she'd said, not for a bit – even if she was right, even if being sad was less amusing than it sounded – it would take longer for her mother. All that energy she expended on thinking about keeping Till safe and not knowing how to do it, especially when she seemed to court danger, to seek it out, to dare it to come at her again.

Criticism of each other's daughters had always been off-limits. It was too dangerous. It would take a couple of weeks silence and no one saying a thing by way of apology or understanding to brush it over.

They – Zoe and Zuleika – might have been a planetary

system. It wasn't that Till disliked their orbit, but she didn't want to become part of it – she was too young for that; she wanted to be herself.

Each afternoon Till prepared for the night to come. It was one of her chores, like bringing in the washing from the line she'd hung from water tank to wood shed. She filled the wood box with whatever was lacking: big pieces of log and smaller branches, and even some kindling to get the fire going again without needing to go outside if by chance it burned out. A chair and a quilt drawn up to the fire and Birdy warmly wrapped at her feet and a lamp and a book kept her safe. Even a sad book could be a comfort. Why was that?

The light – blue and thick – folded around everything and came from everything, as if darkness itself had revealed it, paler at the ticket office window in the room that by habit had become her bedroom. She had not decided, only seen at once that the configuration of window and hidden corner beneath and to the side of the deep counter window and its cantilever shelf and heavy door and the big box lock with its great latch made it safe; animals know the safest place, the place they can hide in the corner of, shelter beneath, and kick out or bare their teeth and snap from. There was Birdy before the fire and a massive door to the outside, the locks on the wire fencing in place. These things were second nature to her; perhaps they were to everyone. Now, in Wirowie, she lay still at night and replayed her evening movements from room to room and window to window around the station, making sure each component, each joint, each crack in her fortress was locked and shut tight. Birdy paced the building with her like a chatelaine with her keys.

Days of Innocence and Wonder

Till watched a young girl on the news holding her big dog afloat on floodwater and a father tying his daughter's hair back, maybe for the last time, he and his wife not meeting each other's eyes, and then waiting for his train to leave for war, his hands over his eyes. This was the world now – tiny images on her small phone, as if seen through a telescope. There was nowhere safe. She might as well accept it, since it was actual, not only a state of mind. And her parents, the helpless soft things. With their ineptitude anything could have happened to Till, which meant that anything could happen in the future and now she was in that future, and she couldn't shake the thought that things were coming at her. She was as prepared as she could be. If things got very bad and she started shaking, she turned the light on, but this made everything else, especially the outside, darker and she was careful not to look towards the window. She had to stay awake after that.

Sunrise was her favourite time in the world; it was hours until she had to worry about night. She let Birdy out for a wander and pottered up to the end of the platform and back again – the release of it, the grass brushing her legs, the chill, the pink light spreading. Oh it was beautiful. And now looking at this pure place and the untouched light she saw how ridiculous her night terrors were. Here was her shelter, her home, the station, the stairs down to the tracks, the paddock grasses creeping closer, creeping down the line, the soft morning sounds – roosters for god's sake – and later a few early people coughing in backyards while they had their first cigarette. There was no badness here. She'd go back to bed and sleep and sleep as if she'd been felled. She'd survived again. She should be used to it.

*

Sometimes she wondered whether she'd taken up singing when she was at school because going out singing took up so much of the night; she had people around her talking and laughing and there was noise all the time, not all of her own making. Sometimes she grew weary of that. Some nights she wasn't home until three or four. Only two hours until dawn in summer. They were good times from that point of view.

Tundra and Mr Oldham offered Till some work. They weren't as young as they used to be, they said, and since they cared for their grandson some of the time it would give them some flexibility. Till didn't altogether believe them. It sounded rehearsed. They didn't look at each other when they spoke and Tundra's casualness did not quite ring true. It was the way they looked at her, as if they saw something she didn't intend and in fact tried to conceal. She said yes. They were good people flinging the cloak of their shelter around her. She found this out the minute she was permitted behind the counter; the place ran like clockwork.

'I think you're being kind,' Till said to Tundra after the first day.

'He worries about you.'

'I can look after myself.'

'You need a few good people around you in any town. We're okay for a few years yet, me and the old feller. He's a good one. You want one, if you're that way inclined. Not my business and I am not asking.'

Till regarded her steadily.

'I might have heard one or two things.'

'Oh,' Till said.

'Now, pet. Just taking an interest. Not a bad thing, not from my end. I don't spread news. News, information, comes my way and that's where it stops.' She puckered and zipped her mouth, and winked.

'You two are dangerous.'

'Tell me,' Tundra said, and threw back her head and laughed. She became serious then. 'Word of advice. There's a policeman in Peterborough had a broken nose. I make no comment about any of that, the part you might have played. You're not the first to be fooled by him. Oh no, pet. Not the first by quite a mile. Tread carefully. The law doesn't look after us all. Sometimes we have to make our own justice.'

Till had worked that out already.

She began to see that their kindness had another reason, which was to tell people thereabouts that she had Tundra and Mr Oldham's support, that they approved her, that people should treat her well, though it might have been coincidence that people began chatting to her outside the shop as well as in. It might be that they had seen her around enough times for her to have become familiar, or familiar enough at least. Mr Oldham and Tundra embodied something that Till felt should be aspired to, which was about a refinement of human spirit and way of being in and approaching the world. She felt foolish thinking something so sincerely, but it is what she thought.

In Peterborough one day, walking beneath the shop verandas, Birdy loping alongside, a weathered man called out, 'Greyhound lady, ay? Heard of you. People talking about you.'

'Oh really?' She looked around, uneasy.

'Can't trust 'em.' He nodded at Birdy.

'She's on a lead.'

'Chase a sheep to ground. Worry 'em to death, tear out their throats.'

'Well.' And she gave a long pause before she said, mildly, 'I haven't seen any sheep around, except you know, a long way down the road.' She thumbed south. 'And she's not running free.' She waggled the lead at him. Birdy regarded him.

He stared at Till, looking through her city way of pretending to be pleasant with an undercurrent of sarcasm and she was suddenly ashamed. It was not far from her old boyfriend's ways.

'Like stopping a steam train. Can't stop a greyhound, love, not when they get going. She's not always this dainty lady, is she?' Birdy chose this moment to lean against him. His hand dropped to her head and began stroking. 'Well, you like that, don't you?' he said.

Till waited a moment. 'Tell you what, you see her chasing a sheep up the street, drop in at the pub, let me know, and the beer's on me.'

'Heh heh.' His chuckle stirred up his lungs and he coughed, about to spit, and looked at Till and stopped himself. 'I'll hold you to it, mind.'

'Wouldn't expect you not to.'

'And I'll see you again, little miss,' he said to Birdy.

The woman at the coffee shop in Ororoo got chatty and remembered her order and asked her to say hi to Roy and Tundra. It was just little things, people smiling, things like that.

*

On Monday morning the shop had hardly opened when Bev came in looking for a screwdriver for the back of her fridge. A rat or mouse had electrocuted itself in its workings.

'Stinking up the place like the dickens,' Bev said. Tundra disappeared down an aisle to look. Bev stared at Till, arms folded across her front. 'Didn't expect to see you here.'

'It's my job.'

'Not because I don't keep a clean home, don't go thinking that,' Bev said.

'How would I even know?' Till said.

'Taking over this town too? Does Tundra know what you're up to?'

'I'm not up to anything.'

'Does she know about the mess you're making of the station? Ruining it? Have you told her that?' Her voice was shrill.

'She knows I live there. I never hid it. She and Roy don't mind.'

'It's not up to them to mind. They don't live there anymore.'

Tundra came back. She put a hand on Till's back, resting it there for a moment. It felt warm. 'Haven't got it, Bev, but I can order it in, no trouble.'

Bev flung her arms up, a hand on either side of her head, and said, 'Oh my god, I can't wait for that, Tundra, I'm a busy woman.' And she stamped back out on stiff legs, throwing out her toes at each step like she wanted to kick someone.

Till and Tundra watched. 'Don't criticise what you don't understand,' Tundra said.

'I didn't,' Till said.

Tundra shook her head, maybe a centimetre one way, the same the other. 'She's got things in her life you wouldn't know, couldn't guess. True of a lot of people.'

'Sorry.'

'No need. The way she is, the way she was then, that's not about you. You were just in her path. You have things in your life you don't talk about. Not my business to ask why.' Her hands moved about on the counter, putting a stray pencil in a jar, wiping the cash register with a dusting cloth she kept for that purpose under the counter. 'The dust today,' she said. 'I'm not asking. You've got your own reasons for moving all the way out here.' She did not look at Till directly.

'Thank you.' Till looked out of the shop door at a car rolling up the street, a little dust flying in its wake, a man shepherding children along the footpath opposite in the shade of the veranda, at a woman and her heeler crossing the road together. 'I'm not asking you either.' She regretted the burst of anger immediately. What business of Till's was Tundra's sadness? Tundra might have no more idea of her sadness than Till did of how she might seem to others. People are often mysteries to themselves, I have observed.

'Excuse me?' And then a little louder, 'Excuse me?' Tundra grasped Till's arm firmly, not enough to hurt, but hard anyway.

'Yes?'

'I see.' She let go of Till's arm. 'You don't know the first thing about this place.' It was as if she'd shut a door in Till's face. 'That'll be all for today. I'll give you a call.' She just stared ahead. She might as well have said, *We don't need you. We never did.*

Till had felt like this once during an earthquake during some lockdown, when all the things she believed solid started shaking, something she felt as much as saw: pictures bouncing and rocking on walls, which were also bouncing, the whole house rattling and thrumming under her feet. She stood there, still, wondering what to do and then it was over and she was wondering what she should have done. Her heart was beating hard.

'Come on, Birdy,' she whispered, and they left, walking around the corner, past the car, down the road. An effect of light spots swarmed in her eyes, like snow, though it was a hot hard day already. She felt almost faint and had to lie down, and Birdy sat at her side looking around like a good guard dog. After a while Till's eyes cleared and she felt steadier. When they came back and got in the car, Till's face in the mirror was white. 'What was that, Birdy?'

Birdy panted and lolled her head out of the window. Till stroked her shoulder and they started for home. Well, she had savings, she could manage. Leaving was a possibility, but she couldn't leave her station. It was hers, whatever Bev thought about it. There were other towns around, other jobs, other people. But she liked these people – maybe not Bev.

She mouthed these words: *I am here, I am here*. She was a city person and she'd moved to a ghost town, and the thought would not become more solid than that. But she felt more solid, like herself she supposed, though unfamiliar, not a person in a costume. The sad growling anger that was part of her had moved off a little way, at least some of the time. She would not easily leave a place that had done that.

Chapter 11

IT WAS AUTUMN now and the growing part of the year was done. Veils of dew fell after sunset and lifted slowly at dawn.

It was never truly quiet. There was wind around buildings and trees, skittering sounds on the roof or outside – but light-footed things that couldn't be dangerous – and all the birds grown familiar now. She knew this place, and other people, visitors, did not. At night, if she peered around the doorway from her bed, Birdy would be in her fireside bed. Birdy knew how things were in the world outside. She pricked her ears, no more than that, and rolled on her back along the edge of her bed, her paws in the air, her teeth shining in the dark, and Till was able to lie down again, and after some time, sleep. She even slept until it was growing light outside. She wouldn't have done that since she was five, she supposed, unless drunk. That didn't count.

An engine noise was something else though, and the roar from outside on Saturday morning was enormous. Birdy was standing at the door waving her tail and looking back at Till.

'What the hell?' Till pulled on her dressing-gown, shoved the hair off her face into a clip and opened the doors.

A man was on the tracks further up, facing up the line,

his back to her, clearing the lines with a whipper snipper. He pivoted in easy arcs – beautiful sweeps of movement like a scytheman of old. Stones flew and whacked into the platform's sides. The dry grass, fine and white, lifted and fell obediently around him, mashed and ruined. The noise was tremendous. A blue-grey smoke and a smell of burned petrol and singed grass drifted. He had dark hair and a strong back and beautiful arms, which stood out to good effect against his sleeveless shirt. He dressed as if he didn't care about the way he dressed or the way people saw him. Jeans and the shirt, rough boots, nothing unusual. She watched for a few minutes.

Nothing in her life had equipped her for this moment, a stranger with nice arms taking matters into his hands on her railway track (as she called it) outside her railway station (as the few people in town mostly seemed to acknowledge these days, by their shy nods and half-lifted hands) just after sunrise. 'Hey,' she yelled, abandoning nonchalance.

He didn't hear. He was moving off along the lines away from her, swaying slowly, rhythmically, with purpose, as if he understood the size of the job and wasn't going to dwell too much on exactitude.

'What the hell?' she yelled again. 'Hey, buddy.' Birdy looked at her and waved her tail and looked back at the man.

Till went inside and got the fire going, filled the kettle and put it on the camp stove to boil, watered the geraniums on the platform – they were flowering nicely. And still he didn't turn. A tree growing out of a fissure in the platform halfway up was doing well. She sprinkled some water on that too. The metaphor tree, as she thought of it; they were both putting down roots. A whipper snipper wasn't going to scare her away. The noise though.

Soon she was sitting in the sun in her sheepskin jacket, a cup of tea in hand with Birdy at her side. The man was well up the line by then, as measured as a machine. He paused three times to remove his hat, swipe a cloth first across his forehead and then across the back of his neck. Till wondered about rushing to give him a drink. *No one likes a try-hard, Till.* Someone should be there reminding her of that. Let it go, she thought. It was an effort, though, to do that. She wouldn't lie to herself. When, finally, the noise stopped, the silence was stunning. Someone from the railway, someone from the council, fire hazard maybe, fuel reduction. Anyway, it was done. She would have offered him a cup of tea; she wouldn't have minded doing that, if he'd passed back this way.

Till strolled up to the end of the station platform. She wasn't looking for him exactly, just checking whether he was still there. He wasn't. He had left a mess of silvered grass fallen up and down the line and had then departed as if it meant nothing, or its meaning was self-evident. The grass was there, it had to be mown, that was all. The stupidity of this sort of activity, the ugliness of the result. She hated disliking someone so quickly. It looked sparse and scrawny like that, and its stillness was troubling. The tracks appeared lower now, more like a canyon carved deep, the platforms like riverbanks. She stood on the edge, the platform's grasses and wildflowers brushing her legs in the wind, not quite calming. It was different now and not hers, and everything was uncertain again. Should she do something about it, gather it up, pile it up or just leave it there? Get a rake maybe and start on it to make clear her claim on this place? And what if he came back and did the same to the platform, cut her beautiful meadow? What if he was from the council? What if Bev had made a complaint about the state of the line or the station or the fencing? Anyway, she was getting proper locks. The fencing's days were numbered.

She looked over her home as fairly as she could when she got back, which was not very, since she loved it. She'd been feeling low since the argument with Tundra and it showed. Inside the waiting room a few stones had fallen earlier in the week and she'd done nothing more than stack them against a wall. It was cold at night and days would soon follow. The only place to get warm was against the fire. Birdy was sleeping in her bumblebee costume on a furry blanket. Wind had its way everywhere. That soft golden dust was drifting again into corners and coating papers and pamphlets blown from shelves and had even driven into the cloakroom. She picked up a pamphlet: *Book your weekend in Adelaide!*

She went to work at the pub. In the evening she watched videos on her phone and took notes and photographs as if she was preparing to write an essay. She'd closed over quite a few holes already. It was doors and windows that were more difficult. It was like a test: if the station stayed up and provided proper shelter she would get through the winter (and maybe also life) unscathed.

It wasn't quite true that he came out of nowhere. He was there one day ruining her meadow, then gone, and another day he was there again, arriving slowly this time, on one of those old vehicles for railway workers, sitting up high with a skinny boy at his side. The kid was alert as a rabbit dog, imperious as a king. And the man who had come and gone sat there too, leaning easy on his seat, the breeze flattening his old shirt to his chest. Till stepped out and walked forward, as if this was the very train she'd been waiting for. She had places to go. She wasn't going to miss him again.

The vehicle was small and moved in a gliding way on the tracks through the dry and flattened grass, making a faint rhythmic squeak. The man and the boy pumped a bar up and down and this propelled the machine. 'Nearly there,' the man called out, and gave a little cry of encouragement. The boy's dark hair hung across his face, which was set to determined. He was breathing hard, and it seemed like he didn't have time for trivial matters of enjoyment or triumph. But at the sight of the platform his face lit up and he punched the air. What a grin. Till couldn't help smiling and even waving. She was pretty sure he was one of the kids who caught the school bus, the one with the red-headed friend. They looked surprised at the sight of her, pausing and then continuing, but slower. Birdy got excited and galloped up the platform, turning when she reached them and cantering back down, her legs and tongue flailing. They called out to her and hearing their friendliness she calmed down, and they all slowed together and arrived at Till's side.

'Hey,' Till said, which the boy ignored. He might have been eight or nine, a skinny kid with curly dark hair, nice-looking, but not happy, at least not now. 'You,' she said to the man, his dad she supposed. He had on a shirt of faded blue with sleeves roughly rolled, and the same hat and the same worn boots, so it seemed almost like the same day as when he mowed and this made him seem familiar. He had a strong face, wide eyes, and from the way his face settled it seemed as if he was predisposed to get the most out of life, as if he went out towards it with hopeful expectation. Of course, Till did not exactly think that at the time but that was the interpretation she settled on, that seemed to best fit.

'Me?' The man touched his chest – like: *I don't know you* – but he almost smiled saying it, as if he was already looking forward to the next thing, and his eyes were bright, waiting, as if they were sharing some familiar joke.

'You're the mowing guy, right? From last week?'

'Right. You saw that? Is this your place now? No one said.' He wasn't happy about it, not mad either, perhaps disappointed. 'I never thought anyone would move in.' His eye moved along a section of wall that Till had repaired, taking in the change. 'I've been thinking about it myself for a long time. Great building, hey.' Maybe he was regretting he hadn't put his stamp on it first.

'I'm sorry,' Till said, though she was not really – not at all, except that he seemed disappointed. 'I only just bought it.'

'Ah,' the man said.

The boy glared at Till, and she could see how in his mind this was their place, his and the man's. There were all these worlds around that no one could see. The boy glanced at the man – what were they going to do now? – and then at Birdy, his face going soft. She was waving her tail and he reached a hand out almost despite himself and Birdy reached her nose out, as if they were in a Michelangelo fresco, across the chasm between them. Zap.

'It *was* looking better. I thought there'd been a working bee or something.'

'One woman working bee.'

'Right.'

'You can come up if you want, survey the estate.' She swept her arm around the platform, the water tank, the peppercorn tree and the station. Even the silos, though in her mind they weren't really her domain. 'Of course, you can come up any time you like. I don't mind. Maybe you'd like a drink and some biscuits? Meet Birdy? This is Birdy.' Now that there were people here she couldn't stop talking.

'Birdy,' the boy said. 'Hey Birdy.' Birdy reached towards him again.

'Well, thank you,' the man said. 'Okay with you?' he asked the boy, who shrugged.

But the boy climbed up to the platform, Birdy bowing her front low and wagging her tail and skittering around him.

'You're being a goose, Birdy,' Till said.

Somehow Birdy broke through the boy's delicate hostility. Till dragged another chair from the waiting room onto the platform and they had afternoon tea in the sun, chatting politely about plastering and whitewashing stonework in interiors, which the man knew nothing about and she only a little, purely through research and trial and error. She was having trouble with the stonework. 'It's like a puzzle, looking around the stones and trying to work out where they went. And they break. Yeah . . .' she trailed off.

The boy, Isaac, went roaming with Birdy up the platform and back and inside the station and out. He had a skittish way about him and was quiet around her. She spoke to him once or twice – you like dogs, nice day to be out with your dad, things like that – but he only stared and went off exploring again.

The man, Ed, just said to him, 'Careful in there. It's not ours, remember?' and let him be.

'Nice kid,' Till said.

Ed nodded. 'He's great. I'm not his dad. Had some things happening in his life. A long story. Another time.'

Another time . . . She couldn't tell if the lift she felt was because of this man or because it was a sign of a connection with this place or because Isaac wasn't really his responsibility. He was something though. She could tell from the way they were together, the boy trusting Ed, Ed keeping a close eye on Isaac, not quite sure of what he might do. All those connections between people – what they meant, what they did. She hadn't thought of them being necessary. Being an interloper and thinking of herself as an interloper was no way forward. An interloper arrived and departed without pause or much effect. People like that made people uneasy, made them cautious. There is no way of anticipating the actions of someone who no one knows.

Isaac came back after a while, leaning against the arm of Ed's chair, picking at a loose piece of wicker, and when it broke free, snapping it apart.

Getting the handcar going and clearing the track had been a weekend project for a long time. It was something they did together, Ed said. 'Isn't that right, buddy?' Isaac nodded, and Till could see the pride in him. There were only a couple of sections of track left. The lines had been dug up and sold for scrap when people began to leave. There weren't enough customers or goods to support the railway. Till had read about it. The other end of this line was some kilometres off to the north. She didn't know exactly where and didn't want to. She wanted it to go forever, to head through the Flinders Ranges and the Northern Territory; she wouldn't mind if the tracks slid into the Timor Sea and passengers ended up looking out at saltwater crocs nosing about their windows. In her mind it went at least to Alice Springs and maybe further, and the same went for the south where it stopped in Burra perhaps, the most important meeting place for Tundra's people, she told her later. Till thought about trains and railways, arrival and departure, the way the buildings kept you safe and gave shelter for as long as a person needed.

Chapter 12

TILL'S PHONE RANG.

'You're late. Thirty-five minutes late.' Tundra didn't bother saying who it was and Till didn't need her to.

'You told me to leave.'

'Didn't tell you not to come back.'

'You said you'd ring,' Till said.

'Well I did, I am now. You're late.'

When she arrived at the shop Tundra started speaking as if they hadn't stopped. 'There's things that have happened around here you can't fathom. Towns run deep. All towns run deep. Where you come from too, am I right? People run deep. Groups of people go miles underground, a long way, into the past in all directions – you get me?' Her look said, *Do you know who I am in this town?*

And Till looked at her, trying to conceal her thoughts, which if they were put into words would be something like: *Do you even comprehend the size of this town? Do you know what town I am from? Do you know I am someone?* But Till's point was weak, because of the nature of Tundra. If you're the queen of anywhere, you're the queen. Till had seen how people spoke to Tundra, how they listened to her and valued her and sometimes took her advice. A man might say he was having troubles with his son, and she might tell them to give their son some room and they'd probably come round, that sort of thing, and it would seem as though they'd arrived at some way forward together and things might go better for them after that. Till understood about respect, but that didn't mean she needed to be a doormat. What did it matter really if Tundra gave her a look? She could survive that. She had neither to curtsy nor to run. She could just be, and see how that went, see what Tundra said. So she stood there, straight, but not as a challenge, just as herself, to see if she was enough.

'Well,' Tundra said.

'Do you know what I called you at first? When I arrived in town?'

Tundra shook her head no.

'The queen. Just in my mind.'

'Ha! You know what I called you?'

Till shook her head.

'Princess.'

Till laughed, even though it stung a little; it must be true what Leiky saw in her. 'That's what my aunt calls me,' she said.

Tundra looked at her sidelong but attentively, from beneath her thick lashes, while she wiped the counter. 'And now? What do you call me now, to yourself I mean?'

'The queen,' Till said simply.

'Killing me, princess,' Tundra said.

And in this way they came to rights. But they didn't talk about their own sadness or ask each other about their sadness, not then, though they did later.

'But what do I do about her? Bev, I mean?'

'Oh, don't mind Bev. It's just her way. She hates everyone, or pretends to. Just act normal and she will too in a bit. Yeah – it can take a while.' Her face shuttered up. 'She's got her reasons. She likely won't tell you. Or she might. You'll find out. But I will say there's good in her. You can count on her. Keep that in mind while you're fuming.'

Bev was outside the ticket office window on the platform and even though it was three weeks since the thing at the garage, as Till thought of it, she felt dread at the sight. Bev's arms folded across her chest and her skinny legs spread in a power stance cast an improbable shadow in the early light. She looked first up, then down the line, and was moving her mouth, apparently in muted speech, though she was on her own. Her hair, which was brown, had been dyed yellow and was turning orange and fraying at the ends as it grew out. (Till had had her own experiment with going blonde and was sympathetic.) Till slid the ticket window up an inch or two – it was moving nicely now that she'd oiled the casings – and Bev's dark muttering came a little way inside. Bev stilled and her head tilted a little to favour her left ear, but she didn't turn, merely stared in a fixed way towards the palm trees and the houses beyond.

It was dark in the waiting room with the blinds still drawn. There was the heavy, wide, reinforced brass triple hinged and latched waiting room door between them. Till had replaced the locks and bolts and oiled the hinges. It was a serious door. She might live to regret the white paint, but it looked good now against the honey stone. And no one could fit through the holes in the walls, except small creatures trying to make their way in the world. She pulled the door open – light flooded in – and blinked and made a veranda of her hand as she stepped outside. She did this in a pretence of casualness that she hoped would tell Bev she didn't care one bit about her being there.

'Oh, it's you,' Bev said, affecting surprise.

What a pair of liars they were.

'Pitiful,' Bev said, as if Till opening the door had activated a switch. 'Absolutely pitiful.' She turned angrily, her eyes sweeping Till. Her nostrils flared.

'What?' Till asked. She could take Bev down if she attacked, or frighten her off, maybe throw her off balance.

'Bottom course is bulging – look at it.' She paused to nod her head at the base of the building. 'Window frames are falling apart, where's your capstone resting, wood's rotted, top of the door, that stone'll come down and smash your little head, nothing there that'll hold, need some more tie stones, mortar's crumbling everywhere – what there is of it. I suppose it was a mess when you broke in.'

'This isn't the first time you've been here to check on it, is it, Bev?'

Bev moved her feet.

'Is it? I didn't break in. I moved the fence to have a look. I could have crawled in from the other side. I didn't want to make it worse.'

'Not your place. I'm allowed.'

'It is my place. I bought it. Never said you weren't allowed.'

'How rich are you?' A jeering tone.

'It was a ruin. I didn't need to be rich. Look at it. No one else was looking after it. You can keep coming up here and sitting on the platform – if that's what you've been doing all these years.' Till's tone made it clear that she had some doubts on that score. 'I don't mind.'

Bev glared. 'I'll go where I please the way I always have. I don't care if you mind.'

Liar, Till thought, then, *Shut up, Till, don't.* She said, 'Go nuts. It's a long platform, plenty of room for us both. I'll bring you a cup of tea if I'm around. I'll get you your own chair.'

'You know, it's the stupidity I hate the most. Don't be cute with me. Just passing through, looking for a new hobby?'

'You're like a dog with a bone. You've had enough but you can't stand someone else having it.'

'You don't know this place, you don't know what it means, and I'm not telling you.'

'And do you know how good that feels? I don't want to know.'

It seemed like the words were falling away from the truth like apple peel and they were getting closer to something. Till was almost starting to enjoy herself, and from the constancy of Bev's volume, perhaps it wasn't so different for her. Till wasn't sure. Looking back, Bev had seemed like some injured animal at Oldham's, one paw caught in a trap she didn't altogether hate, teeth chewing at the paw to set herself free. Almost meditatively, Bev felt across the cuticles of each finger with her thumbs, and feeling loose skin put it delicately to her mouth and pulled off a shred and winced. 'Shit.'

Till saw it then: she needed something – a sting, an argument – to distract from some pain of her own.

'I'll get you a bandaid. Do you want to come in?'

'I'll wait here.' She talked louder as Till went inside and fossicked in the cloakroom. 'Dun't matter. You can buy it, you can do whatever you like to it, don't think it makes it yours.'

Till came back. 'It means I get to repair it. You get to come around. I really don't mind. I'd like you to.' (More lies . . .)

Bev snatched the bandaid – 'I'll do it' – and wrapped it around. All her cuticles were ragged. She began teasing at the edges of her thumbnail.

Till had a vision then, of Bev falling off the platform onto the tracks – maybe (if she were honest) of pushing Bev off the platform. It swept through her and was gone as fast as electricity.

Bev turned her head to stare. 'You can't tell there's no hope for you at all. You going to do it, do it right. You'll freeze soon – like living in a colander. Do you know how cold it gets around here?'

'It is cold.' Birdy chose that moment to come out in her bright blue and yellow bumblebee outfit.

'Oh my god,' Bev said at the sight. 'You been in the shed yet?'

'Shed.'

'Building further down.' She pointed.

'Oh, no. It's locked and the walls are sound. I just left it.'

Bev looked like she might fly at her again even when she was offering help – as it seemed she might be.

'Get Stew. He can show you. I'm saying you should get him in before you ruin it completely.'

Till's eyes began to prickle. She pretended to deadhead the potted geraniums.

'Oh my god,' Bev said. 'Aren't you the precious one.'

Stew came to the door a week later with the keys to the shed, which he and Bev had somehow become custodians of. He was a big man with a diffident manner. His ruddy face rose from an intricate handknitted Fair Isle jumper. The belt holding up his shorts was tucked snuggly beneath his stomach. He wore a

Port beany as a concession to the chill, and workers boots with chunky red socks. Decency and neighbourliness shone out of him, a desire to make life a little more comfortable for her, even to make her feel welcome, but he did it in such a way that she needn't be grateful. How did he do that?

His voice was quiet, a soothing rumble that rolled along. 'Get the stove going first, I reckon. Rayburn . . . You're lucky that's still here. Easier to cook on.' He took in the kitchen table Till had set up against one wall, its camp stove and the small meat safe she used as a pantry standing next to it, and the kerosene lamp. 'Not saying camp stoves aren't good in a pinch – nice set up you've got. Getting cold at night. This'll be good. Lucky you got the other fire.'

He was at such pains not to offend. Bev must have another side. Till hoped she did for Stew's sake.

Stew checked the two stove compartments and moved his hand confidently across the workings. 'Got the spin wheel – lucky – got the damper and flue: gears, brakes, accelerator. They're the main parts.' He opened the firebox. 'Grate there. Connect the chimney. See that up there how it's come loose?' Till looked up. 'That'll do it. Check the shed. Got suh'm back there. Wood. You got wood? Course you do.'

By late afternoon he'd attached and sealed the chimney, given her a crash course in running the stove and the fire was burning nicely. In the shed they found three long green leather sofas like overfed laps that she supposed were from the waiting room. Till went to winkle Ken from his shop and together they moved them inside. They were stately, beautiful and capacious things. Till felt the lustre of possession, the wish to make it nice, as her grandmother said. A rug, paint, maybe curtains, a jug for flowers, a nice lamp, whitewashed stone on the interior.

Not too much though. The walls were beautiful on their own. This was how it crept up on you. She'd started out so free and easy and now she was making lists and dreaming.

It had been a prosperous town once (though on a small scale) but the grand civic buildings and the elegant shop facades had told her that already, and the station would match it again one day. She wouldn't let it down.

Next, Stew inspected the walls and progress and regression. 'Not quite what I was expecting after Bev. It's coming along.' After a lengthy pause he said, 'Help you out if you like.'

It was easier learning in person, which Till did over the next few weeks, watching Stew pick over the stones when he had a spare hour or two, decide against some because of their fault lines, getting the pieces in place without rushing it, the puzzle of it, getting a quiet rhythm going, feeling it as much as seeing it. He wielded the little hammers, tap-tapping with skill and deftness. She tried to mimic it.

'There you go, tha's right,' he said encouragingly.

Briefly she remembered the city conversations about skills to offer in the end times. Stew would be the most important person for miles around. They mixed mortar and trowelled it into the gaps neatly, brushing them off, then with a wet brush so the stones sang and it began to look right. Her early attempts looked experimental now, but they touched them up so they almost matched the rest.

'They tell a story of their own,' Stew said kindly. (There are some notes on the subject at the end of this book if you are interested.)

Till looked through ruins for new lintels of sound and hefty timber or massive stone and if they were too heavy, got Ken or Stew or Ed, whoever was around, to help. It felt good to use these old fragments and scraps to build and renew something. Daniel Defoe would approve, she felt.

There came a time the building was holding out the wind so well that she didn't need her puffer jacket on indoors at night, which she counted a victory. She pulled Birdy's bed up to the stove, and a sofa in close, which Birdy preferred, sitting up on a blanket like a queen. It was strange thinking of how far she'd come since last winter. She could see how it was in the past. When she was in that past she had wanted to think of other times. It was difficult to live in the present. So often people live in hope and expectation of the future or regret or wonder at the past. The idea of now was slippery and indistinct.

Chapter 13

Brunswick 2020–2021

IT IS WINTER in Melbourne, clear and bright and very cold.

Till is reading a prison memoir she found in her parents' shelves, *The Man Died*, by the Nigerian writer Wole Soyinka. There is a passage about a man, the Grand Overseer, who speaks with Soyinka in prison. Outside, in the Nigeria of the book, the sun is weak, the air is filmy and there is a lull in the wind, which is called the harmattan – a cool dry wind that comes from the Sahara in winter and fills the air with the dust of degraded land departing the ground. That word, harmattan. She can feel it in her mouth. It is about something wild and relentless in her mind. She watches a news report from Nigeria on harmattan induced conditions, and the problems for airports, and the news anchor and the weather expert utter the word as if it's nothing special at all. Oh, she loves this word.

Immediately, she adds it to her list of words that she loves deeper than love, whose sounds are perfect, about which her feelings are elemental. Samarkand, Damascus, Kamchatka, Svalbard, Harmattan. Only a few. She recites them sometimes for reassurance. Whatever else, she has the sounds of these words – Sva Da Ka Cha Ba Sa Ma Ka Ha Ta – consonants followed by quick exhalation, as if drawing breath after near-drowning. Some people feel this about a voice, a note from a cello, the *Dido and Aeneas* lament that her father loves, something she knows without asking or him mentioning because of its familiarity to her. She thinks of Zoe: 'Have you seen this lily, Till?' To be near any of these things is to understand your true size, which is infinitely small.

This is how being inside the lanes narrows and compresses Till's thinking. She knows she is not in a prison, that her situation is not like Wole Soyinka's. She can say anything she likes about the federal government and no one cares. She can run if she wants to and there is nothing to stop her driving further than she is permitted, as she has already done, or walking all day long, except the law. It is agreed that this is how it is at this time. The oppression is necessary to achieve suppression. It's not so bad. She has felt something like this – watchful, cautious, afraid – for so many years, and now other people feel it too.

That drowning feeling of her childhood. Her parents had tried to reassure with talk of locks, but Till knew that if the locks were secure, it would be the roof that would fail. The man would peel back the tin at the corner just enough to slide beneath and find a weak spot in the ceiling, above a cupboard say. She watched the cupboard in her room, and the darkness seeping from the darkness like mist. When it arrived she would die. It was inevitable, yet she could not make a sound. She was miles from any shore that might save a drowning person. In sunshine she could forget for a while, but eventually a shadow would lengthen, and all the shadows would stretch away from all the things they represented and it would come back, the dread of getting through another night and the despair at all the nights of her life to come.

In the day, when no one was around, Till crept in and made a small bed of folded blankets and a little cushion by her parents' bed, the sort of thing a person might make for a dog sleeping in a kennel or by a door. She made it so neatly that no one could object. No one should see it happening, and then it would be as if someone else had done it, and how convenient when she might need that very place some time, that very night when she woke to the quiet house, or couldn't sleep. How would they even notice it? It was so small and neat and not in anyone's way at all, tucked into the gap between bed and wall. She never talked about it to Annunciata, and neither did her parents.

For years, Till loved to be read to last thing. It held true night at bay. She and George decided on each book, something they would both like, and last thing at night they would read it on the old sofa in the living room. Once they read *Moby Dick*. Till picked it because she knew George liked it (he loved tales of hardship and survival, the pitting of person against a larger force, psychological suffering). It took months, but they read it all, even the Cetology chapter and the chapter about the whale nursery and the calves snuffling around the boat like puppies, which made Till cry and rage and join Greenpeace and become a vegetarian.

'Excellent,' Zoe said. 'Very good work, George.' She had been out the night they started. Usually Zoe was there too, right under a lamp, so it cast enough light for her to see her writing or embroidery. She was quiet at these times, only laughing or sighing or looking anxiously at Till to assess her distress levels. In Till's memory, the fire was burning and the dogs were sprawled in front of it and the lamplight's pleasant glow held them together.

Then, very late, when all the lights were out and her shaking grew too great, her terror overcame her terror, she crept into her parents' room, dragging a quilt with her, and lay at the side of their low bed on her nest, and sometimes Zoe would half wake and put her hand down so Till could hold it and finally sleep. In the morning and many mornings thereafter she would say only that bad thoughts had kept her awake.

They watched the evening news together, with the dogs lolling in front of the fire in winter. Everyone did to get the numbers about disease and death and lockdowns and what was happening elsewhere in the country. There might even have been something reassuring about the monotonous routine. What I mean is that death was on people's minds.

'People used to die of strange things,' Zoe said one night. 'I'd forgotten. Things you'd never think of these days. There was this family at school. There were three kids. The oldest, Verity, had a hole in her heart, inoperable. She was very thin but with a powerful personality and this fabulous dark hair. Verity was going to die, and people didn't like to disagree with her because of that. People respected her and they were frightened of her. She sort of despised people for their sympathy and tact. She used to say, "You don't have to talk to me like that, I know I'm going to die." She came to school sometimes for a break from home schooling and tormented us all. What a pill. I shouldn't say that. We knew we shouldn't then too. Just because you're dying doesn't make you nice. She wielded her life. She was frightened. I see that now. She wanted to be normal for a few hours, or she wanted people to understand her fear because then maybe she wouldn't feel so alone in it. I don't know. She saw through everyone. She was amazing.

'There was this netball type called Lissa, very mean, who came up to her once, and people waited to see what would happen. They were both powerful, like prisoners in a yard. Verity looked Lissa up and down and said, "Oh, *you're* Lissa. Why are you such a bitch? You know everyone hates you." Lissa blushed absolutely scarlet, and there was this fight on her face between, oh, manners and meanness I suppose. "Well you're going to die," Lissa said. It was like a tide went out and a tsunami was about to come in, and Verity said, "Really? I had no idea. At least some people like me." Later everyone was saying Lissa couldn't stop crying, her face was red. We hoped Verity might come back another time to deliver some truths to a few other people. It was like Lissa had been cursed. She never really got her power back.'

'God,' Till said.

'Mmm, but that's not all. Then there was the middle child. Everyone loved her. She was the survivor. And there was the little brother, a really sweet kid, who fell off his bike one day and was run over by a car. Another boy at school, great kid, cut his thumb and died of blood poisoning. Seventeen years old. It was too late by the time they realised. It seemed old-fashioned even then.'

'What is your point?' Till asked.

'Well . . . I suppose that sometimes young people die for no good reason.'

'Is there ever a good reason?'

'Well,' Zoe said. 'I mean that sometimes people die too young.'

'And we have to get over it even when we're five and someone's been actually killed.'

'That is different.'

'It is.' Till's eyes were red and hot. Zoe hadn't noticed.

Evidently Zoe was still in the past, about thirteen years old. 'There was another hole in the heart girl. She was much worse, and she did die young. She never changed the hay in her guinea pig's cage. We judged her for that. We were sorrier for the guinea pig than for her. I'd forgotten that.' Zoe made a face.

'Mum.'

'I know. It's the truth though. Our mother made Leiky and me go and visit her. She was frightened and people were frightened of her. She wasn't supposed to get upset in case it stressed her heart. She was like a little wheezing empress, poor thing, telling everyone they had to obey. Her mother was terrified; she smoked like a chimney to stay calm. The house stank of it. Her fingers were yellow. It was awful.'

'This is not the same as me and . . . me and E.'

'I'm not talking about you, sweetie. I'm talking about the idea of remembering and forgetting and strange deaths.'

'You could forget. I couldn't. And the deaths are not the same.'

'Mmm. It takes time for things to recede—'

'What are you saying, Mum?' Till knew that E would always be with her.

'I'm just remembering. This plague seems old-fashioned, don't you think? Only there are cars and computers. I can't believe it's happening now.'

'Do I frighten you? Do I frighten people? Mustn't upset Till?'

A look crossed Zoe's face, like a bright light.

'I do.' Till put her fingers over her mouth.
'Oh sweetheart, no. No. Not like that.'
'I think maybe yes.'

Zoe just gazed at her. 'Maybe a little, maybe you're right, but not very right. It's this time. It frightens me.'

Chapter 14

TILL AND ED were having a glass of wine in front of the fire, waiting for food to cook. It was the third night they had done this – scattered occasions across several weeks that one or other suggested. Till looked forward to each time with an agitation that was pleasurable, but which she mistrusted and tried to suppress. She missed him betweentimes, but stretched out the time anyway, as if too much of him might spoil her. What if she got used to him? She feared that what they had, which she could not put a name to in any case, might fail her. She feared failing it. It was easier to miss Ed than to go all in and suffer catastrophic loss. She did not think she could bear that.

Each time, she knew he had arrived from Birdy's dancing at the door and then his call. Rain spattered on the roof this winter night. Till was hoping it would settle in, for the sake of her water tank and because there was no better feeling than rain outside and warmth and shelter within with a person you... she did not care for any of the words that came to mind. Let us say liked. She was prepared to admit that. She'd built up a picture of him: the smart kid who went to university and returned to his roots to give something back.

A few girlfriends in his past, one serious, the others not. She understood his wariness, feeling some of it herself.

'People are always trying to save me,' Till said.

'Are they?' Ed said. 'From what?'

'Oh, things. Actually, there's this guy who's helped me with the station. Saved, I should say. I couldn't have done it without him. Look at those walls.' The section on the south wall to the right of the stove gave her particular pleasure since it had been the most damaged. 'I shouldn't complain. Doesn't matter. People assume I'm a shitty driver because I'm young. I'm not a shitty driver by the way. I'm a great driver. Or they think I drink too much or sleep with too many guys. What even is too many guys? I don't do that now. Bad experience. Yeah, that kind of thing.' She looked across at Ed who was gazing steadily at the fire. Who knew what he was thinking. 'Don't think you can save me.'

'I never said I could. I didn't think you needed it.'

'It's just, there's no protection if the world's coming for you. No one can save you and there's nothing more to say about that.' A pause and a laugh – then, 'In my opinion. Anyway, I can take care of myself. Five years of Krav Maga. I don't usually tell people that when I meet them. But I do tell guys sometimes. You look like one of the ones who can take the information.' She lifted her eyebrows and gave a little smile and his face lit up. (He was in trouble, it just hadn't quite hit him yet.) 'Do you want to test me?' It was a trick she played with guys, letting them find out, if necessary, that she could look after herself.

'Are you dangerous?'

'I am.'

'I see. But for a reason?'

'Yes.' She let herself feel, for a moment, what had made her leave Melbourne. That fear, and anger at the fear.

He leaned back.

'Don't make me feel bad that I can take care of myself.'

'Except you told me, then asked me to test you. I don't want to. I believe you. I don't get where this is coming from.'

'I won't be sorry for it,' Till said. 'Don't make me.'

Ed held up his hands in surrender. 'I'm only wondering if, if there's room for other people.'

'Yeah, that is the question.' Till flung the stove door open and pushed some wood in, poked around to settle it, and shut the door. 'You have to face it. We are all alone. You wake up in the morning you have to face it. Every day you wake up and you have to face it. All day long, and then it's night.' She checked the light outside. Early evening.

Birdy was restless, so Till fed her and brought plates and cutlery and bread and other things to the little table before them. Ed poured some more wine. Till took a dish from the oven – confit chickpeas, an Ottolenghi dish she liked – and bread and salad, salt and pepper.

'I think . . . I don't want to lose you.' Ed bit his lip. 'I don't mean we're . . . something. I mean I don't want it to be nothing. This, I mean.' He gestured around vaguely in a way that encompassed them both, the wine, the fire, this place. It seemed like he regretted saying that much. It was hard for him to look in her face and for her to look back.

'Hmmm.' She knew she felt the same. She didn't want to say it though. 'You might. It happens. You don't know when it's going to happen.'

'True,' he said.

She could see he was talking about someone else now. 'Who?' she asked.

'A girlfriend from way back. It didn't work out. She's the

kid's mother. The next guy was the dad. Anyway, she's not around and he is, the kid I mean. He's a good kid. He's great actually. Hard on him that she's missing.' He gave a look like, what do you do about the world? What do you do with what it hands you? That's what it seemed like to Till. 'I'm not pining, if that's what you're thinking. It's a long time ago. It was right that it ended. We weren't going anywhere.'

'So I lose kids and you save them.'

'You lost a kid?'

'No. I didn't mean it the way it sounded. It was a stupid thing to say.'

'I didn't save one. His grandparents did. They're not taking any chances.'

'He's a lucky kid.'

'He's not alone anyway. Funny thing to end up talking about.'

'These conversations are everywhere. If you listen you will find them.'

'Why'd you say what you did? That you had a kid you didn't lose?'

'I didn't have one. I had a friend. I didn't stop her.'

'Yeah. I don't know what that means.' He glanced at her. 'You don't have to tell me.'

'Maybe one day. I like you coming over, don't think I don't, but I want you to know, I'm not asking a question, and if I was, you're not my answer.'

It was as if Till had struck him. She hadn't meant to sound so harsh, but that's the way it came out. It was too soon to talk it out and smooth things over. He left soon after and then she sat in the dark with Birdy, and the sound of rain on the roof.

Days of Innocence and Wonder

Brunswick 2021

The year opened, blinked languidly several times (five days, fourteen days, twelve days) before shutting out the world again for the end of winter and most of spring (seventy-eight days). Till had never lived in such nowness.

She read a book about the kidnapping of two sisters set on the Kamchatka Peninsula. (*Disappearing Earth* by Julia Phillips, if you are interested.) One of the sisters is eight; she is terribly frightened. Till put the book in the shelves, then moved it outside. She put it in the rubbish bin, but it was days until it would get collected. She tore it up, page by page and fed it into a small fire she built in the lane behind their house. When it had burned down and all the words had disappeared, she swept up the ashes carefully, and in the evening when she was walking the dogs, emptied them down a gutter.

The lockdowns were shorter in the second year, but the music never started up. Singing together was the most dangerous thing of all – everyone knew that – and gathering to watch singing was almost as bad. The joyousness of singing, pulling the air into your lungs and letting it out, could kill someone standing near. It was hard to sing again after that. Even singing around the house felt risky. Till did it in her room or the garden or sometimes online with other people. It lifted them up and reminded them and made them sad: all these things.

She walked in the parks with the dogs and helped Zoe and Adrienne with the grocery deliveries. She went on outdoor picnics and sat at a not very correct distance from her friends. They couldn't imagine a world in which this would all be over. They forgot what they had talked about once.

One thing that Till liked: small gatherings of people out in the sun. They looked like waterlily pads on the park lawns – laughter rolling, children out on bikes and skateboards and rollerblades on a weekday. (People were giving up on the rules by then.) It was beautiful to watch. Among them, some people walked with nowhere to go, like ghost people, like people from the past.

Chapter 15

One night, missing Ed, hardly thinking, Till walked up the railway line to the edge of town and began singing, only softly, in a strange little voice across the plains. She was curious about that sound. E was sometimes on her mind out there. What if E or the ghost of E began singing from down the road where purple turned to black, and her voice had grown and changed because she had kept growing? Her voice would be different too.

It seemed as if Tundra saw everything and everyone. Her eyes, a clear and remarkable green, looked and looked away and looked back: *Thought so*, and she said something like, 'What are you thinking?' And Till believed that Tundra would know if you didn't tell the truth in reply, so Till decided to tell the truth a week or two after she went back to work when Tundra rang to ask where she was. I didn't tell you this part before, but I think I should have.

They stood at the door of the shop – Till and Birdy at her side – and waited for what would happen next, blinking into the gloom after the brightness. Tundra was cleaning the pigeonholes, removing each item, wiping each compartment with her yellow dusting cloth before putting things back: sandpapers, builders' pencils, string and so forth. The great enamelled lamps hanging above swayed to the draft coming through the door, and oblique light came in from the high windows. There had always been something alive about this place to Till, and serious and safe, also beautiful, but she didn't know if it could feel this way again.

Tundra looked around, not quite finished, only glancing at Till. She said, 'Something the matter?'

So Till came in and stood at the counter, as if she was just another needy customer, her old self. 'I still don't understand you telling me off like that.'

'This still about Bev?'

'About you, then you telling me to go home.'

'I got angry, I didn't want you around, and now it's in the past. What, your parents don't get angry?'

'Only quietly.' (She sounded pathetic even to herself.)

'I was not loud, I was firm, and you had no right to speak personally when you didn't know the whole situation. That's the first thing.'

The idea of quiet anger did not seem to impress Tundra. She looked at Till as if she was wondering whether she could be bothered or not. It was her 'white people' face, as Till privately called it, since she used it sometimes in the shop while uttering the words about customers who had patronised, insulted or been ridiculous in some way, and sometimes it made Till laugh, even though she suspected it included her sometimes. She knew it did even though Tundra would smile at her.

But Tundra's anger had blown over. She waved her hand about. 'That's all past. Come on now,' she said, fairly patiently, but Till was still uneasy. Tundra put her hands on the counter and shut her eyes. Till felt the way she was sometimes work and a burden for Tundra. 'I see that we have some things we have to say to each other, else we're done. Come back here now, you and me, pull up a chair. We'll sit down in front of the fire, find out our truth.'

There were quiet times in the shop and Tundra believed in being comfortable in such moments. The two behind-the-counter chairs were silvered wicker with curved arms and willow bindings fraying a little where hands rested and idly picked, and were lined with cushions of velvet and silk and polyester and heavy cotton, every colour – the profusion of colour seemed to be the principal point – an aesthetic that was wild to Till and would be beyond her to emulate, but she loved being around it. Till got a chair and Tundra straightened the old red square of carpet back there, and pulled Till's chair in diagonally so they were half-turned to each other. Till settled there like a tightly curled black cat and Tundra directed the ancient two-bar radiator that normally faced her (she felt the cold) so that they each got a little, and in this way the space turned into a fireside hearth in a small room, and it began to feel safe again. Tundra patted Till's arm. Birdy turned and turned before flopping next to Maggie. Till bent and stroked Birdy, and Tundra kicked off her fur trimmed slip-on shoes and rested her feet on Maggie's soft fur, digging her toes in a little.

'I will tell you some things,' Tundra said. 'Bev is family to me. She is part of my family. Her daughter Liz and my son Bear had a baby, our grandson. Isaac.'

'Isaac?' The name burst out. 'Ed's Isaac?'

'Well . . .'

'I know he's not Ed's. I didn't know who he was. No one said.'

'You know him?'

'Yes. He and Ed come to the station on a pushcart, you know. They go up and down the line. They stop in.'

'I didn't know that.'

'He's a great kid.'

'He is.' They sank into their own thoughts for a minute. Finally, Tundra sighed. 'I suppose we all have a secret or two. No harm in letting him keep it.'

Till wondered why Isaac hadn't mentioned it to his grandparents. Perhaps the station was a secret pure world for him that did not contain the ghost of his father or the memory of his missing mother, and perhaps he wished it did not contain Till who made Ed divide his attentions. He had all these things to bear, and he was only eight, and what if she was one of those things.

Tundra's voice broke into her thoughts. 'My son is dead, no one knows exactly how, won't admit to it anyway. Someone else's secret. We have our suspicions, our beliefs, mind. You know where he was found?'

Till shook her head.

'On the footpath on Main Street in Wirowie. We moved after that. Not a mark on Bear. It could have been someone else – maybe drugs, like people say, but we don't think so. He could be wild, but he wasn't bad. But the police were after him. You know the one.'

'You mean Rod?'

Tundra glanced at her, assessing.

'Nothing would surprise me about him,' Till said. She pulled out her phone and scrolled through the pictures and passed the phone to Tundra who went through the photos, looking closer at some.

'He did this?'

'The week I got here. Welcome to Wirowie.'

Tundra pressed a hand to Till's leg and rubbed her shoulder. 'Pet.'

'I looked after myself.'

'So you did. And you're still here.'

They were quiet for a while. Till got up to serve a customer. Tundra began talking again when they'd gone, murmuring rather, as if ruminating aloud.

'No one knows about Liz that we can find out. She's just gone, no one knows where. Imagine what that's like for Bev. She's frightened for her daughter. She can't help thinking the worst. She can't help it. So, Liz disappeared around the time you turned up. Maybe a couple of weeks before. The police don't care. The other thing – outsiders mean trouble to Bev, outsiders changed her daughter, took her daughter away from her, and now she is missing and no one knows where, and we have her and Bear's son. He is everything and we look after him together. He's what we've got left. So I look out for Bev. If she's angry like that, she's hurting. She sees a young woman like you, about the same age probably, she's thinking about her girl. I don't know that, but think about it. Why are you all right? Why do you live in her world when her daughter does not? You see? Because life's not fair, right?'

'No, it's not.' Till saw that she was an outsider still, that's how people saw her after all these months. How many years would it take? She supposed she got it. Just because she didn't mean to hurt anyone didn't mean other people had to agree. She'd changed things for other people, not only herself. It was an old story.

'So you know about Bear and Liz, our hard times. Some of our hard times.'

'What do you think's happened to Liz?'

'You mean do I think she's dead, been killed? If that is what you mean, say it.'

'I mean, what do you think.'

'I think she's alive. Bear talks to me every day in my heart. There is nothing about Liz being gone. So, I don't know where she is or why, but I keep her here.' She touched her chest in her elegant way, softly; Till felt her holding Liz and Bear there.

Till said, 'Thank you for telling me.' She meant: *What the hell, Tundra, what is going on in this place, what happened to Bear, how'd he die, what is going on with the police, what sort of mother wouldn't come back for her son?* but she didn't say any of that. What did she know?

She couldn't help thinking of E then, who no one had seen since the man took her away, or not that they knew of. Her presumed fate seemed the best of the possibilities that people imagined.

If Liz was alive as Tundra believed – and Till could not bring herself to doubt Tundra – and she loved Isaac as much as Tundra said, that wasn't good in a different way. Till's mind (and the minds of countless other people at other times, mostly women) flew across those dark seas, by which I mean fear, restlessly dipping and skimming like gulls towards fish, glimpsing other worlds when the light struck a wave and penetrated the sea's skin: rows of jagged teeth, tentacles, lantern-headed fish drawn from the deep.

People didn't really want to know, and if they did find out they would regret possession of the knowledge. Till didn't want to know everything, but she would like to know where E was and for everyone's sake, Isaac's most of all, she would like to know where Liz was. There was no virtue in wanting to know the depths of human potential, unless to prevent its worst excesses. Even who did it was not very interesting. It led only to the tired word 'monster' and so on. And here she was thinking of monstrous teeth. There are such people. Then what?

And outside the sun still shone on this cold winter day, a chill wind blew, another ute with kelpies in the back went by, a woman passing waved through the door, just saying hi, a young couple came in to pay for petrol, get some gum and some water, and they smiled and chatted a little – 'cute town' and so on – and Till felt like sending them on their way before Mr Oldham arrived and began to work his peaceful magic on them. Even if people didn't think she was local, which logically was reasonable, she felt more local than someone who described Orroroo as cute.

Tundra poked Till with a foot before she could say what she was thinking. When the couple had gone Tundra gave a little smile, which surprised Till. 'Get me some banana bread from the bakery, if you could? And whatever you like, and an almond milk latte and a regular latte for Roy. I would love it if you would.'

Mr Oldham was there when she got back and they moved about their tasks companionably.

Till said, 'We were talking about the police.'

Roy paused. 'Oh, the police. I see.' His expression was kindly as well as measuring and she stood straighter before it. What kind of vessel was she? A damaged one, cracked and marked by dents and scratches. Would information leak from her; might she betray? 'We don't see eye to eye, shall we say. They've got some different ideas about the rightness of things. Things that you might think are good are bad to them. A young man trying to stop police corruption, a woman being beaten by her policeman husband, someone cutting in on their drug deals. Something might start as a sting but end up as a little business on the side. They've been doing it so long it's hard for them to change their ways. Around here anyway. Different elsewhere. Their ways are the right ways to them. That's all they know. Once you see it, it's easier to move around – steer clear of, you know. They're going to do what they do; we try to sort things out our own way, don't encourage their attention. Only speaking for myself.'

'From experience,' Tundra said. 'I told her about Bear.'

Roy put his arm around her, his creaky hand cupping her shoulder, rubbing up and down a little. She bumped her forehead into him and rested it, turning into him.

Roy said, 'Good kid. Had a little trouble. Fell in with a bad crowd. The police put a heel on his throat and kept him there. They don't like young black men. Sometimes they need someone. I should have been . . . I wish—'

'So the law, crimes, all that . . .'

Roy's expression did not alter, but his eyes moved across her face. 'A crime is an action. It doesn't belong to anyone in particular – poor people, young men, runaways, the desperate, the police, the wealthy. Can be anyone who commits a crime. People forget that. Being police, being in the law, doesn't make you innocent. You understand what I'm saying? They might not be on the side of right, only of power. The law might not be on the side of right. That makes things dangerous. Power has its own rules.'

Till said, 'Don't go to the police if there's trouble, is that what you're saying?'

'Go ahead if you want, just don't expect things to go the way you had in mind. You might get help or you might get interference. They are a tribe; first thing they do is have each other's backs. Second thing they do? Have each other's backs. Loyalty first. Very hard for them to go against one of their own; if there's one bad one they do more damage than they should. Might be very likeable guys at first. You might know a bit about that?' He raised an eyebrow at Till.

'A story there,' Tundra murmured, and put her hand to his arm.

'They don't like people taking matters into their own hands or disagreeing with them. Once you hand them something, well . . . sometimes that works out. They can be dangerous, not always, but often enough. In my experience. People can die. Don't like young men, brown people or women, people driving decrepit cars, people who complain about the police. Others too, I'm sure.'

A man crusted with farm dirt and streaked lightly with sweat as if the surface of his body was mirroring the landscape around, slouched into the shop.

'I'n't that right, Bruce?' Roy said.

'Come again?' Bruce said.

'Police. What are they like, around here, mostly . . .'

'I won't say the word,' Bruce said. 'But you know the one I mean.' He nodded at Till and Tundra. 'Pardon me.'

'My point,' Roy said, nodding gravely. 'I should add, not all police. I believe young Scott whatever his name is, is not too bad. I've heard some good. Marian's feller though. I avoid them is my point.'

Bruce cleared his throat. 'They do have their place sometimes, I will say that,' he said thoughtfully. 'They can tidy things up, and sometimes that is necessary.'

Till wondered about Marian's 'feller', who she'd never mentioned. If Marian wanted her to know, she'd tell her sometime. Also whether Bev's normal way of getting to know a person was first to try to scare them off, then to return and insult them, then to offer them help in a roundabout way (if that was what had happened), then to return and tell them they were wrongheaded in their thinking and inept in all of their actions, and this was why. People rolled their eyes at the mention of her, which suggested something, or said 'bitch', but mostly with faint affection or respect. She had looked in Bev's eyes by then, and she knew about Liz and regarded her more highly than other people she'd known in her life. There was no point in flattery, fake curiosity or politeness with her. Standing your ground was the only approach that seemed to work. She was melancholy and furious, which is an unusual combination. Till braced for the onslaught of her presence as a person might face a winter storm. It was invigorating if not completely welcome.

She ran into her another time at Marian's while getting a loaf of the seeded bread she had developed a taste for.

'This is our world and you come in and think you're fixing it. You think you're showing us what we should do. You think you can bring it back to life?'

'I really don't.' Remember Liz, Till thought. Remember that.

'Yes, you do.'

'Bev,' Marian said.

'I don't even think it's dead,' Till said. 'You and Stew are here, Marian. All those kids who go to school, their parents.'

'My parents,' Marian said.

'Self-centred, that's what you are.'

'You should meet my aunt,' Till said.

'Filling the bellows with air, sweetheart, one breath at a time. Stop pumping and the air's gone and it all goes to hell again. You're making it your world. You're making it to suit you.'

'I'm doing my best. I fixed up the station, I have two jobs, and I buy my bread at Marian's. I do my shopping at Foodland in Orroroo.'

'That is a very good shop,' Marian said.

'It is.'

'And you're here.' Bev was insistent on this point.

'Come and visit me at the station. I could use the help. There's a chair there for you on the platform – you know I said I'd get you one? – and a little table. I think you'd like it.'

'I don't think so. What I came to say, girls, is be careful. A woman attacked out of Jamestown. House broken into. You hear me?' She picked up a loaf of sliced white and paid for it. 'Ladies,' she said and departed.

'It'll be domestic,' Marian said. 'Always is.'

'You know,' Till said, 'I think Bev's softening.'

Till was softening too. It used to be that every time she had any hint of feeling for someone it disappeared and she couldn't imagine why she'd ever felt it. It was a few sad weeks now since she'd seen Ed, and she still missed him, and the point of missing him instead of seeing him was not as clear as it had been. Till sent a message. He came over that weekend and when she met him at the door she put her arms around him and they kissed. It was a good kiss. He stayed the whole night through. Till didn't invite him to stay, only let it happen, so he had no idea that it had a particular meaning to her. It was hard for her to feel safe sleeping with a guy. Actually sleeping. She watched him until he went to sleep and set her alarm to wake early to make sure she was not sleeping while he was awake. She would do that. She did like him.

She watched him for a while when she woke up. This is what she was thinking: that people revealed themselves in bed. When she invited someone in she was asking the question, *What are you like?* Sometimes she let things go to find out a little more.

Chapter 16

By July the station had a clean waxed floor, the grain and knots standing two or three millimetres proud of the softer parts, worn pale and velvet soft from the foot traffic of decades, wall holes repaired (painstakingly, with stone Till gathered from here and there and a mortar mix approved by Stew), and wall cavities filled in the waiting room, around windows and doors. Rain had found it all to be weatherproof and the water tank had filled to overflowing. Till painted the architraves white and coaxed the green waiting room sofas back to respectability with some leather restorer that promised miracles.

She sent photographs to her parents.

'It's marvellous, Till,' George said. 'Did you really do the stonework?'

'Some, quite a bit, with some help.'

'Clever you, darling.'

Zoe said, 'You're staying. You're really staying.' She could not quite keep the dismay from her voice.

'Mum, I told you that months ago. I bought it. Remember?'

'But I can see it's true now. The photos—'

'Make it real?'

'It is beautiful, Till.'

Oh, the quaver in Zoe's voice. Hearing her parents being brave... It killed her. But she lived here now.

Tundra came to inspect one Sunday afternoon. 'Not a nice green trim?' she asked taking it in.

'Too matchy with the sofas,' Till said. 'I like white with the stone.'

Tundra tilted her head about a centimetre, which Till understood to mean that she disagreed but would say no more. Marian had also come, bearing the gift of one of her mother's rustware sculptures: a woman holding an old tin watering can over a tree made of rusted sickle blades. 'See?' she said, nodding at the palms, and Till did see.

'It's like those sculptures from that place on the edge of town.'

'Not surprising,' Marian said. 'My parents' place. My mum does them. I'm staying there now, for a while, since... oh well, I broke up with my dickhead of a husband.'

'Your parents' place is the one with the bicycles? I run past every morning.'

Marian nodded.

'I didn't know.'

'You do now.'

It was quite delicate, more of an indoor sculpture than a paddock piece. Till put it on the mantelpiece.

'Do you like it? I told Mum you would,' Marian said.

'I love it so much. I love it. I'll drop in and let her know. Would that be okay, or would she like to come and see it herself, do you think?'

Marian said for sure she would, only her father wasn't well and it made it hard for her mother. 'Maybe when he's a bit better.'

*

Sometimes Till sang around the station, getting used to it inside, and then she took her voice outside in pink early light, at dusk, sometimes at night. She made her eyes up dirty like she'd be singing later, and she dampened her hair and scrunched it and messed it – it suited her that way; it looked more natural than it did naturally, as if she'd just got out of bed – and it made her feel not herself and therefore like singing.

When she sang, she mostly put on someone else, as if that other person (in her mind, E grown older) was a coat, a suede jacket – vintage, something like that – which never felt exactly like her: her size, her colour, her material, her look. But it seemed that other people believed it, and she could go along with their belief for a while, drinking herself into it, watching and feeling their conviction like an anchor. She began to hum, feeling the buzz in her throat and deeper, warm, an instrument getting going. A few words broke loose, then two lines. She stood on the edge of the platform and let them come out, really singing now. The sun rushed down the lines and sideswiped her, warming her, fleeing past. It was enough to be on the edge of it and to feel it on her skin.

It was an old song of hers, a little about loss, but she sang it differently. It was the way it came out, and her voice was unfamiliar, another voice, different from the stranger's voice she assumed and which came out of her easily. Strange how even though she'd been singing in that voice for so many years, which everyone who heard her assumed was hers because they'd heard no other, she still knew that it wasn't hers. But this unfamiliar voice – she let the sound go. It was deeper, piercing and somewhat harsh in its depths. Later that night she wondered about it, and if it might be her own voice, which she had never met before. It surprised her in the way that a stranger can surprise. (I was less surprised.) She wrote a new song and tried it out, sending it up the rail line, and decided to send some recordings to her manager to see what she thought. But she didn't want to lose that little piece of E.

Till thought about E, whose presence she still felt in some way. An old friend of Till's regarded ghosts with contempt. 'Idiots might believe in them; I do not.' She tossed her head. But Till did believe in ghosts. Why dismiss so certainly something you can't be certain of? Of course E was around some of the time, though not in the way of possession if that is what you are thinking. E would just be there, sort of in a corner of her mind, singing in her voice, singing away, just past the edge of her gaze, a shadowy presence. I'm not saying they sang duets. Till didn't always care for the effect now that she was an adult, though she loved E's bragging style: look at me. (How ridiculous to still be jealous.) And people had looked at her because she was so alive, so wonderful, so loud.

Zoe had a way of deflating Till if Till was overconfident or cocky or something, or for her own reasons, which Till did not understand, like she had after that time when Till wouldn't sing for Adrienne on the street. Till didn't know what it was. Zoe might say, and only rarely: *What a shame you're not taller. What a shame you're not curvier. What a shame you don't wear colourful clothes, a little makeup.* Or she would point out another singer much prettier than Till. It was like a sharp little slap, some kind of reproof, and Till never understood it and never remembered to watch out. She forgot and then she had to remember. Some sad old wound of her mother's that she couldn't help passing on. If Till ever had children she would not to do the same. She would remember that; she would make a note about it. At least, she hoped she would.

Once, Zoe said to Till, 'You think the most terrifying thing is the thought of dying. Then you find out thinking of your own child dying is worse. It doesn't seem possible. I am never not afraid.'

'Mum.'

'Not your fault, sweetheart. But you have to keep going. Sometimes,' and here she paused to look at Till, kindly, but from a distance, 'it's nice to have a break.'

'A break?' Till said.

'You know . . . Even going for a walk can do it. Or travelling.'

Or the conferences Zoe went on, Till thought.

'I don't know if it's because of, you know . . . makes it worse.' Delicately, she didn't meet Till's gaze, and anyway, Till was looking out of the window, desperate, suddenly very desperate for a distraction, for her mother not to mention E directly. Her mother needed to forget her sometimes.

'Look at Maud and Birdy, look at them,' Till said. Outside, Maud was jumping at a butterfly and just next to her, Birdy seemed to be smelling flowers.

They laughed together, shakily, from relief that the moment had passed. 'The irresistible lure of possum poo,' Till said.

'I've been here seven months. Did you know that?' Till said during a quiet spell in the shop.

'Seven months,' Tundra said. 'Doesn't seem that long. Well . . .'

Till wished she hadn't said it. It was no time at all. 'I thought

I'd keep moving, I wouldn't stop, you know. It's a surprise. I surprised myself.'

'Uh huh,' Tundra said. 'You've surprised me more than once, missy. A whole railway station. Taking on you know who—'

'I thought she was going to hit me.'

'Oh she wouldn't hit you, she just likes to make people jump. Doesn't like new people. People mostly don't. Everyone has to move around a bit. Unsettling.'

'Did you grow up here?' Till asked.

'Further west, Ceduna, but my family are from around here. My mother called me back here a long time ago.'

'Oh yeah? How long have you all been here?'

'My dad's side, five or six generations. Maybe seven.' She closed her eyes and the fingers of her right hand moved as if she was playing a piano on the countertop. 'Seven. Mother's side . . . some of it . . . about fifty thousand years, about that.'

'Fifty, fifty thousand.'

She nodded. 'Or more, depending. I'm not sure what we're up to these days.'

A couple of people went past on the road: that guy she saw sometimes, the sheep guy; the llama guy from Yarcowie went past from the other direction, his beautiful black and brown kelpies swarming around in the tray of his ute. She looked back at Tundra. 'Tundra,' she said. 'I feel like an idiot.'

'Stop that now. Not my fault. Your feelings and suppositions are not my problem, got it? People like you . . . you're a child, you're a baby, you're hardly born. Come on. Let's have a cup of tea. People coming through soon. Get things tidy. Wipe that look off your face. Won't do business any good. Then wipe the counter.'

'Sorry,' Till said.

'Not my job to make you feel better. Don't put that on me.' Tundra pressed her hand on the top of Till's hand on the counter and patted it a couple of times. Papery dry, warm. 'Let it go.'

'I like it here,' Till said.

'Happens that way sometimes. You arrived here for a reason. We noticed you. You noticed us. We've been keeping an eye on you. My grandfather Frank is here with me. Have I told you that? Every day.' Tears welled. 'He said I had to speak to you. You know what Roy said the day you came in? He said, "You see that girl in black?" I said, "Yes." He said, "She's in trouble." "She's young," I said. "They're always in trouble." "Mark my words," Roy said. He knows what he sees. But we both saw you had a good heart, a sweet heart. Roy got a kick out of Birdy sitting up like a lady in the passenger seat, sticking her head out like she's about to ask for directions. Your car counted for something. He used to have one like it. It's funny the things that count.'

'Yeah.'

And then very quietly, she said, 'He is not here, but he's still here, my Bear. He said to look out for you, he said you might be in trouble. And you knew about Kapunda.'

'I didn't know.'

'But you knew anyway. More important.'

'What did I know?'

'About the bad things that happened there.'

'I knew it felt bad.'

'Same thing.'

Talking with Tundra sometimes felt less like conversation than witnessing the world sliced in a different way, receiving something, absorbing something: knowledge, maybe insight, though the sincerity of the word and idea embarrassed Till, which she knew was her own city problem not a deficiency in the quality described. But she did feel that Tundra had things to say that she did not understand, but wanted to, and she kept listening.

Till wondered about the past and the things that happened and what people now could do about the past if anything.

'I met a woman once,' Tundra went on, 'or someone asked me to meet a woman once, a descendent of an Englishman who had lived in Kapunda back in their early days. The woman had cancer that would never get better. They kept giving her pills. She was going to die but she could get no peace because of the family stories passed down about this ancestor of hers having killed Aboriginal people gathered in the area with his musket during a massacre in Kapunda. She couldn't sleep because of her thoughts. Someone called me asking for help, since my family is from Kapunda, my mother I mean. My father was born in Terowie, my grandfather in Orroroo. They said she wasn't well, couldn't sleep properly, she kept waking up. She needed something. Forgiveness. So I went to see her and the woman said she was sorry and I said, "You feel bad that your ancestors sent bullets into my people. There's no need for forgiveness. They were forgiven the minute the bullet left the gun." Course she couldn't sleep properly on top of a massacre site. Can't sleep on a pile of bones. She didn't need pills. Pills . . .' Her tone was somewhat contemptuous. 'She needed a healing ceremony.

'So they all agreed to a ceremony. I did the smoking, the ceremony. Afterwards the woman could sleep in peace and not long after she rang me to tell me she was ready to die now. She was at ease and this was peaceful for her.'

Everything about it amazed Till, not only this woman being comfortable about dying. She wanted to ask questions, but the way Tundra told it, the whole thing was self-evident: the problem, the solution, and the effect.

Later, Till looked up Kapunda and read how in the early days the Europeans had opened a copper mine and cut through a train line heading north. It might have continued to Till's own station and beyond, which made Till uneasy and unsure whether this tainted her station.

There was the low hill heavily overgrown with scrubby trees and dense shrubs on the edge of Wirowie, its sign – SHOOTING RANGE – and its further sign advising that care should be taken. She noted the passive voice, identifying neither shooter nor shootee, advising no one in particular of anything in particular, though bullets were inferred. They might appear from the ether and hit anything at all. The entire thing was a mystery. And there was the fresh white iron gate with the fancy curls at the top, as if it was the front gate to a charming heritage cottage and a scented garden filled with lavender and roses, grapevines and so on, not to a place where you might be killed by mistake – *Sorry about that. Who knew anyone was there.*

Tundra quizzed Till on the matter of western medicine and western ways, which Till did not feel very knowledgeable about.

'What are pills going to do?' she asked Till. 'I don't understand white people. Why don't they have women's business? No ceremonies? If they had them they wouldn't need pills. They don't do anything.'

'Like a funeral?'

'You don't need a funeral before you're dead,' Tundra said. 'You need something for your spirit.'

Till wondered whether a coffee morning was a sort of ceremony – it had its ritual side – then remembered a particular one from her childhood, which she told Tundra about.

Zoe had taken her to a coffee morning when she was at primary school, some sort of fundraising committee meeting. An English girl had arrived at school a year or two after E was taken. She had a baby sister born in Australia and her mother had given her the same name – E's name, that is – not knowing of the weight it carried and the alertness of people hearing it, the unquiet quiet, the quick movements of their glances, wondering if they had noticed this name that everyone knew not to use. It was to protect their child from something like a curse, as if not using the name was a sort of talisman, and conversely as if the name itself were an incitement to crime. They pitied the mother and the child both, but could not warn the mother, out of pity, and perhaps a little at shame about their superstition.

People didn't really want to hold the baby; they passed her on to the next person as fast as they decently could. 'No, no, your turn,' they said, and when it seemed the baby's mother was becoming watchful, said, 'She's so cute, what a sweetie,' and so on. But they looked at it warily; they couldn't help it.

The English mother sensed something in the animal protective part of herself. It made her critical. She said it was such a pretty name that she was surprised not to have come across it in Australia. It was quite popular in England (she said this by way of casting some colonial shade, to indicate Australians were backward in their disinclination to use a name so pleasing), didn't the other parents agree? With quick calibrations the mothers declined to take offense – she was right after all; it was such a pretty name. Who among them was going to say it would take a couple more generations before people forgot what happened to the other E, the one who was taken. It will come back one day I suppose.

So they only said, 'Oh, what a pretty name', but quietly so they didn't incite the visitation of a malign spirit. One reckless woman said she wished she'd thought of it. Everyone glanced sharply: *Are you mad? Might as well conjure a spell to summon the devil, or evil, or that man, whoever he was, who stole E away.* Names matter. But I have said that before, and if I have not, I will have more to say on the subject later.

They'd forgotten about Till listening in a doorway to the conversations and to the hum in the silence, longing for the moment to pass smoothly, and thinking of the nights she didn't sleep because her parents had not shut the window but only the flyscreen, which even the most half-hearted person could pierce, even on the second floor. The ladder was against the shed. Till knew exactly where the ladder was, believe me. It would be the smallest matter to move it from there to the side of the house. George and Zoe had left the window like that. There was no trusting anyone. Everything came back to this. She had to learn to look after herself and she had to live long enough to learn how to do that. You couldn't tell anyone all of this in the daytime.

That Englishwoman and the baby with the name disappeared. This is the way it appeared to Till. They were there, then they were gone. No one spoke about it. It was a relief to Till – to them all – but no one talked about that either. There was no need to watch that child and fear her and hate her a little too, feeling the superstition while also feeling sorry for her. The hate was Till's. It came to her sometimes, with curiosity and shame.

'What happened to that woman?' she asked Zoe once.

'What woman?'

'You know. The one with the baby.' Surely she would know, and immediately she did, she saw it on her mother's face.

'They went back to England.'

'Nothing bad happened to them?'

'Nothing bad. It's just, I don't think she was very happy here.'

Till said, 'It's good she could go back.'

'Yes. Why'd you ask?'

'I just wondered.'

When she finished the story, Tundra said, 'What was the baby's name?'

'I can't tell you,' Till said. 'I can't say it.'

'That's because you need a ceremony. I told you. Oh my god. White people.'

Chapter 17

Wirowie

THERE WERE THE rusted bicycles of many sizes at the Andersons' up ahead, strung up like the corpses of trophy hunters: dingos and foxes and feral dogs and cats, always reminding Till of the last wild thylacine tied to the fence. They were an old vision heading towards decay. There was a smallish heap of scrap metal at the side of the house too, which looked like an installation on its own.

The Andersons' place wasn't really in town, but neither was it out. Till followed her familiar running route up Main Street until it became a minor street then a dirt road. It was where the blocks got larger and the connection to town more attenuated. It was the last such place before the side road headed through country for the highway.

Till often paused to see if there were any more of the strange sculptures, and now that she knew who lived there, sometimes stopped in. Mrs Anderson only made one or two a year, Marian said. There were a couple of pieces around town – an emu high-stepping through someone's cactus garden, a dog with its paws on a fence. Birdy snuffled through the roadside grasses along the fence line and set the horse galloping and they ran alongside each other in similar style, one free and one fenced, and Birdy lagged and caught up and raced ahead. 'You're an idiot, Bird,' Till told her when she came back, tongue falling out and eyes rolling so their whites showed. She sat in the shade of a wattle and panted. What a clown.

Some of the sculptures were amusing, some sinister. The swaddled doll in a bassinet with a sign attached to the front – *Was it the dingo though?* – made Till feel strange. Taken together they suggested a maker of eccentricity, but they were the product of Mrs Anderson's imagination.

'I always wonder who they're for,' Till said. Mrs Anderson was cleaning her kitchen at the time, fussing over some persistent ants that wouldn't get the message. You could never know what was going on inside a person.

Mrs Anderson kept wiping away the dead ants. 'Same as for any art. For the person who needs to see them. No one. You. Maybe just me. They take my mind off things. That's always welcome. Like that one I did for you. Those palm fronds. They were finicky things. Oh my goodness, the time they took. I loved doing them.'

Like Zoe leaving Till behind, walking away for a break, she thought. 'They are amazing,' Till said. 'I look at it every day, all angles, close up, far away. I love it – thoroughly.'

When Till had shown Mrs Anderson a photo of it, she said, 'Oh my,' and gave an almost secretive smile. She liked it herself, but a habit of country reticence stopped her saying more. 'Isn't everything for someone? Even if they don't know, they know when they see it.' She turned from the shelves to look around. 'Who are you singing for?'

'Pardon?' Till's voice sounded sharp, just from surprise.

'We all hear you out there singing your heart out. Doesn't matter if it's for no one or someone. We can hear it anyway.'

Till blushed. 'Oh, that.'

'I like it, if you want to know. We sit out on the porch for the show if the wind's blowing right. We take something from it.'

'I didn't know.'

'No harm in it. We all do. People like it. We're short on entertainment.' She looked out of the window at her sculptures, very still. 'My ideas have dried up. You know, Len . . .' She went back to her cleaning.

Mr Anderson was dying, Marian told her. They were waiting and trying to stay busy so it didn't seem like waiting, and trying to be hopeful for his sake despite there being little hope. But what else could they do?

'Yeah,' Till said.

There was a new sculpture a week or two later. A woman in black, a wide open mouth painted red, dark hair streaming back, standing on some railway tracks with a tall black dog. Till liked it. She didn't mention it to Mrs Anderson, just said to Marian, 'I always think the bicycles are a bit sinister.'

'They were jauntier in their younger days. Things change. Their meanings change. They move away from whatever made them.'

'The same with singing and songs.'

When Till finished school she declined any further study. But after a year of singing – just filling in for someone, the older sister of a schoolfriend, not because it was her dream – she went to university to find out about the shit in her head, as she put it. Childhood trauma, PTSD, bla bla bla, so it had been a waste of time after all. They had words for it that they draped around the whole mess like theatre curtains. What a fraud she was. No one had taken her. She had been safe. One year of that had been enough.

All the time, Till kept on singing, then tried songwriting, and she had some success. She didn't really care about it, or the summer of her feel-good collection and her big hit, the last of the old fashioned feel-good summers before the fires and disease. She sang because she could sing and perhaps also because she wondered whether E might have become a singer.

She, E, had a sweet voice. Everyone said so. She remembered all the words and people liked listening to her. They sang together in the playground while hammering pieces of wood together and building cubbies and skipping and tea parties. Maybe E would have been an engineer, or a politician or an activist or a perfumier, but in Till's mind she was a singer, as well as other things, and all of those things had been obliterated.

Till could not comprehend all the rooms of her life that had been taken, all the details never to exist. How was there room for anything else in the world but the cavernous spaces that people walked so delicately around and along slender walkways between the cavernous spaces that were barely safe underfoot, trying all the while not to jostle anyone passing or scrape a tender place or wonder too much about the empty rooms spied, spied, spied, and wondered at in passing. She would think about just one day and everything that happened, and all of those days, the people that travelled through them as the days travelled through time, the arcs intersecting, and her, E, removed from it. The things and the people her removal from life must have changed. And she was one person.

There was a tree on Flemington Road in the lesser-known outer reaches of Parkville, a vast eucalyptus with smooth limbs of a marvellous subtle colour that she looked at when the lights were red. Somehow it flourished on a concrete island surrounded by nine lanes of traffic, tram tracks and bicycle lanes. Till loved it; birds did too, magpies and rainbow lorikeets especially, and perhaps smaller birds invisible from below. It was life to them, shelter, food and lookout. From up there they would have surveyed vast pastures of concrete and asphalt and the machinery of human life and the trees of the nearby park. The Roads Department (if that is their name) wanted to alter the merging of lanes to make it safer and the tree would have to go they said. People launched a campaign with petitions and protestors, banners and all of the accoutrements of anguish and disagreement. It turned out that a lot of people loved it. It didn't matter though. The department understood people and felled it in the middle of the night while everyone was home in bed. Till saw the void that it left, people weeping, birds flying unimpeded through the space it had shaped, bewildered, homeless and adrift.

Till still loved that tree years later. Creatures of all kinds miss things beloved even in their absence. In that way nothing is ever truly gone. It is loss and the space it occupies that I speak of. All Till could do was give E her voice as she remembered it when she was five and how it might have become. She could no longer remember where this idea came from or when it became definite, only that she sang in a mimicking voice that became habitual and that enough people believed it was hers and came to expect her to sound that way, so that eventually she believed them right. It was no great effort.

Only Leiky said to her once with a wondering look, 'Nice song. Funny though. I don't know, I suppose I always expected your voice would be deeper. Not quite you somehow? Some singer you like?'

Till thought, but did not say, *Why yes, Leiky, it is the song of this ghost child, my dear friend, who also liked to sing.*

It was a bright voice with a 'great pop sensibility' her manager said. It was the truth. People liked it, and Till quite liked that. Only she could not feel comfortable about it. It made Till feel strange to hear a recording of herself (since it was not really herself) and even after all those years no one else knew it.

Once Till saw Mrs Anderson moving from one sculpture to another, adjusting a hat, pulling at a metal arm, tying a kerchief about a freckled boy's face, and the quality of her peacefulness reminded Till of her mother wandering the garden first thing in the morning, last thing at night, plucking off a yellowed leaf, deadheading a rose, watering the pot plants. The sinister became wholesome beneath her hands.

Till chatted with Mr Anderson if he was about, sitting on the Anderson porch. One evening he was surveying the sculptures and the solitary horse and its water trough in the sea of sparsely grassed dirt on the other side of the road and the sun setting across it, elemental as that, and he was part of it.

At sight of Till and Birdy, he raised a pipe with one hand and a cup of tea with the other, almost with gaiety, and said, 'Girls are inside if you're after them. Welcome to pass the time out here for a bit if you like.'

So Till and Birdy did. They didn't have a lot to say, but this seemed to suit Mr Anderson, who was a quiet man of faded beauty. He must have been devastating once. He coughed and rubbed his chest and gave it a soft punch as if telling it to settle down in there. His skin was like fly-specked antique silk and his eyes were as pink as one of the salt lakes from down south, small discs of watery blue swimming like rare fish beneath the surface. Mr Anderson was dying. Till didn't need anyone to tell her that.

'She's a good gel, my Marian,' he said in his dry paddock voice. He said the 'l' in gel in the old South Australian way, as if it had a 'w' that went along with it – gelw – which Till loved, as she loved it when her grandma asked if she'd like some milwk in her tea. 'Not her fault what happened. You know.' He waved his pipe hand around in a few circles and the smoke lagged behind.

Till lifted her nose to the tobacco scent like Birdy after something unfamiliar coming in on a wind. 'What did happen?'

'That feller of hers.' He tapped his pipe on the arm of his chair. 'If I was what I used to be I wouldn't be sitting here in this chair, no I wouldn't. I'd be off. I'd be having a word. I'd be having more than a word. I'd be, I'd—' He lifted his foot and moved it in the arc of a kick, a trembling shadow of that. His tartan slipper fell to the porch floor and then his toes couldn't reach it and he slumped back, spent and dejected.

Till picked it up and he held out his foot like a good helping boy. It smote Till. She wanted to cry and couldn't help thinking of George and when he might need such help.

'Very cool slippers,' she said. 'Bet you didn't get them round here. Bet you had to order them, or, no, bet you got them in Adelaide, didn't you. Slippers like that, blue and yellow tartan, don't grow on trees.'

Mr Anderson chuckled and wheezed and looked down at them. 'They'll see me out, I suppose.' He punched his chest again and knuckled some moisture from his eyes. 'I'm done for, take me out the back and shoot me, good for nothing now, can't protect my own gel, can't protect my wife.'

'They'd die for you right now. No need for you to do anything but sit here in your fancy slippers charming the town's ladies. It's enough for them.'

'Turned into the sort of old duffer I used to laugh at. Young ladies coming along to flatter me. Used to wonder where their pride was. Told myself I wouldn't stand for it. Well, I was a fool, I'll tell you that now.'

'You're not a fool.'

'There you go again.'

'We keep finding out about ourselves is what I think. It's hard to imagine what we might be one day.'

'Wish I could say sorry to them.'

'They might have been thinking the same as you now. They used to be you and things have changed, and they're sorry for their own past thoughts, looking at you thinking, *You'll find out, mister*. I'm sorry for mine already. Way ahead of you.'

He coughed out a laugh and punched his chest. 'Now look what you've done.'

'Don't think you'll be getting a sorry from me.'

'Still.' He turned to look at Till. 'Do something?'

She nodded.

'Keep an eye out for my Marian. He . . .' Mr Anderson punched a soft fist into the palm of his hand.

'Nooo,' Till said.

Mr Anderson raised his eyes to her. 'No forgiving that. You watch out for him. Marian's former husband. Terrible feller. Police. Not one of them would turn against him, not one would lift a finger for our Marian. What is the point of them?'

'Police.'

'Yup.'

'Young guy?'

'Young enough. Head like a bullet.'

'I think I've seen him.' His muscled back, his heavy neck, his square hands, his eager cock, the reel that seemed to play in his mind as he went about his business. 'You like that.' And Till: 'No I don't like that', and a twist of her body, a headbutt to his nose, a hard knee to his groin, a roar: 'bitch, bitch'. Yes, she'd seen him. And later there was Marian in her fancy dress in the shop, presiding over her loaves of white sandwich bread and Coke and speaking in that strange proud bitter way to Till, 'Word gets around.'

Mr Anderson clasped Till's arm, and his hand was so soft, so removed from any of the work that she knew was his reason and meaning that she had to stop breathing so she didn't sob. She nearly choked on it.

'My advice? Avoid him. Made trouble for some other folks too. Something bad inside. It's what he likes.'

'I'll remember.'

Till wondered a lot what made men angry with women. Some men, she supposed she should say. Some men, not all men. She asked a man once and he said it was in the Bible and people believed it and that was why, but Till said that was only writing, recording something that existed. The man started getting annoyed with her, as if she was being uppity, out of her lane, too big for her britches, a know-all bitch for questioning his in-his-mind perfect explanation. She could have had a fight, but why would she? It wouldn't change his mind. She just looked at him until he recognised his anger and began justifying it – and then she walked away.

*

The next time she saw Mr Anderson, he was tucked in a hospital bed pushed up to a window so he could look out. Marian and Mrs Anderson were holding his hands. But it seemed like he was already travelling down a road they couldn't see, and Till remembered E skipping away, not knowing about the road before her.

The time after that he'd been laid out.

And then there was the wake at the Chamber of Commerce building on Main Street, a great grand thing with moulded pillars on the facade, high ceilings of pressed tin, the enamel paint yellowed with age, and dark wood panelling, and more people than Till had seen in a long time, from places Till hadn't heard of. The ends of dirt roads, the other side of troughs, over a range of hills, into several valleys, from saltbush country beyond the line. People had liked Mr Anderson, and they found things to laugh about in the tales they told. He'd helped people out with their heavy work if needed, mended roofs and cut wood and so on. He'd been a good worker.

What a strange thing it was how many roads, how many lives could lead to a quiet man's funeral: the desperate woman sobbing – no, wailing – near the sandwiches, beyond polite grief, Till here from Melbourne, Mr Anderson's stricken wife and daughter and a son who'd arrived from the city, the people from a spiderweb of places. People from Wirowie too. The old man on his porch who Till sometimes saw out running. 'You,' he said.

'Yes, me,' she agreed, and invited him to visit the station one day since he expressed some curiosity about progress, and he said he would. Bob Finch was his name.

'Going okay, I hear,' he said, 'so Stew and Bev say. And Ken.'

Stew, in freshly ironed khakis and a crisp white shirt, hair slicked neat with water, stopped to ask if they'd seen Bev, who was walking down to meet him there. But they hadn't.

There was Mrs Anderson some way off through the throng, quiet, a small neat woman with short silver hair, capable hands, and clothes she was not comfortable in – a flowered shirt that she touched the unfamiliar sleeve of as if it was emblematic of this hallucinatory day. How odd, these colours – flowers she'd never seen the like of around here, and on her – and this fine impractical cotton (from a lifetime with her mother, Till knew it was a nice poplin not a poly blend). It made her a stranger to herself – she was more accustomed to her workroom jeans and overalls and soft plaid shirts – and perhaps she wondered if her husband would recognise her if she died right now and arrived in heaven in this rig, if there was such a place, if they worried about such things, if recognition existed. Best to be yourself maybe. But it was a distraction, which might have been one of its purposes. So Till's thinking went.

Grief is hard and boring. People don't tell you that. Misery and leaking eyes and feeling dreary and lost without that person, and people's pity and kind lacerating questions and curiosity, and the flowers and casseroles and cakes and biscuits they bring is all tiring. But it is so nice of them, even though everything tastes of nothing and all the flowers smell of nothing, and they are all disgusting, loud and unnatural, and you miss the person and you can't make it stop or take a break except if you sleep. It is frightening to wake up and know it all again, and to have to live it again never knowing when it will end, or if. Maybe it never does for some people. Till knew this even though she didn't have the words for it when she was five. She could see Marian and Mrs Anderson learning it now, quiet and dumbfounded together.

Two police came in, young guys walking slowly, thumbs in their belts, a tinge of menace as if grieving people might foment a riot from sadness, a clot of darkness in the poor light. One of them was Rod, who Till had experience of, who Marian had other experiences of. Marian had also seen him, judging by the miserable anger on her face and some old yearning – wanting him to be something he was not, hoping for it despite everything, hating him and remembering when she had not and so on.

A low sound like insects stirring rose from the crowd. Marian's mother lifted a hand to her cheek, then her mouth. What etiquette manual could prepare a person for such a moment? Marian saw this and sadness and pity scudded across her face, wind over wheat. She pulled her mother close so they were hiding in each other. Till was too far away, but she imagined soft words, anything to stop this aloneness that was Mrs Anderson's now and that Marian could not protect her from. Till's cheeks were wet too. God she was such an idiot. What kind of loser . . . It wasn't her dad. But even this harsh talk of her mind did not help.

Rod swaggered through the people, making for Marian and her mother. He reached his hand for Marian's arm. She jerked free. Everything about his face went mean. His mouth moved fast, and very clearly, as if she meant for everyone in the room to see and understand this, Marian replied 'Fuck off', with good separation between the words. Everyone could lip-read. He looked like he'd been slapped. Red anger suffused his face, and filled him. Till had no doubt he would have struck Marian if they were alone, but he could do nothing except say something harsh and turn and make for the door, the rage coming off him as random as sparks, making people flinch and draw back.

And then a late arrival, Till assumed from his ironed chinos and shirt, came to the door and bellowed, 'Help. Get scissors, a knife, something sharp, anything,' and looked into the black void behind him. 'There's something here.'

A tidal movement swayed in his direction. Till ran around its edge to the kitchen and snatched a knife from a cake (*Len Anderson, RIP, Beloved Husband & Father*) and ran back. People were gathered in the darkness outside by then, encircling something, which a few of them worried at in the shadows, pulling and yanking and snatching with no clear purpose, the light from the doorway pouring over them putting Till in mind of the attendees at Rembrandt's anatomy lesson. Till burrowed through the warm sweaty bodies, all unwilling to give way, to give up their sliver of view.

'Knife. Knife. I've got a knife. Let me through. Knife,' she shouted, and people did make way, reluctantly, looking for the knife, suddenly impressive outside when a moment before it had been merely domestic, which she held down straight against her leg. They pulled away and grew quiet at the sight of it, as if they could taste the cold iron on their tongues. The right knife can cut flesh as well as cake, something that's easy to forget.

The thing on the ground was long, bulky, tapering at one end. It was warm and that made it disgusting. It wasn't meat, or an animal, not exactly. A person then. Its head moved and a muffled groan and a desperate wail came out of it, like a muted engine, and then a snuffling hunger for air. Marian bent to the head and teased and pulled tape loose from its mouth. There was a humming murmuring of people and calls of advice: that's it, come in from under, careful, oh my god, you're okay, and so on.

Till began sawing at the tape that bound the person's arms to her body. She put a hand on the person's shoulder and looked into her wild eyes and saw it was Bev. 'Hold still if you can. Don't want to cut you.'

It was hard afterwards to make events into a sequence, to make the cloth of the night lie straight and flat. Events seemed to rise out of nowhere, puckering the fabric, making it billow incomprehensibly.

First was Bev's scream – a short one, Till was fairly sure about that. There was the moment when Bev's face was revealed, wild with distress and rage. 'Please,' she said. 'Oh please.' When they freed her and she could stand she didn't know what to do. She batted people's hands away and stared around, desperate and not quite steady. Stew crashed through at a run and she threw herself at him and was saved. Tenderness existed in her and Till couldn't look away from the strangeness of the sight.

The policemen thrust their way through with their pouty chests, hands clutching the implements hanging from their belts. See this, their bodies seemed to say: my whistle, my truncheon thing (*oh, Joe Strummer RIP*, Till thought), my pepper spray, my taser (on the last two of these, Till was not sure, but they were at any rate larger than the whistles) and began asking questions. Till wasn't paying attention to the words. It was everything behind the words which she did not understand at all. Rod, whose body she knew a little and didn't want to know more, shook his head – slightly, as if in admonishment – at Bev. A person would hardly notice, but Till did. And Bev loathed him. It might have been a fight behind the shelter shed – no, more vicious than that, a wildlife documentary, two fanged, clawed creatures pacing around each other looking for their moment from the way everyone watched. This innocent town, innocent as the city, as anywhere. Till began listening.

To every question Bev answered, 'I don't know. I didn't see. I didn't hear. I didn't see him. On the side of the road. Somewhere on Third Street maybe, I'm not sure. I don't know how it happened, how I got here. I don't know. Out cold maybe.' Her voice was a monotone.

Stew rubbed her back and her shoulder and stroked her hair. She leaned against him.

Finally, when there was nothing for it but to stop, and people were getting restless (things were more dramatic on TV), the other policeman, the fresh-faced one, arranged to visit the next day – 'to locate the crime scene' – and gave her his card.

But there was one other thing: Rod saw Till and then Marian close by, close enough for him to see that they knew each other. Well, people don't like to be judged, and if he hated them – one for overpowering him, the other for leaving him – they hated him in turn. There was nothing he could do. He was vulnerable in that moment and could do nothing is what I mean. They knew what was behind this facade.

Chapter 18

'Rod,' Marian said.

'Yeah,' Till said. 'I'm sorry about that, with him. I didn't know he was your . . . I wouldn't have, I mean. I had no idea.' Till could not stop the distress she knew was on her face.

She had arrived at the shop at opening time, Birdy in tow, to see Marian, because they had things to talk about and because it was bread delivery day and life went on. What a wholesome thing that sounded after last night. They were sitting on stools behind the shop counter (almost below it, the stools being so low) and the coffee machine – that shrine to past hopes – a place that seemed to suit confidences, being as concealed as the shrub shelters Till and E had once tended and whispered and made plans within. Birdy had leapt pantherlike into the box window casement the minute they arrived and now lay in a pond of sun. Marian had promised to order Till a seeded loaf and Till had promised to buy it. They were pulling pieces off it now and eating them slowly, talking about what they would like to put on it. Till wanted butter; Marian wanted honey.

Marian had ordered three loaves of seeded, three of white, it turned out. Also six litres of milk. When Till asked her why, she said, 'Because you never know. Live in hope, hey?'

It seemed like an absolute truth to Till, not necessarily about bread and the bread people chose, but about the way people surprise. But there did not seem much point in saying it.

'Dad told you? He did, didn't he?'

'Yeah.'

She began to weep, softly. 'Everything?' She wiped the tears away impatiently. Very slowly, unconsciously, Marian's hands fluttered across her body. She touched her forehead and cheekbone and put her fingers over a closed eye, and ran her hand over her head and clenched a palm against her arm and scratched an ankle and rubbed her legs and finally wrapped her arms around her body, her head tucked in low, and all of it unconsciously. She became a small person, and she was a tall woman really; she was magnificent, and he had made her this.

Till said, 'I don't know. He told me a few things.' She took Marian's hand in hers and held it, soft, and Marian allowed it.

'I wish he hadn't said.'

'Sorry.'

'No. It's all right. It's just humiliating, you know? Someone else would have said something. I'm amazed they haven't already, the way things get around. Yeah, not a nice guy.'

Till said, 'I wish the coffee machine worked. I'd like a coffee.'

'You know, I don't know if it ever did.'

'It must have.'

'I suppose. One of my worst investments.'

It was the only investment Till could see. Perhaps some paint had been applied at one point. The shop had for sale the fresh loaves of bread on the shelves, five bottles of Coke, three litres of full cream milk and three litres of skim milk in the fridge, also some aged packets of jelly crystals in one of the long lines of empty shelves. There was no one around, not a car passing, not a person, no sign yet even of Ken arriving at his collectibles shop. The muffled sound of cockatoos nearby drifted, and the roosters shouting from each end of town, sunshine flooding everywhere.

'We'd broken up, mostly. It's on him not you. Just a shitty guy.'

'We never did it.'

'Oh really?' Marian's eyes went wide. 'That's not like him. He's a guy who gets his way.'

'He got a broken nose instead.'

'Hah! That was you?' Marian slapped her leg and laughed.

'I'm a good fighter. I can look after myself. Your dad wanted me to look out for you – you know that?'

'You?' Marian said, her eyes moving across Till.

'Yes. Maybe he heard about the nose from someone.' Her seriousness seemed to persuade Marian. 'I said I would, so you know. Bev, though,' Till said.

'Yeah. Mum's going around later. There was some trouble with her daughter before she went missing. Always something going on.'

'Tundra told me. I had no idea.'

'It was a mess. I never worked it out. Rod was investigating. It's all gone quiet. Drugs . . . it's always drugs.'

'Poor Bev. But who would do that to her?' There was something weird about it to Till. Binding someone rather than beating them up. That would take time. Then moving them and dumping them. 'Some control thing. Do things happen around here?'

'No. Never. It's quiet, so quiet apart from the odd feral. Kind of an outlier town. Everything happens in other places.

Not enough people to cause trouble. A few homeless people squatting. No one would care. I suppose they still have owners, but they couldn't sell them. People don't mind that. Not enough of us to mind. Yeah, I really have no idea. Something about her daughter maybe, some warning? But she didn't say anything about a warning. Her legs weren't tied. They must have walked her in.'

'She doesn't know anything.'

'Says she doesn't.'

Bev's eyes had rolled as if she were livestock being branded. The terror that quivered through her. Everyone's horror. There was the memory of the shadows, and for a moment Till got her old sick feeling about night. What if someone had been watching – so her thinking went. The hard light of day revealed everything, or seemed to, and was a comfort for those reasons. She concentrated on the verifiable: the last box on the shop shelves, the line someone had drawn with their finger in the dust, Birdy's wet nose, the child's handprint smeared low on the shop window, the Bushell's Tea poster curling at its corners, its faded red highlights.

Marian made them each a cup of tea and Till began fiddling with the coffee machine as a distraction, pulling levers, poking around its mechanisms. She did a search for its make on her phone and watched an instructional video in concentration. 'Got any screwdrivers?' she asked Marian, 'unless you'd rather I didn't.'

'Why not? Pretty sure the warranty's run out by now.' She clattered around in a drawer and found a few and Till began dismantling the machine, laying out the parts on the counter. It was like a beast after slaughter. Why did she think such things?

Marian watched. 'I should have got Dad in. He might have

liked it. Why didn't I? I wanted to be independent. I don't know. It doesn't matter I suppose.'

'Coffee always matters. It smells good. It's enticing. Make it a coffee destination. The first time I came in here I thought it was a coffee destination. Who owns the shop?'

'Me. My mother, I suppose, but yeah, me really. It's been in the family forever. Absolute sinkhole for money, like everything around here. Poor Ken.' They looked reflexively across the road to see if he'd arrived, but it was as still as a museum installation. 'And what did you end up getting? A bottle of water. You coming in kept me going for a week at least. "Could I please have a soy latte?"' she mimicked. 'Oh my god, when I got home.'

'Well, the sign was on the footpath,' Till said.

'What a dill,' Marian said, but affectionately.

'Your dad said something to me once.'

'Did he?'

'"You must be the Melbourne girl, right?" Only just stopped himself laughing. I loved your dad.'

'Yeah. Everyone loved him. I mean, they really did. Oh my god, women.'

'Really?'

'The lady crying over the sandwiches?'

Till raised her eyebrows.

'I don't know if they were ever a thing, but in her mind they were. I suppose they might have been. Hard on my mum. People love talking. His kindness was devastating.'

'He was a very charming man.'

'He was my dad.' She couldn't help crying then, and Till couldn't either. Misery loves company. Someone said that to her once. Marian sniffed and leaned forward to wipe her nose on the skirt of her dress. 'Sorry.'

'Traditional purpose of skirts. Of course if you sold tissues here . . .'

Marian laughed – 'I'll start a list' – and cried a little more. Till took her hand and stroked it and sang a few lines of 'No Woman, No Cry', which I can't tell you any more of because of copyright, but you can look it up very easily. Till did not sound very like Bob Marley.

'People have been listening for you,' Marian said.

'Oh yeah?'

'Yeah. Wild singing.' A pause. 'That's Bev who says that, if you want to know. Apparently,' she added tentatively, as if it was also a question.

'Oh. Wild. I don't know about that. I'm singing anyway. I don't think I'm going to stop. Bev hasn't mentioned it to me.'

'Maybe she likes it,' Marian said. They both laughed at that.

Sometimes Till and her parents had heard the zoo lions roaring when the wind blew from the south, and she imagined the lion getting the man, and the strength of her wish made her feel it might come true. Even thinking it was somehow a responsibility. It was a person's life she wished to be extinguished.

They stopped talking when a police car came into view, slowly rounding the corner in front of the shop, sliding past the window – briefly, Birdy raised her head – and down to the next corner where it made a right onto Third Street. No rush about it, as if it was trying to catch people off guard. Till and Marian were at the door by then, then outside on the street watching.

'Well,' Marian said.

They wandered down, just a casual weekend stroll the day after a funeral, the day after the strangest crime in a scarcely inhabited town. People like to project a story about themselves; it gives some sort of cover if someone accuses you – saying 'ghouls', 'busybodies', for instance. You are prepared. Eagerness would be unseemly.

The police car was parked on the road further up, past grasses and weeds and a pile of scrap metal on the left, a stone house on the right, its fence weathered into strange muscular remnants, like beef jerky. One of the police, the sidekick, walked along the asphalt, pausing to look at the dirt. He spoke on his phone. Bev and Stew came out and they began their vague wandering together. Once, the policeman who wasn't Rod squatted and poked his finger at something on the ground, the way they do on cop shows, but tentatively, like he was copying something he'd seen. Rod gave him a soft boot as if he'd embarrassed them both with his industry, and he stood and they looked down the road, saw Till and Marian, and walked away along the road in its endless direction west, hard against the verge, scuffing at gravel and stones.

Mr Finch was sitting on the big shop step when Till and Marian got back. 'Minding it for ya,' he called out. 'Came for some bread.' He stood creakily and came in and soon he and Till were poking about in the coffee machine's entrails.

Later, Rod and the sidekick came in. 'Business booming as usual,' Rod said, and when Marian and Till simply glared at him added, 'Nothing to say?'

Marian said, 'You're the one who came in, so it seems like it would be you who wanted to say something.'

'Came by to warn you about something.'

'Oh, a warning. I've never had one of them before.'

'I'm warning you,' he said with menace.

'Once again . . .'

The dreary exchange kept unfolding, coming out of them in pieces formed and fitting together like worn-in machinery. Everything about them except the violence was here. Till could not now remember what had appealed about him late at night, pissed, in the dark, without words. Just those three things presumably. He might feel the same. His eyes sheered away from the sight of Till; he didn't meet her eyes.

'Just tell us then,' she said.

'We don't have to tell you,' he said.

'Right. You're doing us a good turn.'

His face coloured up at that, but he wanted to deliver his message, he wanted them to feel something.

It was this. A woman had been found two weeks before, he said, bound and suspended from an old water crane at the railway station at Yongala, which, like Wirowie station, was closed. She'd been there overnight and for a little of the day before, and was lucky to have been found, the police said. She had hypothermia, was covered in bruises from a beating and in terrible distress. ('Screamed like a banshee apparently,' Rod said in a jaunty tone, 'once they took off the tape.') The station was on the edge of town and not often visited. It was a passing railway enthusiast, of the type that occasionally turned up on Till's front doorstep, that discovered her. Bless the railway geeks and tourists if you ask me; don't complain. It was just as it had been with Bev, apart from the beating and being hung up. The woman knew nothing at all; she had been caught unawares while walking. Investigations were underway, Rod said. A random prank, the police over that way said. ('Pretty fucking random,' Marian said later, 'and not what I'd call a prank.') Or an old boyfriend, or some drama following her from the city to this quiet place. Marian made a humphing noise at the word 'quiet', and said, 'More like dead'.

They wouldn't say who she was – just a townie taking advantage of cheap property.

'Nothing wrong with that if no one else wants it,' Till said, for the first time in a while feeling her city past. 'Everyone wants some shelter.'

The police were waiting for details of the Yongala attack, the young policeman said. There had been her and now there was Bev.

Neither Till nor Marian had seen any stranger about Wirowie. Where a town is so empty a person can pass unnoticed because there is no one there to see. It might as well have been a ghost who'd passed through. It left them feeling uneasy.

Mr Finch continued working on the coffee machine through this, only agreeing with Till and Marian that he'd seen no stranger in town since Till's arrival. 'I probably wouldn't though. I'm on a side road. Only person passing by is Till, here, on her run.'

The police left.

Then Mrs Anderson dropped in on her way to see Bev, who had rung to ask her to come over. She wanted the company. She wanted to talk.

'Did she mention Yongala?' Marian said.

'What about Yongala? She didn't say anything.'

'Another attack a couple of weeks ago. Police just told us.'

'Oh my god.' Mrs Anderson put her hand to her mouth. 'I'll go see her now and find out. Wouldn't they have said something to her?'

But no one knew.

Till and Marian filled Mrs Anderson in on what they knew, and she headed off for Bev's. Two children turned up, sent by their mothers – small boys with shining eyes and the curiosity of puppies – and each bought a loaf of bread and some milk.

Then Ken came by. 'Bob,' he said to Mr Finch.

'Ken,' Mr Finch said.

'Don't tell me we're going to have coffee here one day,' Ken said.

'Yup. Training pigs to fly in the backyard too. All systems go.'

They both chuckled – some old joke between them.

Till and Mr Finch had got as far as they could with 'The Machine' as they were now calling it; they thought a seal had gone, so Till ordered one and said she would let him know when it arrived. 'If that's okay with you, Marian?' she asked.

'Oh sure. Don't mind me,' Marian said.

Ken picked up the last seeded loaf. Marian told him he wouldn't regret it. He looked at it doubtfully. They filled Ken in on the news, and after he left Mr Finch headed home.

Marian looked around as if expecting more people to appear. 'What a morning.'

'You should have some lollies here, and some icy poles,' Till said. 'That would keep them here.'

Marian pointed at some empty jars behind them. 'Been there. We call them sweeties not lollies.'

'Sweeties. Okay. I would buy some sweeties if you had them. Those kids would. People love having somewhere to stop in. The shop would be like a community hub, like this morning, everyone catching up on the news, buying their bits and pieces.'

'Okay, okay, I'll get some sweeties then. But you better buy them.'

'And icy poles.'
'Fine.'

Mrs Anderson came back some time later, and seeing her, Till was reminded of her sadness, and of Marian's. They moved slowly, almost wading through it. A tide was heading out and they weren't ready; it was like that. Seeing each other seemed to remind them. They shut the shop and began walking up the street and Mrs Anderson told them the strange news about Bev, that she could have answered some of the policemen's questions but wouldn't. The person, the man, who had worn a balaclava, had caught her on the road, and though she'd fought back he had her down fast and kneeled on her while he gagged and then tied her about her torso and taped her face and arms. Then he walked her on Mitchell up Aver or Amelia, she wasn't sure which, to Main Street.

Mrs Anderson turned her head. 'Just there. Probably Aver. He knew his way. The whole time he was telling her he wouldn't kill her, he wouldn't hurt her, but she mustn't talk to the police or he'd kill the boy. He kept saying it and she believed him. He meant Isaac. So he'd been watching them. There was something about him that made you believe him, she said.'

'My god,' Marian said. 'But why do it? I don't understand. He didn't want anything?'

'No. I suppose he just wanted to do what he did.'

Marian shook her head in agitation. 'But what did he want to do? Scare her? Scare the people who found her, who saw her? My god. Why Wirowie? That's it?'

They walked quietly, Mrs Anderson thinking, the three

of them wondering. It seemed as if this hadn't occurred to Mrs Anderson. 'Anyway,' she said, 'it was the thought of Isaac that kept her quiet. He knew about him.'

'Why would he threaten to kill Isaac?' Till said.

'You know him, don't you?'

'Through Ed.'

'There's a lot of pain there,' Mrs Anderson said. 'Bev and Stew don't need any more worries.'

'Ed and Liz were at school together. I don't think they were serious. And Bear,' Marian said.

'Yes, Bear. God he was a sweet kid. *They* were serious.' Mrs Anderson shook her head a little. 'That was a hard time.'

Till looked back down the road where the oxblood colour of the shed and the splash of white writing was still visible, the word BEAR larger than the rest. It was all too weird, last night, this morning, this sunlit day, pleasant now, but chill. The cold evening air was waiting to pour in, fill up the space like water, and she thought about lighting her fire and locking the door and whether she might feel uneasy again tonight, the first time in weeks. She probably would. But she had Birdy. Ed was away on some trip to Adelaide and Sydney for meetings. He'd be back the next day or she might be ringing him now. But she could manage on her own.

'Sorry we didn't tell you,' Mrs Anderson said.

'Doesn't matter. Tundra told me a while ago.'

'Oh, good. I'm glad she did. It's just that everyone knows so no one talks about it. Yeah, a lot of pain.'

'Ed told me about him and Liz. He just didn't mention her name. I should've made the connection earlier. Tundra filled me in. A bit slow. Isaac doesn't talk much at all. He's never mentioned his mother.' What if he just wanted to keep that little piece of Ed to himself, separate and sort of pure, not mix it up with his family – his mother who was missing, his father who was dead. She held that idea up with the way Isaac was, the way he was with her, to see if they made sense together.

There were Mr Oldham and Tundra too, their connections to Bev and Stew through their children, their losses, this one precious child. All the precious children just trying to make their way. Every one of them. She didn't know anything and couldn't help thinking again of the day Bev came into the service station and flung words at Till, and how Tundra had been angry with Till and she'd lain down around the corner while Birdy guarded her. She hadn't talked to them about E and maybe she should. That was a great void that she dragged around with her, all the while giving no sign it existed. Who was she to talk?

Cockatoos broke into screaming in the peppercorn trees near the corner of the arid gardens and kept on after they passed. Finally they – Till, Marian and Mrs Anderson – reached the WWI soldier's memorial on Railway Place and stopped since it was Till's turnoff. She sat on the granite step. They all did.

'I never know what to say to Bev and Stew,' Till said.

'None of it's new to them, remember that,' Mrs Anderson said. 'Liz. She just ran at life. Wild, too pretty for her own good. Sorry. I don't mean that – just came out; it's what people say. She was very pretty, and the way that went was not her fault, not even half of it. Boys were after her. Things went in the wrong direction and it dragged Bear with her, you ask me. Then he had to protect her, and then the police were after him.' She glanced at Marian. 'Sorry, sweetheart,' she said to her daughter.

Marian waved it aside. 'The man's an arsehole. I'm sorry I ever met him. Sorry I brought him into your life. He never belonged here.'

'Bev would say different. Her Lizzie could do no wrong. She didn't really do wrong. We like to think the best of our children. I do think the best of you, Marian. You're a wonderful daughter.'

'Oh Mum.'

'No, don't. I'm going to say it more often. No arguments now. Does your mum say that to you, Till?'

'Yes she does. Quite often. But sometimes if she's been kind of annoyed, so . . . I feel like she's saying sorry sometimes when she says something nice, or she means she's disappointed in me but can't say it so she's saying she likes me despite everything. It's complicated.' What she meant was that love could feel heavy.

Mrs Anderson seemed to feel some delicate solidarity on the subject of mothers, and after a polite silence said, 'Where fault lies is always untidy. Roy and Tundra never blamed her. They blamed the police.'

'Bear? Was it murder?'

'Found dead,' Marian said. 'Rod said it was a deal gone wrong, Bear double-crossed someone, a dealer killed him.'

'I don't believe that,' Mrs Anderson broke in. 'Not the way they'd do it. No way of telling how he died.'

'What about the sign? Who did that?' Till asked.

'Roy's work, though he's never said so,' Mrs Anderson said. 'He believed it was antifreeze I think that killed him. Leaves no trace, he said. I don't know if that's right. The police made council paint it over – I heard that from Ruth at the council offices; she's in my knitting group – but someone always noticed, came by in the night and painted it again. In the end the police gave up.' She nodded her head a couple of times. 'Sometimes Len did it before Roy found out, save him the trouble. Yeah . . .' her voice trailed off. 'Roy called it keeping the flame burning.'

Till stirred her stick around in the dry leaves at their feet. 'I thought it was about a dog the first time I saw it.'

They laughed a little at that.

'That sign. It's like it's sort of baring its teeth, like there might be something behind the door.'

'Not completely wrong,' Mrs Anderson said. 'Roy can be an angry man. I know the way he looks. He keeps himself in check – he's careful. He and Len kept the truth alive. It'll be a lot for Roy on his own now.' She glanced at Till, and touched her arm. 'Oh honey, no need to cry.'

'It should be you crying. Sorry. I'm so sorry. It kills me what parents go through. Losing a child. Oh my god. Sorry.' She wiped her nose on her sleeve. No one minded.

'Yes. It doesn't kill them though. They mostly live with it. Terrible pain. There's more than one way to lose a child, more than one reason for it to be stolen. It's the thought of the authorities stealing him. They're wonderful grandparents, so careful. They have to be. Any trouble from them and who knows what the police might do.'

'You mean Rod. Just say it,' Marian said. 'I'll do it. I'll look after the door. And if anyone asks, you can tell them it was me all along.'

It made sense. This is how it was agreed. It made Till think of those childhood deaths her mother had told her about, how they seemed not inevitable or unavoidable exactly, but as if the world bent in that direction, and it was hard to stop riding that curve.

Chapter 19

TILL DROVE BACKROADS to Yongala in the morning, passing windmills and ruins, climbing through low hills until grey silos loomed in the shallow valley below. It was unease she felt rather than fear, though she sensed it changing, its clammy touch coming towards her. It was curiosity that drew her. She wanted to see for herself the place the woman had been hung, and where she might have died but for the luck of someone passing by. Till navigated her way towards the silos, since they'd be at the station, slowing as she drove along the town's streets. If times had ever been good here, it could only have been for a short while. Gardens and houses, the pub, had the same parched quality, scrawny almond trees choking in front yards, the paint on buildings reddened with dirt and chipping away. Forests of thistles grew on street corners where the mud caught. It was worn out.

She found signs and came to the railway station's widely spaced tracks which ran and ran like highways along the edge of the town. The station building having been demolished gave her a wrenching feeling about her own station and its likely fate if she hadn't saved it. Long platforms, with steps up to them at each end heaved free of the gravelled earth and subsided into it as if their existence continued beneath. Her great-great-grandmother must have left from here more than a hundred years before, walking from the station building across the open ground, climbing the stairs and waiting for the great smoking metal serpent to take her away.

Till and Birdy walked the platforms and the rest of the railway complex, mostly empty now. It had an uneasy becalmed feeling despite its openness. All around was worn out grass and neglected roads that petered into nothing, and scrubland and a few dead or dying trees and low, sparsely treed hills rising in the distance, which brought to mind concealment and watchers. Birdy seemed to feel some of this and stayed close by. The silos presented a grim appearance under the flat grey sky. And there was the water crane the police had spoken of, concealed at first behind a stand of trees near the northbound track – a shock when Till came upon it. It looked like a gibbet.

It was very tall, several times her height. The woman's attacker must have known of this place, if they did not find it by chance, and prepared the rope for its work. He might have flung rope over the cross bar and pulled her up, he might have drawn a four-wheel drive or ute in close, rested a ladder there and climbed it, he might have put a ladder against the water crane, he might be an acrobat, he might have shinnied up. And did the woman's feet touch the ground, and what was she hanging by, and how well could she breathe? Till couldn't help wondering and trying to picture it, the person who found her, the woman's state. There were houses nearby, she'd driven past them, none of them in view of the station, and it wasn't a local who found her. The station didn't mean anything to the town except the forgotten past. It had a bad feeling.

She didn't know why she'd come now, what she hoped to

see, what anyone might hope for, a sight of themselves, their own worst fears perhaps, one side or the other of an equation about life. Or was she, Till, the same as any other person, wanting to witness such a place, gaze at human potential and her own fears. It was nothing really, there was nothing to see, only things to imagine, and she did not like the directions that imagination sometimes travelled, and she left.

At the shop, Till told Mr Oldham and Tundra about E and what had happened and they were very nice. It seemed the time. She didn't know why. Nice is not always a weak word. They were exactly right in what they said, not making her relive anything or give uncomfortable details or recount her many feelings on the subject, or sympathising in a way that would make her weep. Till was grateful. They considered her before their own curiosity. That is what I mean by nice. 'I wanted you to know,' Till said, and they thanked her.

'It's terrible to lose a child,' Tundra said.

'I'm so sorry about Bear.'

'You've heard more about him. I hear it in your voice.'

'Only a little. It was not like gossip. It was filling in a picture because of Bev and what happened to her. And about Liz.'

Tundra and Mr Oldham had heard from Bev. She had rung to tell them to watch Isaac carefully, not to let him out of their sight, which they said they wouldn't. He had been staying with them the night before the attack, and since, and only Mr Oldham had gone to the wake.

'I'm so sorry,' Till said again.

Roy brushed the words away with his fingertips, rubbing them together and releasing them.

'I love that name,' Till said.

'Not his real name. You probably realised.'

'No.'

'He was such a round little fellow, with thick hair. Wasn't it, Tundra?'

'Beautiful hair, our boy.'

'And eyes.'

'And he was such a strong boy.'

'Sturdy.'

'Yes. Our wee brown bear. That's what we called him.'

'Old family nickname. Suited him.'

'Everyone called him Bear.'

'Everyone. He was so funny. A livewire, you know?'

'Bear.'

It hardly mattered which of them said the words. They were so familiar to each other that either might have said them, these quiet whispered thoughts and comforting memories that they shared, had shared often in the past.

'Maybe a dog would be good for him – Isaac, I mean – his own dog to look out for him,' Till said.

Mr Oldham and Tundra looked at each other. A silent conversation took place. You would have to know all the history, the words that had been spoken, to know, but Till knew it was happening. It wasn't her business though.

'It's a thought,' Tundra said.

'It is,' Mr Oldham said.

Till remembered her beautiful lurcher, Daisy, who had saved her life night after night for years.

'You and Ed,' Mr Oldham said. 'He's a nice feller. Always was.'

'I suppose,' she replied.

'We knew you knew him, but we didn't know you were, you know, seeing each other,' Tundra said.

'Who told you?'

'Oh, you're a cagey one. It was Ed himself. Came through this morning all lit up.' Mr Oldham laughed, and she and Tundra did too and that was not what she had expected of that afternoon. Mr Oldham knew her well enough to know she was cagey and to make it into a joke, and she knew them well enough not to mind.

Just the thought of Ed . . . She was seeing him that night.

Sometimes people arrive in your life. You don't deserve them or not deserve them. That was Till's thinking the first morning that Ed came into view, even though they didn't speak for days. She had a better impression of his arms than his face. It seemed like she had been waiting for him in one way, but she had to move herself, change the course of her life to be in a place where someone else's life could come across hers. Sometimes you were in the wrong place and sometimes the place worked out. Nothing for it but to be grateful, to thank fortune, to gather up its goodness and to live.

Ed had bought a little place on the other side of Yongala, a while back now – beautiful country, cold in winter though, he said. He wanted to show her. So they found a day when Till wasn't working and they drove there. She could hear in his voice how much it meant.

'The secret is to slow the water down, not to steal it,' he said as he drove. 'Then things can grow, they're waiting to grow, to come back: grasses, trees, water plants, reeds, water creatures. Birds have come back. It's like it was all waiting.

There's this guy who's advising me. He's teaching me to read the land.'

He had missed her, he said, that was what he mostly wanted to say. Till said she had missed him too. She didn't try to pretend otherwise. It was a strange feeling. She had been judging herself for thinking about Ed more than Bev's troubles and the weirdness of everything, though she had thought about Bev too – also Marian and Mrs Anderson. She wasn't a monster. She couldn't pretend any more that she and Ed didn't matter. It felt precarious – she might have been balancing on some thin wire – but it was exhilarating too.

The folds in several hills fell towards this green trough, which was as bright as a Christmas beetle. Tall thick reeds swayed in the water. A large waterbird lifted and some small parrots and finches dithered through. Insects darted. They walked and talked. The green was a wide ribbon that drifted down the shallow valley, the water slowed by rocks and boulders. Small trees and shrubs flourished near its banks.

Long ago, creeks had thrummed with birds – vast numbers, people said, all singing in the trees. Till couldn't imagine the noise of it – birds she'd never even heard of, hundreds of species, which she'd read about in one of Zoe's old books. Some of the birds stayed in one place. Others passed through. In the terrible drought of 1896, birds drank from a farm trough, hawks and tomtits and other species side by side connected in desperation and, filled with water, went to roost in nearby trees. Once, a flock of small birds fell from them after over-drinking ('like ripe fruit', the book said) and died. People dammed the creeks and felled the trees and missed the birds and lizards when they went.

'It's beautiful,' Till said, meaning the country there, stupid inadequate word. She meant that it was life, and it was sad because the land wasn't whole. She wondered whether something similar might be possible with a town to stop it running away. Wirowie had stopped her running.

Till liked Ed. I have said that. She liked the way he kissed her thigh and hip and waist and breasts. It made a soft sound. She waited for it each time and it made her close her eyes and smile and shiver.

'What did you think when you first saw me?' Ed asked.

Till stroked the hair on his forearms, one way then another. 'Nice arms.'

'That's it?'

'That's a lot. Good arms are very rare.'

He laughed.

'How about me?'

'I don't know.' He lay back and shut his eyes and opened them again, and blinked. 'You were like a little black cat, next to a huge dog. It was just weird and funny – in a good way. And then it was you, and I felt like I knew you. Of course I didn't, but I was so happy to see you, like, there you are, I've been waiting for you.'

'I am way more superficial. I went out and yelled at you like I was fifteen hanging out of a bus window trying to get your attention. Yoo-hoo! I scream-offered you a cup of tea and you just kept on with your very important whipper snipping. So romantic.'

It was such a pleasure talking in this way. It was the deepest comfort. She would never have enough of it.

Till supposed she might love him. Once love is involved the possible and impossible become too much entwined to be pulled apart. Even the most delicate approach will end in distress. Best to go on and see where it ends. It's what people do. She wondered if she might one day love Isaac too. She was afraid of failing him and this made her cautious in the matter of love. Sometimes you let people down; it happened. Not because you were careless or stupid or unfeeling, but because sometimes you couldn't see all the pieces right, or you didn't know what they were, what people were like. Knowing that, how would a person risk it? She couldn't even use his name out loud, only in her head. What malign spirit might hear him named and know him? What might it do? Superstition, you might say, as if scoffing diminished the thing, but so what? Superstition is real in its way. That is its power. It's not wise to mock such things or to treat them lightly. And don't look at them too directly. They don't like that. One night Till felt she saw someone moving around in the dark in the station. She and Birdy lay quiet, covered in black, invisible, watching the shape, whatever it was. She never knew if it was corporeal or of the spirit. That is the sort of thing I mean.

Brunswick 2021

She remembered three other things that happened close together.

Once in late autumn or early winter the year before, Till came upon a man near the corner of a lane, who began fumbling at his fly as she approached. Just an ordinary guy with a little fisherman's hat on, in the inner north, miles from beach or river. Had he been hanging around the lane waiting for someone? She sped up and roared, 'Put that away now, mister, or I'll snap it off.'

A little shriek, then a rancorous voice emerged from him – 'missy, smack your bottom, heh, stick it in, little slut, slit your throat' – and so on, tugging frantically.

'I mean it,' she roared and ran at him, Birdy alongside, and he turned and fled. 'Fuck off, loser,' she screamed, and he did fuck off. From all around came the clamour of backyard dogs. She was shaking afterwards. I mention this in case you would like to observe later that this impulse had always been there.

After that she kept a small switchblade in the inner pocket of her jacket. If something unsettled her – like the terrible groaning and beating from the other side of the fence she once heard – she put her hand to her breast and felt the hard knife there and was reassured. The times were making them crazy, each in their own way, or at least had given them reasons to express their strangeness.

Not long after, or shortly before, Till wasn't sure, she came across a middle-aged woman with short dark hair sitting on a camp chair by a little folding table at the opening of a one-person tent in a lane, between two gates. (I mention the gates in case you are wondering whether she was a nuisance. People living there could get in and out if they wanted to. She wasn't a problem at all. And there were public toilets not far away in the park if you are wondering about that.) Her view ran along the lane and from her tranquillity, her stillness gazing up the avenue of fences and overhanging trees, she might have been pondering the Swiss alps or a tropical rainforest or a mountain gorge. She had a tartan patterned thermos at her side and drank from the white lid–cup from which steam rose. She nodded at Till and raised her mug casually as you would someone passing on a walking track. *Lovely day for it.* She was gone the next day. Till had blundered through her home.

Around the same time, or perhaps a year before, some people without a home pitched a tent in the park. They had two big-headed dogs tethered to a pole hammered into the ground so they could move in and out of the tent at will when their owners were elsewhere. They attacked local dogs if they approached to investigate and people complained to the council. They didn't like these outsiders. Even their dogs were the wrong kind. After a week or so they left too, the council having found them shelter.

People mostly look after themselves and the people (or creatures) they love. Till regretted not offering the woman in the lane and the camping people a room and a hot shower, even if they declined. They came to mind again when she met those other women without hard walls at their backs. They had each other of course and that was something.

It was time blurring, even while it was happening, that she found hardest. And looking back how would she recall sequences? How were you supposed to remember when the world and all its markers had become untethered from life? A few months later, people would hardly remember what they'd done in those years.

Till, dressed in black, and Birdy, black, start walking at night. Till is pursuing invisibility. They leave softly by the back door and the side pathway and the side gate and hug the shadows along the street until they turn the corner into the lanes and can start walking freely. Till is learning to master her fear the way they all do in these times, walking its dark passages, alert for distractions, trying to keep fear at bay. It seems more dangerous at night, but it is less dangerous since if Till pulls her black face mask up and leaves her hair untidy about her face, no one could see her. She can hardly see Birdy when she leaves her side. 'Birdy,' she breathes, and she sees a flash of the white of Birdy's eyes. It is hard and a discipline to keep moving along when you can't see around you.

And once they hear a dog whimpering and once they hear a cat screaming. A leaf crab-walks along the ground. Creatures move in fruit trees, mostly birds, but also possums and bats. A currawong, enormous in flight, sweeps around a corner and flies at fence height all the way down the lane, cornering again at the end. It is a secret world; this is the birds' road. No, the bird is a daytime memory. Or it is a bat and a memory of night. Sometimes she remembers things from a long time ago.

It is different in the day. In the daytime, Till's mind drifts, but not towards memory or anticipation. It drifts in blankness. It will always be like this. It's as if she is shut into the present, and life, future, past have been stripped away. There are fruit and fences, Birdy loping, boyfriends fallen away. No smoky eye makeup to create the illusion of the night before. Her face is bare.

I don't altogether understand everything I see and hear, but I am a good noticer. My mother told me that a long time ago. I didn't notice all the things I should have.

Chapter 20

Wirowie

ISAAC STEPPED OFF the pushcart with a small cat carrier, which he set on the platform. Ed came behind. Isaac opened the door and reached in and there was a puppy, a tiny rag of fur that looked like it had been used to mop more than one floor. He squeaked and trembled but he liked Isaac, who picked him up and held him close. The puppy pressed into his neck, a good sign. Isaac shut his eyes for a moment.

'Is it your dog?' Till asked.

'Yep.'

'Very cute.'

'He's orright,' he said in a gruff voice, like softness would be showing them too much.

The puppy saw Birdy and squirmed to be let down, and the boy put him on the ground. The puppy writhed its way across to her in pure abasement, flinging itself onto its side under Birdy's nose, and they had to laugh. Isaac told Till about the names he was considering. She said they all sounded good.

'You know your grandma and grandpa are my bosses?' Till asked Isaac. He wanted to know which ones, so she told him and she said she knew Bev and Stew too. 'Bev keeps an eye on the station, and Stew taught me how to do the stonework here.

He got the stove going and showed me how to work it. They're pretty great. I couldn't have done it without them.'

Isaac's expression flickered his feelings: pleased and resentful, proud and contemptuous, but a little less than he had been. Everything was on the surface with him. He hadn't learned to conceal himself. Watching the way Ed was with him, Till's mind flashed to a small boy she'd seen learning to ride a bike in the park the year before. When he fell his father shouted at him to just stay on next time, and when the child fell again and began silently weeping, his helmet sagged to one side, the father jerked the bike upright and shoved it at him. Behind his expression seemed to be another five generations of angry men and his own sad child self.

George never spoke much of his childhood, which he had spent on a farm in the hills outside Adelaide. It had been one of his jobs to kill the chicken for the Sunday roast each week, and to catch them if they ran away with their necks spurting blood. 'What did you do when they did that, Daddy?' There was something on his face, and he didn't speak for a moment and then he said, 'Well, I caught it, Till, and it died. It was dead already,' and he stroked Till's hair and said, 'It didn't hurt it. It didn't know.' She would like to know if he held it gently while its neck was bleeding, and stroked its glossy wings and the soft feathers on its neck. She hoped he had. She asked why he'd done it. It was only that he had no choice. 'My brother and sister liked to prove how hard they were. It pleased our father that they could kill without flinching. He wanted me to be a good countryman one day, not shame the family.' (Why would a father want to break his gentle son? George would never do that to her.) His father's disappointment was part of him. Where did choice come in? Till had never felt that

George passed on that disappointment. He knew Till had lost something. There was a break in her. This was who she was now. There was only moving on.

All this was flickering like a speckled shade through Till's mind that afternoon. Also Mr Oldham's regret that he might have been too tough on Bear.

The puppy got tired and had some food and water and went and took over Birdy's bed. Birdy sat on the sofa with Ed, looking down disdainfully. Isaac helped Till make a cake for afternoon tea, very serious, reading the recipe from her phone. 'We need cream,' he said. 'Have you got cream?'

'I do.'

'And icing sugar? And strawberries?'

'Yes,' she said. 'I do. I'm pretty sure. Better check the fridge.'

He flung the door back. 'You do.'

'We will not be disappointed then.'

They had the cake and were not disappointed. But Isaac saw Ed kiss Till in the kitchen while they were washing the dishes. He didn't say anything, but he went outside and after they left, Till found the little tree growing from the fissure in the platform pulled out and tossed aside to wither. There was no saving it. It was a bad end to the day. But the tree and how to make things right with Isaac were not her only preoccupations.

Till and Marian and Mrs Anderson and Bev could not stop wondering what had happened to Bev. A slow conversation looped between them in different configurations (Till and Marian, Till and Bev, Mrs Anderson and Bev reported back to Marian and then Till or directly to Till) and bound them together. They could not make sense of it. There had been nothing sexual. Was it about power, they wondered, or maybe fear. 'It's always power in some way,' Till said, and people listened to her.

The part Bev found strange was that he wasn't interested in what he was doing. He just had to do it. 'Like a parcel getting wrapped,' she said, nothing more than that. If it was something to do with Liz and drugs and delivering a warning, wouldn't he have mentioned it? It was the motive that the police had decided on in the absence of any details or information from Bev, and having decided, had gone quiet. Bev had no news, except for the aside that the woman from Yongala had gone back to Adelaide. It was too quiet, too empty out here.

Bev was uneasy leaving home and walking down the road where she was attacked, and for a week or two, Till and Marian and Mrs Anderson took turns visiting. Stew didn't know what to do for her or what to say. He stood in doorways wringing his hands or rubbing his arms and making cups of tea, saying what he'd do to that man if he ever got hold of him, but he seemed more frightened than anything to Till, seeing the change in Bev. She was like a planet knocked off its orbit and no one knew what she might do or how they should be in her presence.

Till heard her parents' agitation and fear when she told them what had happened. Always before, phone calls were filled with renovations talk and what to do about leather sofas and about Maudie, whose arthritis was getting worse, and how Birdy loved the country, and about rugs and hot water systems, and weird customers at the pub or the service station, things like that. What could she say to them now when she was worried herself and trying to tell herself it was all okay?

'Two women, you say,' George said. 'You're sure you're safe?'

'Oh yes. Stone walls, big locks, huge dog. I'm fine.' She was not fine. She was not sleeping well.

'Till,' Zoe said.

'Really, Mum. I can always stay at Marian's. Mrs Anderson invited me.' She didn't mention the woman in Jamestown.

And what could her parents do in the end? Nothing. Till had decided to stay.

The shop wasn't the best place for an eight-year-old on the weekend, Tundra said. She had brought Isaac and one of Isaac's friends visiting for a change of scene one Sunday, dropping in at Bev's first. The two of them, Isaac and Robbie, were like small puppies tumbling around, and Isaac's puppy tumbled with them. The puppy was called Tex now, after some football player. They ran up the platform, past the spot where the tree used to be. Isaac looking at it on his way past. He came back subdued.

'Grandma said you went to their place,' Isaac said.

'Grandma Bev?'

He nodded.

'I did.'

'What for?'

'To see how she is. She hasn't been around for a couple of weeks. She likes to keep an eye on things around here so I wondered.'

'Did you, did you say anything about me? Did you talk about me?'

'I told her you were a champion cake baker.'

'That's all?'

'Did you have something in mind?'
'No.'
'I said you were good on the pushcart. Is that okay?'
'Yeah.'
'Okay then. Anything else?'
He shook his head.
'I think we're good then.'

They took the pushcart up and down the line for a while, its effortful squeaking marking their departure and return, and from the sound of their cries, his spirits had recovered. Later, they made another cake, a different one. Till wondered whether she should have opened up the subject of the tiny sapling. Was he inviting that? She had no idea.

Bev began leaving her home again. She felt all cooped up, she said. She took her dog with her everywhere, a big heeler called Wayne with a watchful eye and a ready nip, and she'd fetch up at the station, knocking on the waiting room door or the ticket window to get Till's attention. 'A change of scene and I'll go back. I don't trust my own home, my own street, my own town,' she told Till.

They'd sit before the fire on a cool day and outside if it was sunny. It was the end of winter. Grasses were fresh and green, mornings were sharp in the nose and clear, and afternoon warmth brief and tied to the arc of the sun. The golden light came in aslant, and the great palm trees sent enormous shadows across the southbound line and the centre platform. If Till wasn't there Bev went on her way, though Till told her she was welcome to stop for a while and offered to get her a key so her destination felt safe.

'I wouldn't be comfortable on my own. I need people around. I can't see anyone from here. It's knocked the stuffing out of me, that's the truth. I don't feel myself at all.'

Till could see that in her. Her voice was thin and reedy and she was always cold. The long brown alpaca cardigan she wore each day was wrapped about her and knotted at the waist as tight as could be, and she wore a big kilt pin high up to hold it snug under her chin. She sank down into the sofa as if it was shelter as well as comfort. She'd lost weight and her swaggering way of being in the world. She left no wake. It made Till feel tender towards her. Bev would hate that if she knew. Her sorrows and wounds had risen up and she'd lost the way of concealing them.

'I can't find peace about Isaac. I worry about him the whole time. He's with Roy and Tundra for a bit. I was that frightened about what might happen to him I wasn't sleeping. Who would want to hurt Isaac? He's a good kid.'

'He's a great kid.'

'That was a good idea of theirs about the puppy.'

'Yeah. And who would want to hurt you?'

'I have my enemies. I thought you were one.' Then, after a pause, 'Sorry about that.'

'Hah,' Till said. What she meant was that she understood the town as territory and herself as an interloper of unknown origin and intent, but there was no need to say it. 'Anyway, we're friends now. That's what I think.'

Sometimes Bev removed the pin and fiddled with it, testing the point on her finger, looking at the dent she made to see if it drew blood.

'Good idea,' Till said, which startled Bev and made her almost smile. 'Good to have something like that about you.'

Till pulled the small switchblade from her pocket and released the blade, snapped it shut and put it away. Very fast. It was something she practised in spare moments: clean removal, clean release, speed. 'Like that. Something people don't expect. Make sure it's sharp.'

Bev didn't say anything at first. 'I suppose you have a reason for that.' She nodded towards Till's knife pocket.

'I do.'

'Well, that is strange. I should be surprised. Why aren't I?'

'We made a cake. Did I tell you? Isaac and me.'

'Oh really? You're not going to tell me about the knife are you?'

'Probably not.'

It didn't really matter. Bev could not stay with the thread of talk and Till saw how the thing that had happened to her was beginning to stretch out, that the aftermath would stop being something that would one day be done. It had become the life and world that Bev inhabited now, that they all lived in.

Till knew how that went. Fear soaked into you; it was you, and eventually you could not remember who you were before. She had begun feeling its touch and her own old fears again. Ed was away and the station was quiet and dark. She bought some new lamps and came inside earlier, not only because of the cold, and was filled with misgivings if she arrived home at dusk or in darkness and used her phone torch to light her way from the car park, around the side, past the water tank and the corner between its curve and the station wall. It made everything beyond the light worse. There was no lighting all the darkness. She tried not to look towards the water crane further up, since it so resembled the one at Yongala, and once inside checked the locks more than once and listened for sounds outside, paying attention to Birdy's attention. She hated that this was happening.

She walked Bev home late in the afternoon after a visit, and on the way back saw how the sun seemed to be plummeting towards the horizon and walked faster.

Till's big summer song – the one from before the fires – came on in the pub that week and she began singing, almost like a reflex, but softly, and moving around almost dancing. Then she was really singing because she was at home and she felt light at the memory of carefree times, as they seemed looking back. She sang the old hit, still pulling beers and serving. It felt prematurely nostalgic. What a time that was, no one knowing what was to come. It might have been a decade ago.

Someone whooped. People began to realise it was Till's song, and who Till was, and wanted more. It felt good to sing again, even the old songs she didn't much like.

Afterwards on the street, a wizened old man with watery eyes stopped her. Maybe he wanted to talk about her singing.

He said, 'Got yourself a poacher's dog.'

'Excuse me?'

'Go out at night with it, check your traps, poke about, can't see a dog like that at night, specially a black one. A walking shadow, can see everything, and if it's still it's nothing at all. Handy beasts if they know what they're about. What are they again?'

'Greyhound.'

'Greyhound,' he said. He shut his eyes, seeming to savour the word. 'Tha's right. That's what people said.'

'Oh, they did?' That old unease . . . people watching.

The slightest nod. 'Wondering whether you knew what you had by you. Better to know. A good-sized beast. Fast?'

'She is.'

She sang each week after that, on Friday or Saturday night. Birdy had her own following, bringing back memories and strange bush events with packs of hunting dogs of people's childhoods. The wizened man sat with Birdy, to keep her company, he said. The other man from months ago who swore she'd chase sheep and was still waiting for this to happen sat with them. Doug from the motel where she'd stayed way way back, and where she showered for months, was an old friend of Birdy's these days. It suited them all. The men's faces would soften and they would murmur to Birdy between sips of beer, and chat and reminisce and listen.

E's voice (as Till imagined it would have become) was showy, with a bit of glissando and some fondness for embellishment, and she sang in that voice. E would have been a showman. Using that voice felt close to a lie now but it would be hard to let go of that piece of E. The week after that she said something about the voice of an old friend of hers, not mentioning that she had died long ago, and sang a few songs in that old way and then a couple of songs in her own voice, the one she sent up the railway line. Annunciata once asked, 'What allows life to proceed?' It was a place to start.

Till began walking in darkness as she had in Brunswick. It was a discipline, like underground diving, which she had read about during the years cooped up. Could she control her terror enough to face the thing she feared, to be inside the passages of deep darkness. Could she stop the panic that would make her drown. She was filled with dread. Soft shoes and a small knife and her black dog were all she needed. Each night she made herself quiet and still, she whispered the words and made the sounds Sva Ba Cha Ka Ha Ma and so on to the end, several times through, as long as it took to settle her breathing, and felt her heart and the pulse in her neck: steady.

From the doorway she watched a fox daintily toeing its way along the sleepers, snuffling into corners where track met wood and a slow lizard or some beetles might be found. It was easier to see movement: a fox's tail tip flickering, the way a creature altered the texture and density of darkness, rats dragging Birdy's discarded bones away to strip them of sinew and flesh. What I mean is she was the watcher then, not the prey.

When she was ready she placed her hand to her thigh, and Birdy rose. A black greyhound has a particular presence, especially at night, being so much part of it that they seem to merge with it and dissolve and expand until they are night, they are darkness, they are stealth and danger. Poachers dogs.

Till looked at Birdy now. 'No hunting tonight, Bird, just looking.'

Birdy's teeth were reassuring. They were the only things showing – if a night was warm or there was a need for ferocity – also the white rim of her eyes. Her eyes glowed in the dark, just a trick of the light, but it gave pause.

They left the station and walked slowly along fence lines, beneath trees, down the long thin shadows of Stobie poles. If it were day she would have spoken to Birdy. Birdy didn't care about her night silence. A smattering of laughter or music or TV drifted from houses: human rustling. There was only home or a long drive or wandering in the dark around here, and lights and people behind curtains, their shadows waxing and waning in movements of domestic shadow puppetry and all the ancient tropes – love, grief, anger and all the rest. Some people didn't care about concealment and the illusion of shelter – who would bother looking in; why would anyone be about? – and she watched them making hot drinks, standing before pantry doors, talking to other people, sitting with their feet up, scratching and yawning.

She went up Mr Finch's road, past his house and paused to look through the window. Ken came through a doorway and walked to Mr Finch and put his arms around him from behind. Mr Finch reached his arms back and turned and they kissed the way old lovers kiss. They loved each other. It was beautiful, also sad. Who was she to say that? Their secret might be part of it. They didn't look sad. It looked warm in the yellow light and cosy wherever she went. But she could not help noting how provisional the shelter. A small stone shatters glass, a boot foot breaks a door.

It was not easy. Each night she had to make up her mind to it. The wind might be soft, or stirring, lifting her hair, leaves and branches, Birdy's ears, the grasses. Seeing poorly made her listen. By the wind on her skin she determined temperature, direction, steadiness, sound. On a cold night their breath lifted cartoonishly. Torchlight would only blind her and make her a target.

As a child, Till never considered her parents until the night she heard soft noises, murmuring, suppressed laughter. She might have been ten, lying in her little nest on the floor, and they all lay there silent and aware, and George said to Zoe, only to her, and very softly, 'Oh well'. This was how she found out she was not the centre of everything. Now she knew that Zoe and George had to bend their lives around her brokenness and keep that a secret from her, as if they'd been whispering behind her back. It was humiliating. She turned away from them then, to pay them back for their kindness in concealing her from herself.

One day George brought home a dainty brindled puppy. It was a lurcher, he said, a hunting dog. The puppy turned tall, imposing and lithe, and there is always something about a brindle that gives pause, as if back in their family line there is a more savage creature that camouflaged itself in flickering shadows and bided its time. Till observed that people gave them space and that other dogs were cautious. She called her Daisy.

'Daisy,' Zoe muttered, watching Daisy charge through the herb patch, the dahlias, the pots of flowers, snapping things as she passed. 'You don't think Destroyer might have been more apt?'

'Every child should have a dog,' George said, 'and some need one more than most.' That was the end of the discussion.

This might have been after she stopped sleeping at her parents' bedside. After that, Till watched Westerns overnight from the deep, old, green velvet sofa in the living room downstairs – anything she could find, sound turned low, Daisy at her side, and together they got through the night. She plunged down the humming avenue of greenish light into deserts and canyons and shootouts between cigar-chewing men with hats pulled over narrowed eyes. Later she wondered whether the landscapes reminded her of road trips. At dawn, she dozed for a while, got up, had a banana and went to school where she finished her work and slept, head propped on the palm of her hand, until the bell rang. It was as safe as lying in the car at night watching shadows.

Till and Annunciata talked about her trust issues – that adults could not be trusted at all in Till's view – and what would make her feel safe. Till said she would like to be able to punch hard, very hard. Annunciata said okay and talked to Zoe and George. So she learned how to fight and if it did not altogether remove the fear, it gave her the hope that it might one day. An instructor once said that she fought with true desperation, which was a rare quality. Till said that each time she fought she pretended she might otherwise die, because one day it might be true.

By moonlight one night Till noted the accelerating ruin of a house on Wirowie's westernmost street and went back the next day. She kept an eye on the houses along this stretch. There was something about the in-betweenness of its state: its fine collection of rusted ironwork, its collapsed walls and ceilings, its sloping doorways revealed and the chimney exterior fallen away to leave its intricate insides as exposed as an anatomy drawing, say an autopsied womb: here is where the baby lay. Lean-tos of weathered board added at the side, one to another, were like so many falling dominoes. Car tracks led from the side road along the house's fallen front and its water tanks and turned the corner of the house and disappeared under an ancient peppercorn tree.

It would have been a respectable house once; the interior chimney work was very fine. The facade's empty slope-roofed doorways led to darkness. A new room had fallen and there was a pile of chimney stones to pick over – beautiful colours:

honey, ochre, cream, butter, caramel – which she might be able to use for the station. It was abandoned, so no harm done; no one would care. From some courtesy, she preferred not to be seen trespassing or scavenging, as people might think of it. No one was around so she went ahead. They were good-sized stones, not too chippy or brittle, and she began a pile, treating them carefully, looking them over. It was a good feeling doing this methodical work. Birdy poked around, pausing to sniff, to look.

Then there was a moment: Till stood and looked towards the house's empty doorways, and Birdy's head lifted and her ears pricked and she looked too, taking a step, and there was a quality of a shift in movement or in the depth of darkness somewhere inside. They had to leave. Something wasn't right. She felt it, and Birdy did too.

'Birdy,' Till whispered. It was enough for Birdy to hear and she came even though she wanted to look some more. 'Come on,' under her breath, and then louder to sound normal, not frightened or suspicious or wary. 'Come on, Birdy.'

Brunswick 2021

Something Till hadn't thought of for a long time.

One cold evening lockdown walk in the lanes, she and Birdy heard a heavy blow and a gasp of breath on the other side of the fence. The night was drawing in and there was only sound, and the feeling of different people living their incomprehensible lives – as close as touch yet unreachable. The person did not cry out even after two more heavy blows. Till, heart pounding, pressed close to the fence, pictured two people on the other side silent for the shame of it and the rage and whatever else might keep a person silent. Terror, defiance. Behind the fence, a cockatoo screeched and beat its living wings against its ironwork cage, the only witness.

It was quiet then, as if both sides of the fence were listening. What did she do? Nothing. She did nothing again. It was at night on distant backstreets and hidden pathways that you found out the truth.

There was one more thing.

It is spring, true spring. The fruit trees are flowering all up and down the gardens that back onto the lane. The air is sweet with the blossom of plums and quinces and persimmon, also a few apples. The new leaves are like the beginning of time. They are so fresh.

Someone has painted red hangover veins below the Groke's eyes, and now it is sadder and perhaps even desperate. Till stops, the way she always does, as if it is possible to comfort an inanimate painting on an iron fence that someone occasionally embellishes when she is not there.

Each day that week there are changes. Another Groke appears, this one mostly black, with a smaller, longer one at its side a few fence panels along. The two of them might be playing tennis. A ball flies between them. The ball changes to a knife. The knife is in the side of the new Groke. Droplets of red fall from it. A car travels down the lane behind them, at a distance. Till can feel it before she turns. It is slow and silent. She walks at her normal pace, Birdy close at her side, and when they turn the corner to reach the street, and the car is hidden from view, she and Birdy run fast, and double back up the side of someone's house, and wait.

It is the last lane walk.

Wirowie

What would she say – *Hey you, you in there?* If there was someone, what of it? Strange people lived on the periphery of any number of these old towns, washed up by life and its circumstances and their own actions and things they are escaping. Looked at in a certain way, she was one of them. The only difference was she could afford the repairs.

Sometimes the body knows, but also, sometimes the mind turns away. It might have been a cat in the house or a possum, if there were possums there. It might have been anything.

When Till was a child, sunlight, laugher, company made her forget the terror of night, obscuring it as well as any cloud. She believed if she could rekindle that feeling in darkness, strike a match and light a candle – she meant metaphorically – it would be well. But darkness fully inhabited would not admit light. Fear and darkness travelled together towards her in the quiet of the house. What if her mother and father were not sleeping but had died? What if bad people came in windows, or through the roof, through that little door in the ceiling? What might be there? She asked her father about it once, casually, because how would she mention or describe the people who might live in that unimaginable space? What if he laughed? (She would never understand such laughter.) He didn't laugh at her. He said it was such a small space, no more than forty centimetres high, and he showed her how much forty centimetres was with his arms. He got the ladder and they looked in the little hole in the ceiling, shining a torch around. 'It's insulation, rats and possums. That's all,' he said.

The next night Till rang Marian to see if she'd like to come out roaming, since she would like the company and maybe Marian might like the mystery, but she didn't answer her phone, and she didn't answer the next morning or at lunch. And when she did ring, it was Mrs Anderson beside herself with fear. Marian had disappeared. There was no sign of anything but her absence. Till went out to her car to head up to the Anderson place and found a piece of paper folded and tucked under a windscreen wiper, which she opened unthinking.

It was a small note, computer or typewriter written: CONTACT THE POLICE *and* HER MOTHER WILL DIE. And there was a map of an area west of Yarcowie, and a circle on a road, and longitude and latitude.

Chapter 21

It was a ruined farm on a dirt road cutting from the highway through to Yongala, and although larger in scale, was like all other ruins thereabouts: walls collapsing, roofs fallen, old barrels rusted in the yard, trees once kept alive by kitchen water. They saw this from the road. There was no other car around. Mrs Anderson had insisted on the police despite Till's misgivings – Mrs Anderson didn't care about her own life – but there was no sign of them. The one big gate was locked and the wire fencing stretched unbroken on either side. It was terrible to get out all the same, to expose themselves in this way.

It was a desolate sort of place – more desolate than others, I mean, and the sky was low and grey and smudged. The sparse weeds were coated with dust. A blighted almond tree with some cankerous disease of its bark had flung out sparse blossom on its one living branch, which reached across a path. They stooped under it, all the while shouting 'Marian, Marian'. Flocks of pigeons exploded from window cavities. It was hard to make that much noise when instinct said, *oh be quiet, be soft, be cautious, don't even breathe*. But they had to, so there was just the shouting, their own clumsy footfall, wind surfing through the trees and then more clamorous shouts and their silence when they stopped to listen. There might be a banging sound. The wind was turning blustery and rattling loose tin so Till wasn't sure.

Till wrenched a long iron bolt from a length of shattered timber in their path, picked off clinging splinters and hefted it and put it in her deep thigh pocket. You never know. They heard nothing in particular and went slowly, except after a bit, an irregular banging intruded, incoherent but deliberate. More of their dreadful noise, Mrs Anderson half-sobbing, as they picked their way past and through the ruins of buildings: the farmhouse with its pressed metal ceilings collapsed and a kitchen stove with its door fallen open, windows out and shutter swinging, a long open-sided shearing shed, vast blocks of stone at the corners, huge tree trunks supporting the tin roof, mostly fallen, a large barn (Till noted in passing the massive stonework batters on the side, the long string courses, the fine stonework, the careful infill stone), twists of rusted wire tripping them, this beautiful honey stone and the banging, and suddenly they were upon a section of massive and wide square stone edging, a little more than knee height, of a vast rendered stone tank six or seven metres deep and as wide.

Mrs Anderson grabbed Till. The banging continued. They looked over the edge. Deep in the shadows, on piles of farm rubbish – bales of wire fencing, tangles of machinery, roofing tin, and old beds, broken timbers, garden waste, bushes and weeds – Marian sat kicking her legs against a piece of timber, awkwardly since they were taped together, looking up, her mouth taped, her arms bound behind her. She was near the top of the heap, but still metres below them. Her hands and arms were bleeding. She kept kicking, even when she saw them, kicking, kicking, as if she'd stopped thinking herself real and could not imagine they were in the same world.

'We're here. We're here,' Mrs Anderson sobbed.

A ladder lay on the ground exactly parallel with the wall, not thrown aside. What sort of person . . .

Till was thinking *dungeon, septic tank, cellar*, and Mrs Anderson, as if she knew Till's mind, said, 'Water tank. They would have been thinking the drought would end. They'd be ready next time. Death traps, these things.'

'Oh.' Till felt foolish. It would have had a lid surely, though how would it cover such an area? She imagined living alongside that vast waiting body of water and reckless children running around and a lid with a small hatch opening onto the darkness and closing overhead and nothing but cold water. *Just concentrate on Marian, just that.*

They lowered the ladder and Till climbed down on shaking legs. Mrs Anderson held the top steady since it threatened to slide and it was just junk and rubbish and waste shifting around beneath it. Above, she heard men's voices and almost screamed and lost her footing. They might send Mrs Anderson down too before taking the ladder. Heads looked over. It was Rod and the other guy.

The tape was tearing and fraying anyway; Marian would have freed herself eventually, probably. Thinking this made it almost bearable to Till even though she knew it was unbearable. She, Marian, might have been able to pile things up high enough, then pile up the rubbish and delicately climb it and catch the edge and pull herself over it. That might have been possible. Till took out her switchblade and cut Marian free and put it away quickly before Rod saw it and took it away.

The sound Marian made – a sort of animal growling of

disgust and horror. She pulled at the shreds of tape. Till tried to help. She was frantic to get out of here too. She rubbed Marian's arms, and draped her jacket around Marian's shoulders. So stupid. They'd forgotten to bring water, a blanket, anything. Marian was shivering with cold and she had wet herself and this humiliation in front of Rod when she reached the top made her furious.

He looked disgusted and couldn't hide it, and he was angry. 'Come on, let's go,' he said. 'Let's get out of here. We'll get you home.' The shutter started its banging again, a doleful sound. 'Food and water, a shower, and then we can talk.'

He bustled them, his hand around Marian's arm up high, almost dragging her along so she was unbalanced. There was nothing Till could do except hate him more and keep up with them. But Marian wouldn't go in the police car, and they couldn't make her with Till and Mrs Anderson watching.

Marian got in Till's car. Rod stopped there. 'It'll just be some prankster. Young guy. Look at her.' He nodded towards Marian shaking on the other side of the car window. 'He'll get tired of it.'

Sensing their attention, Marian turned to face them. Mrs Anderson said, 'It is not a prank, Rod. There's nothing about this that is like a prank. It's someone dangerous. It won't end here. This is not the worst of it. You should know that. You're police. I shouldn't have to tell you. Look at the state of my daughter, your former wife. Look at her. Does that look like a prank happened?'

'So it got out of hand. She's a tall woman. She'd take some handling.' A faint smile formed – remembering handling her, thinking she deserved it. It meant something like that. Oh, Till despised him. She hated herself for being tricked by him.

'Three, maybe four women now,' Mrs Anderson said. 'Leave aside your connections to two of them and do your job, or people might start talking. Do you understand me?'

'Don't tell me my job. You understand me?' He jabbed his head forward so Mrs Anderson reared back. 'You understand.' His voice was a fist; his words were blows.

'I think we do,' Till said.

So Till drove back to the Andersons' and the police had to follow.

Much later, after all the police business was done, and Marian had eaten and drunk, which she could only do in tiny biting sipping amounts, she said to Mrs Anderson and Bev and Stew and Till, who she wanted nearby, 'He said this one thing. He said, "It's the Cherry Ripe girl I want." Who the hell is that?'

'I'm so sorry,' Till said, but she was on her own in the car by then. That's the way it is. Sometimes you stay. Sometimes you have to run.

She wondered for years how she would know if she were living in a time of innocence, innocence being a state of grace in which you loved people and people loved you with mostly unblemished constancy, without shadow of hurt; when shopping for pleasure and beauty (alongside more utilitarian shopping for sustenance and so on) continued almost unchecked, except by dwindling funds; when children could hold pet funerals that contained death and sadness in small pleasant containers and rituals; when you lived in one of those pockets in history where people mostly stayed healthy and lived for close to an allotted time, and mostly were educated, and mostly had shelter, and mostly had some choices, even if these things were not equitably distributed; which is to say a small and astoundingly privileged corner of the world in which you were oblivious more or less to your good fortune. She was learning now that she had been living in such a state in this ruined town.

When you felt the framework tremble, the ideas shake loose and begin to fall, leaves, confetti, dandelion seeds, eucalyptus pods, feathers from exploding pigeons, rafters and ceilings, the roads dissolving, the wind howling the truth, then what was the point of it all? She felt the cloth of life shredding, its edges whipping. If you had to leave in an emergency – rising waters, burning city, breaking earth, howling wind, mass deaths – what did you take? And if your car failed, the fuel ran out, what would you carry? She'd left with as little as she could bear to carry and be bothered to pack when moving again. She had left with her dog once. She could do it again.

Chapter 22

All Till could think of was flight, since the action of flight itself, being in a car that was moving fast, meant safety, comfort, all the old words. It was to spare everyone in Wirowie too. She had brought that murderous danger into their pleasant world and they, oblivious, had welcomed her – eventually, at least. There was nothing to be done but remove herself and the sickness that followed her. That's what she told herself at first. To be clear, mostly it was to save herself since this was her life's habit. In saving herself she was saving everyone else, since she was the Cherry Ripe girl, so she was doing the right thing anyway.

Of course she left. It was late already and she drove only to Doug's motel in Peterborough. The motel, FOR SAL in January, was now OR AL. Weeds were growing high around posts and doorways. He hadn't been at the pub of late, and she had a hot water system these days. Slowly, he wheezed to the door, his terrier, Mini, darting and rushing around his feet. He was attached to an oxygen cylinder and his lips were almost blue, but he seemed to expect to survive the night, so Till asked for a room.

'Thought you might be considering buying,' he said, chuckling phlegmily, and coughing in a way that just rolled the gunk around until it sounded like growling. Till laughed too. They were old friends these days, from the pub and because of Birdy. He wheezed off and returned with a key and a dish of dog treats for Birdy. 'You bring Birdy in too, don't worry about her.'

She would not cry, she would not, but she did not understand the world at all. She said 'Thank you so much' and he said 'You're welcome' and she said 'If anyone comes by looking for me you haven't seen me, okay?'

'Understood,' he said abruptly, without further questions, which made her wonder about his past. This town, all towns, all places, she supposed. There is time to have so many lives. She'd only seen this one small part of Doug's life. He might have been a comet blazing across the mid north in his day. She would make him a cake when all this was done, and she would ask about his life.

So she slept fitfully, and very early rose and kept driving, frantic now to leave this world behind. She drove fast and randomly. Once in a while she passed through a town, her car cleaving it in two, leaving on either side slices of lives: a young couple walking a pusher, a boy slouching down a footpath with a kelpie scouting his way, a woman wrestling some sheets in the wind. They pulled her arms up, the wind was so strong. Yarcowie, Caltowie, Canowie, Booborowie, Terowie, Willowie, all the places where water used to be.

Late in the morning she looped west – to her, the true direction of journeying and flight – and calmed enough to slow and briefly stop on the banks of a wide dry riverbed and a shallow floodplain. It was evenly but not thickly scattered with redgums, three or four or five times the size of any she'd seen before, an ancient remnant civilisation that persisted, cathedrals of the tree world. How many must there have been once.

She felt observed – no, more contemplated. Was she a threat or just one more newcomer? Till didn't know. Birdy was alert, ears pricked and head up, gazing around, looking for the thing that Till could not find words for and might wonder about forever. To see those trees was to understand the meaning of the word reverence.

They bought food in a town facing a treed hill that rose steeply and close. The town seemed to hunch over the heavily treed creek at its base – guarding it, Till supposed. Everyone would have needed that water. Clouds lifted like smoke signals from behind it, white above the dark trees. The pub was old whitewashed stone, double storey, with a post and rail veranda of ancient, wide, long-muscled timber. People must have sat there at day's end smoking pipes, drinking beer or spirits or . . . her imagination petered out. And whatever else they drank. Perhaps they looked at the dark hills wondering who was looking back and what they would do if they approached. They might have done more than wonder. It seemed probable. The massive stonework courses of the pub's facade, divided by split tree trunks, told a story. It was a fortress. If she survived this day she'd look up the town and find out, if she could, what happened there to leave it feeling this way. There were always people wanting to do bad, and that left marks on a place.

It was an effort not to keep turning and looking back; looking back always marked you as uneasy. It made people prick up their senses and wonder why, or told a person who was hunting you that you were found. Still she looked back and saw nothing. Her fear didn't leave, but somewhere in her was a small space where she could think. Some reckoning was due. Things could not go on in the same way, and she was almost ready for it.

Almost. She headed west through steep hills scattered with grass trees then saltbush and thickly growing trees in a dry creek that the road and a railway line cut across. The road was against the grain of everything; that was its purpose. A sign way off to the side said **SALTIA**, like something from a Western, all that remained of a whole town and its station. She was leaving her world and entering another. It was like her long-ago drive through bushfire smoke into clear air and a place separate from her childhood, and untainted. This place felt slippery and concealed. She didn't know its safe places, or if there were any, or if she would need them. It was her expectation though; she could not imagine otherwise.

Turquoise parrots flashed past in stunning glitter. The road sloped down to salt plains and the hard wavering light of late afternoon. Till narrowed her eyes and continued. She might have seen a car on the salt flats of Port Augusta, floating behind her in the shimmer, and again on the other side of town. That didn't mean it was him, but it might be. That might mean he didn't know where she was, only supposed that west was the continued direction of her flight as it had been before. She was half-blinded trying to make sense of the vision. There was a car she might have seen more than once on the road. She wasn't sure. In the luminous grey it seemed like the road had disappeared into air or water or salt plain, she couldn't tell. Cars hovered above this absence and it felt like she was dissolving too.

Sunset – a great sweep of orange, lingering pink, then darkness. Her eyes were drifting shut and the wheels found the edge of the road more than once and she yanked the car back. Birdy began whining. Till pulled onto a side road or driveway and drove along until she found the entry to a paddock gate and pulled in. It was that or crashing. She and Birdy ate a little and drank a little and Till got out the quilts and they curled up. It was like the old journey, humming darkness around, blurred as felt, stars and a sliver of moon, and quiet.

Birdy slept. Till did too for a while, then woke thinking of trees, those beautiful old giants from out of Wilmington. Till could have lain down at their feet and died if it weren't for Birdy. She dreaded what was to come, whatever that might be. One of the things about dogs: they tether you to life. Had George known that when he brought Daisy home? Children had a similar pull. They need you – how can you betray them? Yet she had left Isaac behind without a word. What kind of monster . . . She didn't like to think of that, even if he wasn't hers, and she wasn't sure how much he liked her. He had reasons to be cautious with his affections. Maybe he did like her and she was frightened of that. Maybe she liked him and was frightened of letting him down.

Yet last week Isaac had drifted slowly, reluctantly along the platform to see her. Till was sitting at her outside table with Birdy at her feet. She had her guitar, and was singing and playing quietly, running sounds and words around like stirring a stick in the sand. But she felt self-conscious if she wasn't performing and put the guitar aside. When Isaac reached Till she said hello. He bent his head and lifted it and said hello, then bent it again and moved his feet, scuffing them through the small shards of stone that lay about. And she remembered again, again, that Isaac had lost his mother and had never known his father that he could remember and he kept going. She wiped her eyes quickly, fiercely, before he saw.

'I brought you a tree,' he said.

'A tree?'

'For you. To plant. You know, where . . . the other one was.'

Till waited to see if there was more, but he was waiting too, and the sun kept shining on them.

'Can I see?' she asked. 'Would you like to show me?'

He opened the supermarket bag he carried and drew out a newspaper parcel, long, rolled around and around into a fat tube with three red rubber bands holding it secure. He unrolled it with clumsy tenderness, not sure of the right way to do this and how to take enough care. Till pictured Bev or Stew wrapping it, perhaps walking him down to make sure he got there safely. Strange things were happening and there were the police and their hostility to consider, and he was the most precious thing in the world to Bev and Stew and to Tundra and Mr Oldham, this beautiful wiry boy, the braveness and sadness and faint belligerence that were part of him, the adoration that he sailed on unawares, that kept him afloat.

It was a small eucalyptus with glaucous leaves so finely edged in a dark red that you might miss this perfect detail.

'Look at that. I love it. Where do you think we should plant it?' Till asked.

They chipped at the crack in the platform, hacking away to create a good hole where the seedling would fit and they dug some soil from outside the station to fill it and carefully planted the tree there.

'Water?' he asked.

'Yep. It'll need looking after for a bit. It's a tough spot – a good one though. It'll cast a beautiful shade in summer in a few years. They grow fast when they get going.' She told him about the tree in Melbourne that she had loved.

'They cut it down? They really did?'

'They really did. It was huge.'

'And what about the birds?'

'They had to find new homes. I hope they could. It was right near a big park with lots of trees, so I hope they were okay.'

'Oh.'

'Yeah. Anyway, here's a tree we're planting, so that's something. Thank you.'

How did people live with the weight of children? She'd seen those adults in the park screwing up their lives without a pause; fathers disappointed with their children's kicks; children dumbfounded with grief at their failure to impress, all gathering their shattered hearts and persisting.

'It's a beautiful tree,' she said, 'the most beautiful tree I've ever seen.'

Isaac laughed.

'No, really,' she said. 'It's perfect. Thank you.'

They did like each other, she could tell.

Metaphor much, Till thought now, remembering this, and I must say I agreed. She'd ignored that and proved him right. She could not be relied on – still. And all she'd sent Ed was a text message saying she was going away for a while. He was away himself assessing a couple of promising properties for solar and wind way north of the border, and would likely be out of range anyway he'd said, but she hadn't listened as well as she should have or told him she would miss him. At least he had told her in advance.

There were people she loved, and maybe people who loved her. She could not lose them. She had made a whole life, and what might the man do if he caught her now and did whatever it was he needed to do? Death seemed inevitable, more or less, and there would be more death. He was going to keep on. No one knew who he was or his long connection with Till – almost her whole life long. Oh, she loathed him – she was so angry she could choke – and he was still controlling her, pursuing her for whatever reasons he had, which she didn't want to think about. What did it matter why? She had made a life and he was going to take it again. Till thought of other little girls and what might happen and their terror, and the way his actions reverberated. What happened to E was still happening. Death was not the end of violence. Say she went back. It would be a chance versus no chance. She was in trouble either way. Vengeance for E. To spare other girls. These were the important reasons. She could not imagine being free of fear, but she wanted to feel it. She wasn't a child anymore. It was time.

And like that, she decided to turn back, and having decided, slept again. When she woke at earliest dawn she found a route back to the highway and headed east, back through the hills. She drove fast. She wanted only to get as close to Orroroo or Wirowie as she could before something happened. Maybe she could set some kind of trap for him. Enlist some help. Put him down a pit and deprive him of hope, and life.

A thin line of lesser redgums meandered down a creek bed to the south. They approached and veered away at a subtle shift in gradient. Youngsters for the most part, seedlings remaining from a time when the giants were felled for all the fences and fuel and railway sleepers thereabouts. And the people mostly cleared too, one way or another – guns, disease, departure.

The curved roads fell away, straightening and pulling ahead of her, undulating along the low hills like flailed rope. In her mirrors, the road sections she'd driven disappeared behind the crests of hills like the rooms of a mansion, their doors closing in endless repetition. There was not a sign of the man's car ahead or behind. She might have lost him. But would that be good or bad? She wanted never to see him and she wanted him gone, but something had to mark his complete departure.

The car shuddered and the wind screamed at the loose window seals. Birdy reared up and began whining and staggering about the back seat to stare from every window, the volume of her whine increasing at the swooning pull of a hill's curved bottom and the airy swoop at a hill's top when it seemed they might take flight – oh god, it was wonderful. 'What a ride, hey Birdy?' Till called. It seemed like they were free.

At the top of a hill she glimpsed a car way off in the rear view mirror, and at the next saw it was gaining on them steadily. It could be a stranger, someone going about their business in a car designed for these roads, but she knew it wasn't. One eye on the road, the other on her phone, she rang Ed. It rang out. Then she rang Mr Oldham, stabbing at the keys now, dragging the car back from the gravel verges once or twice, the whole time showing herself terrified to the person behind.

'Yes?'

'Mr Oldham, I need help, please come. Hurry. Someone's following me. I think it's the man who's been—'

'Oh lord,' he said, 'Tell me where.'

'Heading home, south of Peterborough on Cleary.'

'Don't do anything rash, you hear me? Stay on the main road. Keep going as long as you can. If he stops you, string him along now – if it is him. Keep talking. Stretch the time.

Don't make him angry. Don't get smart. Keep your phone on, in your pocket now, on silent.'

'Okay,' Till sobbed.

'You hear me?' His kind voice.

'Yes.'

'Okay. In your pocket now. We're here now. Tundra's here. I'll be there soon.'

Neither of them mentioned the police.

How was it that beneath people who had neatly ironed shirts and straight side parts and fringes smoothed carefully from that part, who drove their aged but immaculate trucks of a dusty mid-green no longer manufactured anywhere in the world, down the roads, never wavering over the line even though there was no one coming for mile upon mile, might be someone capable of anything. And if it was true of him, might it not be true of anyone, of her.

Chapter 23

He was behind her, and at her side a minute later. When he looked across she knew it was him. She should have contacted the police in Melbourne, or at least told her parents when she first saw him in the park. But what would she say? That a man with a particular walk had put his finger down and it reminded her of the grey man of her childhood who she could not remember. More of that old embarrassment and shame. And what use were the people around here, who they would surely get in touch with. What would they say? *Did he approach you or threaten you? Did he say anything at all? No, nothing.* And then what?

Perhaps if they were switched on and didn't think her an hysteric, if they remembered the story of the girl who stayed, whose friend did not, perhaps then they might have paid attention. But that would be saying the fear was real and then she really might drown. It was not so bad, was it, if she'd just imagined it? She could get through each day by cutting it into little pieces like the lacework snippings of bones. No. Let it go.

Or she could have rung someone last night from that paddock gate. She never thought of it. She might have been five again, as powerless as that. The road ahead was empty under the early sky, with deep shadows flying back and pink light filling the world, and there was nothing to stop him, no witness to fear or complicate. If she'd left later there might have been a car or two, a Mrs and Mr Winnebago, as George always called them, and they would stop, appalled, or she could drive along with them at the exact same speed like a shark and a pilot fish, the shark protecting her from larger foe. She wished she'd done a stunt driving course, knew about doughnuts and three-sixties and rolling another car. The cars touched each other with a dreadful scream, but hers being so much lighter and with no power to speak of, she was muscled off the road. The car skittered and swerved in the loose dirt and gravel and grass before it slowed, no more heft to it than a matchbox car, and really she was lucky. There could have been a ditch or markers or road signs, a collision. Birdy could have broken a leg instead of falling in a screaming tangle on the floor. She almost wished for that, for what was to come being taken out of her hands. He pulled in behind and when he opened his door and put a foot to the road she tried the accelerator, thinking to escape, but the wheels just spat gravel and made the man angry. He jumped at the gravel as it hissed and bounced, spitting some out, smearing it from his mouth.

Now she is watching him approach in her rear view mirror, and she is looking at the man who comes along the pathway every day of her life. His finger is down. It is the man from the park all those months ago.

Two memories pass through her, quick as light.

Brunswick 2021

There in the park so far from her childhood, Till had watched this man and the way he moved, and despite her fear she could see how he was misaligned. It was the inside of the man she saw. His outside self, clothing and so forth, was nothing but a disguise, but he would not be alone in that, Till supposed.

The man took a hand from his pocket and let it swing loose at his side, all his fingers curled like small pink shrimps but for the one that was quite straight. Till's heart clamoured; she felt hot, and put her hand to her throat and it was hot too. She wanted to vomit, but that would draw attention, and more than anything she didn't want anyone noticing her in that moment. The man especially. This was a feeling in her animal self, not her mind. Her mind had no idea.

She ducked her head, made herself small and swung around on her toes. 'Come, Birdy.' She spoke under her breath in a low voice, a sound that turns to nothing in air. She stepped onto the grass for the quiet of it. She could hear herself anyway, though the wind was stirring the tree canopies and rainbow lorikeets and musk lorikeets were screaming from the gum flowers above.

Don't turn, don't turn. Her mouth shaped these words. She held herself steady. A second, maybe two, she couldn't help herself, it would be all right to glance back, surely, and she did this. And he was looking, and he raised his hand, his stiff-finger hand, not far, but deliberately, and turned his gaze away. Till swallowed. She would pretend she hadn't seen and she wouldn't run. She turned the corner of a small hill made by the side of an amphitheatre. Now there was land between them. Now he could be anywhere, about to surge over that small hill.

She began to jog. Birdy was surprised, but glided beside her, her long legs reaching. 'Wait, Birdy,' Till panted. And Birdy slowed. There was a thicket of trees there whose shadows and shelter they could rest inside.

They stood quietly. There were signs of people sleeping rough: a couple of filled plastic bags, a rolled camping mat, a folded tarp, very neat. There was the smell that I mentioned before too, faintly faecal, and three tattered pieces of toilet paper further off. It was a lair, a wild place. The feeling of this grew. Till prickled with the danger of it, of having, as she now saw it, broken into a home. She peered out and only metres away could glimpse people in all their colourful clothing, and pieces of broken sky, and swathes of grass, and hear the lorikeets still, just the same as when she was in the open before, and regretted now having gone inside. Birdy got restless and began sniffing around, poking her nose into piles of dry leaves and snuffling, and then started whistling with boredom and need. Finally, when it was too ridiculous and there was nothing else she could think of, they left the lair – the noise of crunching twigs and leaves – and returned to the open and walked home through the park's centre to avoid pathways and people. When they got home they stayed inside.

Much later in the evening, Zoe said, 'What is it, Till? Has something happened? You're being so quiet.'

'What? No.' It was exactly as before. How do you say it? What are the words? *It was him, I know it was, and still I cannot describe him.* She said nothing.

'Why are you pulling at your hands again like that? You haven't done that for years.'

George looked at her then and she knew he had been pierced with memory of a time when nothing really happened at all. Till knew they would still say nothing about it, meaning the thing that hadn't happened anyway. But I will tell you.

2004

One autumn when Zoe was away at a conference or something, Till went to the zoo with George. They stopped at the lions and looked at the stupefied creatures holding their faces into watery sun, blinking and lashing their tails. Till didn't like to watch them like that. In a nearby enclosure the hyenas were locked in vicious skirmishes, snarling and darting, snatching raggedy lumps of meat and bone from each other, playing tug of war with whole limbs. Their muzzles peeled back in thick ridges to show their enormous teeth. She could hear their snarls and strange yips from where she was quite clearly. George put his hand on her shoulder, but she was all right watching this. They seemed alive, unlike the bored lions. She ducked under the post and rail barrier and put her fingers against the wire, hooking them through.

'Careful,' her father said.

She wanted a hyena to come closer, to really see it. One of them swung its heavy head around, watching her, and a little thread formed between them. She bunched her fingers together, straight, squeezed her hand through the chain wire to her wrist, and twinkled her fingers. The hyena came like a bullet. She pulled her hand, pulled, her hand wouldn't come, the hyena was there. At the last moment she turned her hand, squeezed it tight and yanked it free. She was staring into wildness, the hyena's small black wet eyes, the smell of its hot meaty breath, and something thwarted coming off it in waves. Hate and rage. Her hand meant life to the hyena – it brought it to life; it gave it meaning, if only for a few seconds. She had taken that away.

Somewhere a long way off her father was shouting her name, her old name still since she was not Till yet, grabbing her close, fussing and drawing her coat about her as if it was armour that could protect her from all harm, and shaking her, both together, frightened and furious.

She could see as if it was happening, the hyena darting away with its prize, her own tiny paw with its ragged nails, a choice morsel and a rush of life for a wild creature in a cage. She held her hands out to see them, to make sure of them, and squeezed her fingers and pinched one hand then the other as hard as she could. You needed two hands to do that. It hurt, but she didn't cry out. She hid her hands in her jacket pockets and squeezed her fists tight again to make sure of them, thinking about each hand in turn.

'I won't tell Mum,' she said to her father. He shot her a look. He didn't say thank you so she knew she was right. He couldn't agree that Zoe would be furious. But she would be. She would be incandescent. It was a word Zoe liked, and Till liked to say it too. She said it now. 'Mum would be incandescent.'

'Oh, I don't think so,' her father said. Till saw that even he lied sometimes.

Till wouldn't tell her either, but she didn't say it again. When her mother watched Till tugging her hands and squeezing them and pinching and looking, she said, 'What are you doing? Stop it, sweetie. They're all over bruises.' Till and her father's gazes glanced off each other's. She did this for weeks. Finally it wore off.

That is also not quite true. She had not forgotten the hyena's wildness. It was that something else happened to replace it: E.

Birdy had fallen into the foot of the passenger seat, and was stuck there screaming and sobbing, her legs a flailing mess. 'It's okay, Bird.' Till heaved her collar, helping her up, dragging her onto the front seat, her voice shaking. When she sat up again, the man was at her window, his face filthy, his eyes flat and hard.

He mouthed the words 'Get out' and when she didn't he smashed the window, very hard and sudden with a big stone. His face was still. The glass spread about, on her, across Birdy.

'What the hell?' she said. Birdy started up again. Till brushed shards away from her and off her own lap, feeling around the seat beneath them both. If Birdy got glass in her paws there'd be trouble.

'Now get out,' he said.

She got out. What would be the point of screaming in the middle of this emptiness? That drowning feeling again . . . *Keep your head, keep your head, keep your head. Not too fast.* 'Just going to get the dog,' she said. 'I have to go around. I don't want her walking on the glass.'

'Birdy,' he said, not addressing the dog, or even Till, not wanting a response, just to get her wondering how he knew, what else he knew, to throw her off, for his own satisfaction. Oh, she hated him for that. She wanted to kill him immediately for that intimacy.

The man said, 'Shut her up, make her stop.'

Till held Birdy's collar and stroked her head, trying to soothe herself at the same time, work out what was happening, what to do. The knife was in her jacket in the back seat of her car, tossed aside as too warm. (*Idiot, Till, think, think.*) She still had that bolt buried deep in her thigh pocket, bumping against her leg. More than fifteen centimetres long, a centimetre in diameter, a thick square twenty mil nut at one end, a wide loose washer, a deep turn at the other end that would penetrate a skull with only a little effort and resolve. It was a good weapon if she could find a moment to use it. She was glad she'd prised it free in that ruin. 'Never regret not having the perfect weapon; look for something to hand that can be the weapon you need,' a fight trainer once said. It was in her right pocket for her right hand; any luck and he wouldn't see it, sitting on the other side as he did. It was good feeling it there, not comfortable, but comforting nonetheless.

'You don't shut her up, I'll let her loose. You fight, I'll let her loose. Or would you prefer me to smash her skinny head in?' He raised the rock. 'Or I could just shoot her.' And then he held up a rifle.

That changed things. 'No, don't. Don't.'

'You're driving. Put her in the back.'

'What do you want?'

He didn't look at her directly; she saw that he couldn't. His mouth moved as if he was considering which words to release, as if he was chewing them up and he'd come across a big gristly bit. 'Call it unfinished business.'

There was something he'd said that she had not understood so long ago and had forgotten. And now she remembered it. He said to her, 'A bird in the hand, my gran used to say.' And he had gone. Well, they'd be back in no time, he said. 'You wait here now, unless you want to come?' Till shook her head, and stared hard at E to tell her she shouldn't go. E had on her laughing face like it was a dare. Maybe if Till hadn't given that look, E wouldn't have gone. She watched till they were past the brown building, wondering about the bird in the hand, which she had not seen.

'I am?' Till asked. 'A bird in the hand, your gran used to say. Isn't that right?'

'My gran? I told you about my gran? I said that, did I? And you remembered. Did you ever tell anyone?'

Till didn't say. She might not have. She should have.

'It was never the other girl.' He said her name then and Till felt sick and faint. If she passed out it would all be done.

'I thought she'd bring you along. Should always finish what you start. Something else my gran said.'

'And the people about here? What was that?'

'Just having some fun. Send people a-jitter. Which you wouldn't understand. Just looking round, saw that one hanging at Yongala. Gave me some ideas. Different possibilities. Get in now,' he said.

Till helped Birdy into the back. She got in the driver seat. It was still warm from the man, and this was unbearable to her, disgusting, touching his warmth, feeling it meet her. She remembered for a moment the safety of the bread queue and its pleasant warmth. This place was the opposite of the beloved safety of her car, the place that had been her principle sanctuary for years. Again, the nausea. She was frightened she would see his teeth. She pictured them fissured and stained along their lengths like an old whale tooth she'd found once. Pull one out and carve a tiny picture on it – an anchor, a man harpooning a whale, a sailing ship, a tillerman, a woman holding a sword and the scales of justice – call it scrimshaw, call it a story. Well, a person couldn't altogether help their teeth, but I have already noted that.

Till ran her tongue along the edge of her bite – the bottom teeth mostly, since his bottom ones were the more troubling in her distant memory, and unimaginably worse, more vicious in her imagination, the way they jostled for attention.

'Stop that with your tongue, you filthy little bitch,' he said.

Till adjusted the seat and started the car, a hybrid, silent.

'Okay,' he said. 'No flashing lights, nothing stupid, nothing, understand? Or you're gone. Both of you.' He blinked, weighing something up. 'I have killed before.'

As if Till had not considered this. What a fool he was. 'Sit down, Birdy,' she said. 'Now where are we going?'

Chapter 24

NAMES MATTER. THAT is always true. The names of places – the ones that had disappeared, that were here, now, in these grassed valleys and plains, the hills, stories of her great-great-grandmother, things she had read about the times before, what was known or believed or surmised – were hooks in her mind, so it was like she was driving through a story world, a place of myth. They passed a cemetery familiar to Till, a patch of ground set back from the edge of the road fenced with stock wire, red dirt with yellow hills as regular as rickrack braid behind, where she'd sometimes stopped and taken photos of graves, wondering where the people buried there had lived since there was not a building or town nearby.

Especially she had noted and photographed one family plot lined with wrought iron hoops and finials and marble gravestones and plaques resting on the dry mud mosaic flats of red soil. There were several people from a family with the name Duldig buried there, including two girls: Anna who died when she was three, and Gladys who died at five, also Anna's brother O.R. Duldig who died at twenty-four on the battlefields of France. The inscriptions read:

Days of Innocence and Wonder

*Let the little children come to me, for such is the kingdom
of God
Safe in the Arms of Jesus
Rest in Peace*

It wouldn't be so bad lying in such a place. Imagine if a departed person could rise from their grave and lean their elbows on the iron railing and gaze across saltbush or wheat, the lid of blue sky, insects rising and falling between the two, scuttering lizards, the hills – tsunamis of earth rearing towards them, never arriving. It would be nice. Some graves looked like the houses of the plains thereabouts, their edging falling away like tree bark. Some had nothing but a piece of metal hammered into the ground, and a name and a flower and a cross, birth and death dates painted on. But even that was more than E had. It was not possible to look at this without thinking of the many children who had died or been killed or maybe stolen from around here and elsewhere, also missed, still and always missed and always loved, forever.

Days of innocence and wonder . . . did they ever exist? Perhaps not days, but a few rare hours, minutes, seconds. Even when we were on those seemingly timeless journeys, I knew it would end, and it did.

Driving the same roads last week, Till had stopped on side roads or the tracks to properties hidden in the folds of hills. Bluebush and saltbush stretched away on the dry side of the highway; on the other side the wheat was holding on, but further from the road than it had once, and it grew sparsely. The old Goyder's Line writhed beneath her, before her, behind her. She had been driving the edge of the marginal land, more or less, the road unzipping it. What a mystery their journeying had been to her when she was small. Everything the outsiders did was against the grain of the land. The mystery, reading the old records of the past, was that they loved what they were destroying. But thinking it beautiful wasn't enough. It was still happening.

Till let Birdy out and they walked up and down a little way, Birdy sniffing, and she, Till, in her own way sniffing. It smelled of nothing, or only bright cleanness, of something just departed, of light, and apart from the irregular hiss of wind through the grasses and flag irises that were flowering then, it was quiet. There was not another living creature that she could see, though she had once seen a lone emu gliding away through the wheat and arcing up a hill at the sight of her car and the feel of her gaze, as otherworldly as a dinosaur. She was used to the bones, only stopping to identify them by species, or to admire their intactness or particular beauty.

People used to live here – hundreds, thousands moving about and pausing, gathering together, meeting, celebrating and dividing. To read about them from the scant records, the things that people said and noted down, they were there and then, over only a few decades, just gone as if they were the end of a wave disappearing into sand, ghosts walking through a wall into another room. It was an old story – disease, dispossession and murder, outsiders having their way . . . That it was sad was the most they would concede, but as to personal responsibility or shame, there was no need for that. It was the Europeans before them, the squatters not the pastoralists, who were the bad guys. They were off the hook.

Perhaps the way people thought was changing.

Till asked Tundra about it once, and Tundra said, 'Not many of my people still living on Country. Here and there.'

'But are there others?'

'Oh yes, south and west, on Ngarrindjeri, Ramindjeri, Nukunu, Kaurna land. I say, you should come back, we belong here, we've been here thousands of years, we are part of it, it's part of us, but they say it's the place of killings, it's not safe. Everyone remembers, everyone knows. I tell them that's the old times, from before, not anymore. It's all changed. They don't do that now. It's still our Country. They don't believe me.'

Till thought of Bear. She thought of Liz and how the police didn't care. She thought of Isaac and the fears of his grandparents that he'd be stolen from them. Things hadn't really changed.

Ed had been there when she got home only a week or two ago, before what happened with Marian. He was about to head on a trip up north again. He had a key to the station, but some reticence or courtesy made him wait on the platform. No hardship in that, sitting in the sun with a tin mug of cool tank water at your side, your elbows up on the seat back, hands hanging loose. He swatted a fly, and blew it from his mouth when it came back – pfft, like that. So neatly. She loved it at this time of day. She'd made this place what it was, or returned it to its old self. She had bandaged its wounds and splinted its broken bones, she had anointed its skin and applied concealer. It was a golden thing, and there was Ed bathed in sunlight, ridiculously beautiful to her and totally unaware.

'I watered the tree already,' he said as she walked towards him, Birdy loping at her side.

'My hero.'

He smiled then in a pure way, as if he couldn't see all the stuff she dragged around, the great rusted greased clanking chains and manacles of her rage and sadness and regret. Anything she said seemed to delight him. Imagine that. She hadn't failed him yet. She wouldn't think about that, just kept walking. His eyes widened at the expression on her face, determination or ferocity or something along those lines judging by his alertness, and when she got to him she flung her bag to the ground and climbed onto him. He put his arms around her and kissed her neck.

'Do you want to go inside?' he asked.

'I don't mind really.' She paused to put her hand against his face and kiss him. 'A cup of tea would be nice.' She laughed.

'You' – he was laughing now too – 'Till.'

'That's my name.'

Later, much later, back outside, she said, 'I should tell you about my name. It's not really Till, or it wasn't in the beginning, for years actually.'

Ed opened his eyes lazily. 'Matilda?'

'No. Tillerman. I chose it. It was from a song I heard at kinder, or it might have been school. I think school. I only heard it twice and I loved it. I always hoped they'd play it again.'

The teacher had been looking for another one about blackbirds that they were learning for the end of year. Till liked the Tillerman song, for the sound of it, and for one line that gave her a good feeling. She didn't have a word for it, it was only a feeling. Now she might say comfort, joy, but it was joy with knowledge of lack of joy, of loss. It came after something. There were piano chords, laconic, melancholy and sparse, and a tired voice wrung out of a strange place. She ran the few words in her mind now, the only ones she knew, not even sure of the tune, though she hummed a little under her breath, watching Ed leaning back on the platform in the evening sun, picturing a playground with people singing for the love of it while children played for the love of it. They played to their heart's content. She loved that song, and she'd only heard it twice in her whole life.

Ed said, 'Tillerman,' surprised.

'Yep. Weird, I know. Some old song.' She wished she hadn't mentioned it now. It wouldn't be the end. It was a name that had questions trailing in its wake. There was something confessional about even saying it. 'I just let people think Matilda. Sometimes I get Tilly. Not keen on that. I had another name before.'

'What was that?'

'Doesn't matter. I don't use it. I'm only Tillerman now. Well, Till.'

'Cat Stevens, right?'

Till swung her head around. 'Pardon?'

'Your parents were fans? Or no? This is so confusing.'

'What?'

'The singer, Cat Stevens, who sang the song "Tea for the Tillerman" that you got your name from?'

'You know the song?'

'Grandparents were hippies. Folkies, greenies. They ended up on a bush block. We went there on holidays, singing around bonfires sort of thing. It's kind of old.'

'You sang it?'

'Not this one. I don't *know* it, know it. I just kind of know of it. You could have looked it up. No one mentioned it to you?'

'I'm just Till. Tillerman's only in my head. It's private. My parents like classical and jazz, a bit of Dylan. I don't talk about my name. I don't talk about it at all.'

'Okay.'

'And now you know.'

'I won't tell anyone. I'll probably forget.'

'Not a joke.' He was really finding out now what sort of person she was. 'It is so not a joke.'

She began to tell him more things, all in small pieces, adding things slowly when she remembered. She was sobbing at the end, which she hated; it was hard to stop. He held her.

She said, 'How do we live with the pain? It just pours out of us, we wade around in it, it smears all over everyone, you can't get rid of it, I hate it, I don't understand it. Like, shit happened to me, unbelievable shit. I shouldn't say that. I get to live with the shit so I'm the lucky one. My friend . . . I can't say her name.' Here, she tried, she did try. 'She didn't get to live with it, she died. I had another name once. I can't say it though. Doesn't matter because it's not my name anymore. Till's my name. It was my idea. Did you know that? Imagine the responsibility of that. I mean, who was I, five or six years old, to be choosing my own name. What a thing for a kid. But there was no other way. I know that. I was glad of it. It saved me.'

'Why, why . . .' Ed said.

Till could see he didn't even know what question to ask. It was that weird a situation. It was hard thinking about this . . . thinking about it. She didn't know the words for it, but she was used to that.

She walked up the platform a way. Birdy kept an eye on her but didn't follow. Till came back. 'I never thought. I didn't even know the words, just the sound of them, and tillerman, that word. I don't even know the tune properly. I like it though. I liked it.' She hummed a little, goofing it up because she felt foolish now, and wanted to recover the mood, and he smiled, and she sang a little more, about the singers singing and hummed the rest.

'Ah, "sinners" and "sin". Pretty sure.' (Again, I can't tell you the line because of copyright but you can look up the song 'Tea for the Tillerman' online and listen to it to your heart's content.)

'No.'

'I think maybe yes?'

She glared at him.

'Hang on.' He took his phone from his pocket and tapped and the piano chords came out, the beautiful sad chords, and he was right.

'Bastard.' They listened to the end. 'Again,' she said, and he played it again, and this time she sang. 'I can't believe that line. It was because it was beautiful. I thought it was about innocence. It's about the truth.'

'I'm sorry.'

'No, it's okay. It's stronger.'

He kept on sitting there in the late sun, his legs stretched out, crossed at the ankle. His face was lit up – did I mention that he was a beautiful man? I see that I did – and he turned, squinting into the sun. 'It's a good name.'

Till said, 'I'll tell you about it all one day.'

'Okay.' He didn't ask more questions.

They sat some more, Till with her eyes closed. She was remembering the Name Day, and the visit to the therapist, Annunciata, when she was five or six. No, six. She'd started school.

Carlton 2004

They – Till, as she became, and George and Zoe – had parked near the Carlton Gardens and walked through them and along Victoria Street to Annunciata's office. They held each other's hands, Till in the middle, to keep her safe. It seemed the thing to do. Once, she would have run along and come back and brought things to show them, or raced ahead to press the button at the lights. It was not for love, although they did love each other. Maybe they blamed each other. Till didn't know what for but she felt it. They were worried. Now Till wondered if it was just to stop themselves from drowning.

Then they said they were going to have 'a little talk about how things were going'. And when she asked 'What things?' Zoe said 'Oh, you know', which Till did not.

George said, 'How you're managing.'

The mystery of what adults meant, the deceits of their language, the way they wielded it to make themselves feel better and left others to do the dirty work. Even George. It was the worst revelation of that day.

It was winter, and ragged leaves from the plane trees were still plunging to the ground, leathery things like desiccated bodies. The leaves on the ground, brown things, moved and scuttled in the wind and crunched under foot like the bones and carapaces of small creatures: quails, mice, cicadas, crickets. Zoe avoided them or shuffled through heaps. George stepped on anything in his path, even kicking a few, acting carefree as a boy, trying to cheer them up. Till could only see this now.

It was a quiet room with walls the colour of butter (which is subtler than margarine, and beautiful) and soft chairs arranged in a circle, and the therapist's name was Annunciata, which was a new name to Till. She, Annunciata, said they could call her Anna if they preferred, since her name was a mouthful, but no one did that day, and Till never did in all the years they met. She loved it.

The aesthetic considerations were just a backdrop to Till's outrage. She would choke on it, she could vomit at the betrayal. They were going to make her think about things, things . . . She was only a child. She remembered this encounter often, later, the rising nausea and shame, embarrassment and many other things rushing towards her at impossible speed and yet they all sat there like it was a Quaker gathering, which Till was not to experience until many years later, fictionally and vicariously while bingeing on *Fleabag* during the unexpected reversion of society to the distant past with a technological overlay (during the times caused by the thing that people preferred not to name or recall), which would have made this present futuristic, speculative, science fiction from their times. It would all have been speculative from her own childhood for that matter. She had only recently found out that her parents had grown up without computers or mobile phones, the pitiful things.

She found a cobweb in a corner to watch so she could think and not think. Children might not have all the words they need, but they recognise them the minute they meet them. They are like old friends or nightmares, no less understood for being unknown. She despised adults for the burdens of participation they placed on children without asking. One day she would have the words to say this. All of her thinking about her feelings and adults were just to hold this moment at a distance, and she knew it; she did it on purpose. Suddenly, she felt older and was aware of it, and the session hadn't started.

'What would we like to talk about today?' Annunciata asked.

As if the therapist's voice was a starting gun, Zoe said, 'She won't answer to her name. Not at all, not even at school. She won't talk to us if we use it. She doesn't say anything, just goes to her room.' She shot a wild, actually, an angry look at Till.

George picked up Till's hand and held it.

Quietly, Annunciata said, 'I wonder why that might be?' She said it in such a way that it was as if she was just wondering herself, and Zoe understood, but Annunciata didn't act like Zoe had been stupid not thinking along these lines, so she did not have to add this to the sum total of her feelings, whatever they were, which Till still didn't know or understand. It was also clear to Till (as she became) that they had been talking behind her back, which was something that she hated almost more than anything. She could never defend herself against their words.

Zoe said, 'It reminds her?'

'I wonder if it might.'

'I see. Of what?'

'He might have used it.' Here, she delicately looked at Till, who said nothing, but she didn't feel bad about not saying anything. She was thinking how the world wouldn't look after her, that she had to look after herself. She trusted a moving car, locks, having a lot of people around, even though she also didn't trust people since even kind people failed. They didn't check fences, they left windows open, there were spaces in their roofs, they left people on their own, they didn't check on them. But she couldn't say it. Zoe would think she was ridiculous. She would say *Don't be silly, S—* Oh, Till had almost heard in her mind the name her mother kept using.

'We might never know.' Annunciata spoke directly to Till then. 'You don't need to say anything until you're ready. You're in charge. No one should make you.'

They sat quietly, looking at each other, waiting for understanding to settle, to understand what it meant. That old before-girl was gone. She might not come back. Already Till felt her falling away. She was shoving her away as hard as she could. She could not wait to be free. She wanted to kick her.

'Oh—' Zoe was weeping. She had begun to say Till's old name and stopped herself. The day before she had taken Till by the shoulders and really squeezed them, and she might have used a harsh tone when she said, 'Answer me, S—', using her old name, and had shaken her, but not too hard. She, Zoe, didn't think it was too hard. Zoe didn't like to think badly of herself, Till could see that. Till was the only one who could tell Annunciata about that, but she knew she wouldn't ask. Even so . . .

'What should we do now?' George asked.

'Well, identify the problem. I don't mean what happened. The particular problem here, apart from not using her old name, which seems like a good idea?' Her face turned into a question for Till.

Till nodded.

'She needs a name, for school and things. We have to call her something,' Zoe said. 'I mean it's ridiculous.' Her voice got that angry shrill teary sound. It was like being squeezed again.

'I wouldn't say ridiculous. Self-preservation perhaps would be a more helpful way to look at it. I agree, a name would be good. Maybe not immediately, but she will need a name.'

'What?'

'You could ask her,' Annunciata said. 'Ask her what her name might be now, what she would like. Maybe she would like to decide? Something you're comfortable with, beautiful.'

She lifted her eyebrows – a question – at Till. 'Maybe not today. Something to think about for you.'

'Okay,' George said.

'Madness,' Zoe said, though in a less confident voice than usual.

Annunciata nodded. 'Does it matter though, really? What allows life to proceed is the question.' (It was a question that made Zoe look very thoughtful.)

One day she came home from school and said, 'Till.' Her parents learned to used it. She said she didn't remember, if people asked where it was from, only saying that it wasn't from Matilda. (She didn't even tell Annunciata, but she didn't mind.) She couldn't trust anyone with that information for a long time. It felt safer.

Much later, when she did fine arts at university and looked at annunciations, she saw her therapist as an angel bearing lilies (*Lilium candidum*, symbol for purity, innocence, spring, beautiful things, unchanged for centuries – millennia for all she knew), bringing them to her, bringing wisdom, or news or something. A lack of judgement. A therapist called Annunciata should probably change her name. It was too much really, but Till liked it then and for years after and even now. It was perfect. Beautiful Annunciata who stood up for her and saved her life.

Chapter 25

Near Wirowie

It was fifteen days since she'd seen Ed. More than anything she would like to see him, just catch a glimpse. He would see her trying to catch his eye and would give her that sidelong look and widen his eyes and smile like she was purest delight to him. That's what he was to her. If she saw that look just once more she would be okay, she could manage what came or if she died it would be enough to have seen it.

Till began reciting in her mind the names of people she cared about, and was surprised when Bev came to mind. Oh, Bev would have some words for this nobody, if she met him again. She would tell him some truth. And Tundra and Mr Oldham. They would finish him off. They would despise him. He would cower before them if he met their gaze. And Marian and Mrs Anderson, Ken and Mr Finch, and Zoe and George. Zuleika would stab his throat with one of her gleaming thumbnails.

Outsiders had brought nothing but destruction and sadness to this place. She had to include herself. She saw that now. Benign intent was no excuse, yet people cared about her, the very people she had brought harm to. Till wondered if she was letting them down again in this moment. He had a gun.

Should she crash the car? No knowing the outcome. Birdy galloping up the highway on her own . . . And there was the gun, and a gun is an unfair advantage. It neutralises another person's skills and suggests power in the carrier where there is none of any real sort. It is an admission of weakness while still being a strength.

Till felt him looking at her.

'You've changed,' he said. The change did not seem to please him. He looked behind at Birdy. 'That's a useless dog.'

Till drove, heading down the road in the direction he wanted, towards Wirowie.

'You hear me. Something to say about that?'

'Not really,' Till said. 'She's a good dog.' She wanted to say also that she loved Birdy, but already she had said too much, made Birdy a target maybe.

'They are not bad animals. I had a dog once. Shepherd. A biter.'

'Never trust a shepherd, my dad says. There are some good ones, some not. You don't know until you know.'

'Say that again and I'll shoot you.'

'We'll crash then,' she said. 'Don't you want to live?' She gave a little shrug, like whatever, it was nothing to her. She didn't care if he lived or died. She would kill him if she had the chance.

'You want to know how I found you?'

'No.'

'Your mother got careless, heard her talking at that cafe around the corner from your place. Oh yes, I know where your parents live. "My daughter" this and that. Stupid.' He looked swiftly at her and she knew he believed she'd ceased caring, which was not true. It was that she'd stilled her heart enough to think. She was walking in shadow now, and she put her hand to her heart. It was steady. 'Got to Peterborough, asked around for a girl in black and her black greyhound. It was that easy. Not very smart of you.'

It was quiet again, just the hum of the road. Till loved South Australian roads. Driving on them was a great pleasure to her, though less than usual in these circumstances. The way her mind was drifting. Actually it was better that way. It kept her body steady and her mind clear.

He said, 'You want to know where she is? I bet you'd like to know that,' taunting her again to regain something. He meant to kill her then; he didn't care what she knew.

'No,' Till said. 'I wouldn't.' But she couldn't help herself. 'She was a really great person, you know? She was funny. I loved her. I think she might have been a singer. What a sweet voice she had. She could harmonise. Five years old and she could harmonise. Do you know how rare that is?'

'You shut up now. Shut up. Stop that crying. What a baby. I'm going to tell you for that. I dumped her on your street. So you could keep each other company. Over a fence in a ditch, right there.' He inscribed a square on his leg and tapped a spot at its edge.

'In a garden?'

'That old factory. It's still there. Wrapped her up. Musta done a good job.' He grinned at that. 'Want to know what I did? I—'

Till pulled the car left and the gravel spat and the car swerved. The man yelled and turned the wheel back, and now the car lurched and wavered.

Till steadied it. 'Tell me anything else, and I'll make sure it's the end.'

'Bitch, fucking bitch.' He jabbed the rifle into her side.

Till pulled away from it, but held the car steady. 'I mean it,' Till said. 'Do not tell me. I don't want to know. They'll find her whatever happens. It's the last factory, and they're developing.'

'I don't think so.'

'They'll be clearing before they build. Pretty sure they are already.'

'Shut up.' He banged the rifle stock on the floor and fumbled at the rock in agitation.

Till began thinking the words, Samarkand, Damascus, Kamchatka, Svalbard, harmattan, then sounded them in soft breaths: 'Sa Da Ka Cha Ba Sva Ma Ka Ha Ta.' Her heart and her breathing steadied again.

'What are you, crazy? What is that?'

'Words.' Thinking to distract, Till said, 'Why'd you stop? People have been wondering.'

'I read that.' It seemed to give him satisfaction. 'In jail for a little crime for a few years.'

'How many?'

'Fifteen.'

'A lot of years. Not a little crime.'

'I didn't do it, just didn't want to stir it up. Fifteen years is less than life. Slings and arrows. Time to make plans.'

'You had some reading time,' she said. But before he could reply, the sign for Wirowie appeared and the moment passed. She didn't care what he'd read. Evidently it had not saved his soul or pricked his conscience.

'This is the turnoff,' he said.

Till looked in the mirror hoping for a glimpse of green: Mr Oldham and Tundra's ute. But they'd be half an hour behind, and how would she stretch that time out.

'Turn off then. Head to the station. Past the caryard. You get a good view from the front row cars. You know the ones?'

'I do.'

'Light blue Ford Thunderbird, Fiesta-red vinyl, porthole window. Get there early enough, no one sees you. They never do.' He shook his head – the stupidity of people. 'Not too fast now.'

Till eased the accelerator. 'You've got a fedora, right?'

'A good hat.' And then, 'How do you know that?'

'I'm a noticer.'

'You never saw me sitting there in the car. I saw you.' Taunting her.

She would be dead soon, yes she would. 'And why are we coming back here?' When he said nothing, she said, 'You want people to find me? Shock them?'

'Think you're so smart. I want them to see what you deserved.' He turned his head in a gliding way that already seemed familiar, as slippery as an animation, to see how she might react. Never trust a person with a shepherd: another thing her father said.

You know this, but I will tell you again. He had turned his head and looked back, E had been skipping at his side in her red coat, bobbing along on a cold midwinter day. E had looked back and waved. *Oh E, I am sorry.* Till hated that he was right. 'You'll be sorry,' he had said to Till, using her name as it was then, then twice more, a sort of teasing song, which she hated to hear. He knew how she'd feel. 'You're the one missing out – not this one.' And he used her name and grinned and Till saw all his teeth. They were different in her mind.

She waited for E to come back but she didn't. She remembered his finger then, her hand through the wire fence at the zoo, the hyena's hot breath and fury. He might have said something to E, she remembered his voice, his sweet friendly voice, a little louder than it needed to be if talking to E, working to hold her attention. He wanted Till to hear, she understood now, had been trying to entice, keeping the pretending game going for this little time more and lulling E along. Never since that time had she uttered her own name – she couldn't make herself; she had felt nauseous when other people used it. It was deeper than superstition. And E's initial was as close as she could come to uttering her name, and even then almost always in the quiet of her mind.

Why hadn't she screamed then gone for help why had her throat closed where had her words gone?

She had read about drowning. People who are drowning don't scream. They gasp, their arms flail, their throats close, they might be deathly pale before the water begins to slip inside. People watching might not realise. Till had failed E and she died. No one could say anything that would make that untrue, even if a five-year-old should not be responsible for anyone's life, even if other people had failed her too. Sometimes one mistake can cost a life, and sometimes it's a blizzard of human errors. In all those years she had not been treated roughly by men apart from the policeman, that bastard, that shithead, that creep, Rod, Marian's former husband. She had sometimes felt the beginning of fear and the possibility of things going bad. Not like this though.

*

They tied Birdy at the station's outdoor tap. The man agreed to a blanket and some water for her, since who knew how long she would be there on her own. He could care a little for a dog. Till took as much time as she could fussing over these small tasks. The man did not take his eyes from her. When they were done, he pushed Till quickly down the platform, along the meadow path, along the roadside to Main Street. She noted in passing the man behind her with the gun and the statue of the man with the gun standing nearby. She didn't bother hoping that someone would appear and save her. She could have an hour long midday nap on Main Street without being in any danger from traffic. The cockatoos screamed and tumbled in the palms; beneath them Till could hear the man's agitated breathing, puff puff puff, like that. Then down the street until they were at its centre, a sort of stage swept clean by wind, where Till waited for the next thing, which must be death. She looked at the gun.

'I prefer a knife.' The man held a knife up and felt about in his pocket with his other hand. A hanky. He spat on it and leaned towards Till, reaching with his hand and she reared away. 'Your face is filthy. Come here. You can't outrun me,' he said.

'I'm fast.'

'I've got the gun.' He patted it at his side, as if it was his old shepherd, the biter. 'So you know, I can shoot. I have no reason to lie.' But he stopped with the hanky.

The knife was his preference, the gun was for backup. That was useful knowledge. She was thinking again now. A knife was survivable, wasn't it? He moved it sinuously. It might have been a numbed limb returning to life and he adjusting to its heft and balance, returning it to himself. He raised his other hand and pointed at Till, holding out that finger and pointing with it. She couldn't take her eyes off it.

Till remembered the way he'd used E's name – almost jaunty, as if exercising rights. Yes, E was his in some way. She could tell he liked that. And then he used Till's old name, reclaiming familiarity and right, a way of making her small again and confused. That smile and easy way of his. Till vomited, suddenly, leaning forward to save her clothes. It splattered on the ground and a little on his shoes, which were different from his old ones – grey vinyl with a diagonal zipper on the outside: easy on, easy off, zip zip, he had said, working his own zip. Till hadn't been that impressed, her own shoes having impact-activated sparkly light heels and Velcro straps. Her hair had fallen forward and she tried to catch it all, but couldn't. Some bits had caught the ends of her hair and now it was foul and wet at its ends, sodden black string. She pressed it against her front with her sleeved arm and rubbed. It smelled sour. Her old name. Well, it wasn't hers any longer. She should have been sick on him.

She was five again telling E to come away and staring all the while, and E was laughing because she was a livewire – nothing more than that, and nothing wrong with that. Why shouldn't a girl be bold? Till wanted to be bold, and look what had happened to her. 'Idiot.' Oh, she'd spoken the word.

'What did you say?' he said, then into her face, 'What did you fucking say?'

'I was talking to myself,' Till said. She wasn't in the main street of a ghost town. She was still watching E, how she rushed forward and snatched at that finger and darted back, and how the man laughed and his eyes stared. It was a joke but it was serious too. His mouth moved in the laugh but he never stopped staring. E didn't notice that, so she rushed and snatched at his finger again. The gash in the wire was growing, its edges were curling, every day it was larger. His whole hand, his whole arm could reach inside now.

Everything conspired to make it seem like something from long ago even while it was happening. The colour and emotion of it faded, and the smattered images became foxed and old-worldly as her great-grandmother's mirror, as if Till had been hovering above watching a piece of theatre, something ancient and emblematic. A man with a knife gripping her arm. The long bolt in her hand now. The knife fallen. Her kicking it away and the man screaming. Him raising the rifle and flailing it. The hesitation: how to steady a person and shoot with an implement so long, whether to let her go and take a shot as she ran? Something crossed his face – irritation and disbelief. He hadn't planned it well at all. And there was Birdy, tall and black thundering towards them, the piercing sound of a shot and a bullet skittering and missing. Then this problem: how to ready the next bullet with Till feeling her chance, strong and young and angry, heaving her arm free. She hit him again with the heavy bar, more certainly this time. Birdy, dear Birdy had arrived at their side, prancing and wriggling all around her with excitement, getting between them. She had found Till again. Till's voice was high and sobbing, 'Birdy. Good girl, Birdy.' And the man bellowing, 'Fucking dog, bitch,' lashing out with a foot at Birdy and hitting with the rifle so she yelped and backed away and came back, and him trying to hit Till with his rifle now; he couldn't fire with his damaged hand. Oh, it was a mess.

Lucy Treloar

    Someone was approaching from a distance: Zoe running. Till must have died because it made no sense. And a ute in an old-fashioned green coming behind her: Mr Oldham.

Chapter 26

AFTERWARDS, IF ONE of them were asked, none could say who or what put an end to it: the bolt Till smashed into the man's head, Zoe shoving him away from her daughter, Mr Oldham's ute striking him as he staggered unbalanced or his head hitting the road. Whatever the truth of it was, the man sprawled to the road face down and drew his knees up one and the other like a baby learning to crawl and slumped with his knees caught under him and tipped sideways. Red began to spread around his head. The bolt fell to the ground at Till's side. She and Zoe clung to each other.

'Till?' Zoe said. She barely glanced at the man on the road.

Mr Oldham braked and wound down his window. Till went over and spoke to him. He got out and put a gentle arm around Till and they walked back to Zoe together.

'Till. What's going on?' Zoe said. 'We should, we should call . . . emergency services, police, ambulance.' Her words came out on huffing breaths of distress.

Was this the impatience parents felt sometimes when their children had no idea? Till looked at her mother and it made her feel tired. There was so much she didn't know. 'This is the man who took, took . . . who killed E. It's him. He's been here doing things. We didn't know it was him. He came after me. He's here because of me. He found me and he's been hurting people. He wanted to kill me.'

'What? Call the police,' Zoe said. 'We have to. Call the police,' she said to Mr Oldham, who looked at her steadily.

First there was the man, who despite everything was not quite dead. His chest still moved.

'We'll wait a minute or two, I'd think,' Mr Oldham said. 'He's been making threats against my grandson too.'

There were things Till might say to the man: *You know you did wrong, don't you*, and in her imagination he nodded yes; *Fucking arsehole, you deserve to die*, and he nodded yes; *You killed my friend*, and he nodded yes. And after this agreement from him she was finally at peace and he was dead. She didn't say anything though. She stayed in his sightline and she saw that he knew she was alive and she supposed he knew he wouldn't be for much longer. He blinked once or twice as if clearing his vision, checking its ability to reveal the truth, marvelling at his mortality. She said nothing and did nothing. None of them did.

The heat in Zoe and Till had burned out – it would be indecent to kill him in cold blood – so they waited until his fingers stopped moving against the asphalt, which was only a few minutes more. This was the worst bit: deciding not to help or give comfort. It went against the grain. What I mean is, it was a choice not to help, not shock preventing them, though they were in shock.

Here, now, Zoe told Till later, she noticed that the ends of a few of his fingernails were roughened from his scrabbling; shreds were lifting. Police might notice that if they came to examine him, she said, and wonder what they were doing while he tried to gain purchase on the asphalt. The undamaged nails were otherwise fastidiously kept, filed to a half-moon curve, and rather long for a man. But who would pick up and hold the hand of a dead man to file his nails.

'You know I used to peel your tiny fingernails off with my teeth,' Zoe said. She moved her mouth a little and tapped her front teeth together. 'It stops you cutting too deep. Blades are dangerous.'

'Yes they are,' Till said. 'Where'd you come from this morning?'

'Kapunda.'

'Must have started early.'

'Couldn't sleep. I wanted to get here.'

'Oh Kapunda,' Till said, and that was all. She might save Tundra's stories of the massacre for another time.

A few flies had begun to investigate the pool of blood and the man's head and his grey pants where he'd shat himself. Taken together, there would be some cleaning up. Still, there were only the same few people there. Hours might go by before Ken arrived at his collectibles shop. Was there anyone they could leave to discover the man?

'Not Ken,' Till said. She could see Mr Oldham was thinking the same. Who would destroy his sweetness? It wouldn't come to that.

'Need to talk it all out, I reckon,' Mr Oldham said.

Zoe started up again but he looked at her kindly and patiently, sorrowfully really, at her ignorance and her innocent belief in the institutions of law and so on. It communicated something and she became silent again. The man stopped moving and his eyes dulled. None of them was willing to touch his eyelids and conceal his dead gaze. He had become a problem that needed solving. They moved out of his sight-line, just walked away a bit without any of them needing to say why. It was more comfortable that way. They made some calls.

'Oh god.' Till's eyes were bright suddenly and she was as pale as if the blood had drained from her too. She sat on the edge of the high shop walkway, and hugged her head to her knees. Her legs bounced and jittered. She straightened, rubbing her hands down her thighs, pressing them, holding her feet against the gutter, but the shaking would not stop. She shook her head rhythmically. Birdy came to her side. Till put an arm about her and stroked her slender head.

'Sweetheart,' Zoe said, and sat beside her and pulled her close.

'Dad?'

'He sent his love, so much love, he said. Maudie's not up to travel.'

'Oh Maudie.' The thought of her getting old . . .

'I know.'

'Mum,' Till said. 'I have to tell you. He told me. Him.' She pointed her finger without looking at the shape on the road. 'He told me where E . . . where he left her. He said in a ditch at a factory, the one up the road from your place.'

'That's what I'm here to tell you. So you weren't alone when you heard. I thought it might be on the news. They're doing tests, but the police think it's her. Her parents are sure. Something she was wearing.'

'Her red coat,' Till said.

'Found her while they were demolishing.'

'Oh.' Till sobbed then; she wailed.

'But why did he tell you?'

'Because I'd be dead anyway so it didn't matter, so I knew that we'd had her company all this time. Know what he said? "Wouldn't want to split up the girlies." I can't . . . I can't . . .'

'No. Oh sweetheart. I want to kill him again.' Zoe wiped her face of tears but they kept on and she gave up. 'I'm glad she was close. Oh, that's a weird thing to say. Sorry. Her parents. How do they go on?'

'They just do,' Till said. 'People do.'

'Yes.'

'I love them.' Till did not mean love. She meant pain she wished she could not imagine and did not want to witness in them but knew she would have to sometime. And should she tell them what he said, how she tried to crash the car to shut him up, to spare herself the truth?

Two people came hurrying along from the west arm of the crossroad: a solid woman with pecking step and a man in a worn old shirt. 'Bev and Stew,' Till said, 'thank god.' And then a tall red-headed woman with her hair streaming back like Boadicea, and a dignified woman, lean as rope, came towards them from near the monument. 'Marian and her mum, Mrs Anderson. You'll like them,' Till said under her breath and Zoe did seem reassured. Mrs Anderson in a button-down skirt and a neat checked shirt seemed the most wholesome thing in the world, to Till too.

Zoe stood as they came closer, wiping her hands on her dress and pushing back her hair as if about to open the front door to dinner guests. What to do with this awkward body behind them?

Mrs Anderson had brought a clean sheet to cover the man.

Also a ragged old hand towel, 'In case you need to clean anything up.'

Imagine thinking of that. (Till picked up the bolt and wiped it and put it back in her pocket. She didn't want Rod taking it. No need to complicate things. She folded the towel, blood inwards. Wordlessly, Mrs Anderson took it and put it in her bag.) She would do nothing – 'nothing' – to help the man who left her Marian in a pit like that – 'like a pig after slaughter'.

'I'd kill him myself, if I could,' she said. 'You sure he's dead?'

Till told her he was and she was pretty sure she was right. None of them would touch him to make sure. The Mrs Andersons of the world hold it together was Till's thinking. They knew what to do. She, Mrs Anderson, and Stew draped the sheet over the man and fastidiously tucked it under his heels and head, being careful not to touch him unless through the sheet. Death is a fearsome thing.

They decided to tell the police the truth, leaving out the man's threats to Bev to hurt Isaac, in case they claimed she'd obstructed justice or impeded the investigation, whatever phrase that might make them sound competent or interested. The phone call from Till to Mr Oldham could not be explained away if they happened to look into it, and E's parents would have to know everything there was to know, Till supposed, though she wasn't sure. And there was his confession about E while Till was driving him to the place he planned to kill her. She regretted not crashing the car. She would like to have seen him frightened. Her driving skills weren't up to making a good job of it. You can't plan for everything.

The police arrived with sirens wailing, perhaps to make a show of the thing, or to bring people out. If that was the case, it served its purpose. It was as if an ice cream van had rolled into town. Out came wizened people in clothes of an archaeological cast, sweet Ken and nice Mr Finch among them, a single mother determined to make a better life and her daughters – one of them the future netball star Till sometimes saw heading for the school bus. The fear she had felt for them back then. (*Let it go, Till.*) The hillbillies from the outskirts of town came into view in their torn-out-sleeve shirts and filthy jeans, slinking along like feral cats. She had never seen some of these people before in her life, but other people knew them. They were quiet was all, or busy, or their lives ran along different paths and times from Till's. It was a living town, but living in the way of the almond tree growing from the Hidden Waters Emporium's backyard – dead along some of its branches, persisting in other places, shooting strongly from one young branch, where it was scattered with furry green nubbins of nuts.

'Nothing like it since 1973,' Mr Finch told Till. He lowered his voice, 'Except for Bear. That was a bit quieter. A good kid. Terrible thing.'

She and Marian saw Rod, and he saw them. People knew who he was, but for now he was a function. The police unwrapped the man's head carefully to take in his face, maintaining a professional impassivity, as if death were a daily encounter for them. They seemed like responsible citizens who were just going about their business of trying to hold their patch of the world together and make sure the right people paid the price.

People in town either believed them, Till presumed, or went along with the whole performance. *Yes, officer*, and so on. Some people might think they were right, that sometimes the shape of a society matters as much as the substance, but I don't think that's true. Tundra and Mr Oldham loathed such thinking. Such facades enabled the rot. Till despised them, but they made sense just for now while they got rid of the man.

When they told Rod about Till's call, he said, 'Why'd you ring Mr Oldham?'

'And not the police? Is that what you're asking me?' Till said, like flinging a match at a tin of kerosene. 'Would you like me to explain why I might not want to call you for any reason at all? Happy to. Wait, I've got some pictures on my phone that might help.'

'Just tell us what happened,' he said. His temper was already up, his face suffused with blood. 'How did that happen?' He looked over at the wrapped body.

Marian took Till's hand and held it tightly while Till told her story.

Rod looked at her, not quite mastering himself. 'So you've got it all worked out. You're a girl detective now? Do you even know his name? And you've just . . . killed him.'

'He ran me off the road, kidnapped me, made me drive his car at gunpoint, marched me up here to stab me on Main Street, wanted me dead. No one killed him. He fell in front of a car.'

'So you say.'

'He said he killed my best friend. He told me where he'd dumped her eighteen years ago. And he's the one who attacked Bev and Marian.'

'Can they identify him?'

'He wore a mask,' Bev said. 'We told you that weeks ago.'

Zoe stepped forward. I forgot to mention that she was dressed in a sooty black vintage Comme des Garçons dress of boiled wool with ragged seams and large buttons, like some rich ragamuffin, an avenging angel. Till wouldn't presume that no one around here knew what the dress was, but she was sure the police would not. The point is that she looked so different, so out-of-town, her attire almost costume-y, that she might have been a visiting prophet or oracle or high priestess. Of course, the truth had already come out by then so her summary of events was more like a closing statement by a lawyer.

She, Zoe, spoke quietly so that they craned to listen. 'This is my daughter, who has lived nearly her whole life knowing her friend was murdered and worse. And you're asking her if she made this up and this is an innocent man on the road. I saw him shoot to kill Birdy to stop her running him down. This gentleman here' – she gestured at Mr Oldham – 'and I were trying to save Till. Her friend's body has just been found, exactly where by some extraordinary coincidence he told Till he left her. I have just arrived here from Melbourne to tell Till. I'm sure you can appreciate that this is distressing news. They're doing tests. Now there is a body here. They will find out who this man is.' She paused to tuck back a curl that had blown across her eyes. 'Till had reasons for not ringing the police. I would like to hear what they are. Perhaps you might have some idea?' She glared at Rod until his gaze flickered away, then cast an eye around at the assembled people, who looked back, expectant.

They all knew or had heard rumours that he had assaulted Till, beaten his former wife many times; had failed to discover anything about several strange kidnappings in the area, including that of his former wife, Marian; that he had a grudge against Bev because of something to do with her daughter Liz, now a missing person; that some people said he had planted false evidence on Bear Oldham, her partner. Of course, that was rumour – no one really knew the truth. And there was the matter of Bear's death. The sign proclaiming his murder was right there behind him.

Rod was rage itself, and he had to hide it. Zoe, and Rod's sidekick – whatever his name was again, Scott, that was it – didn't understand at all.

Zoe said, 'I hope someone's going to fill me in on the rest.' She shifted her attention to Till. 'You said this was a beautiful place.'

'It is.'

'Well, I hope so,' she said.

It might have been the sense of Zoe as an outsider witnessing a private town thing that made Scott, the younger policeman, take charge. It was untidy. It was raw. Things began to unfold in a proper way after that, which is to say that it now more closely resembled the cop shows that nightly screened on almost any channel you cared to watch. People knew what was going on; they understood what was expected of them. What is your name? What is your address? Have you seen or heard anything unusual around town? Have you seen any strangers about? (Everyone said the same: that they had never seen this man before. Except Till who had not seen him since she was five and still could not describe him but still would recognise him in a moment if he only moved: his mouth, his hand, his feet, if he walked.) Where were you last night? And this morning? May I have your contact details, there may be further questions et cetera. All these questions from Scott with Rod taking notes. His pen bounced on the paper in his agitation. He kept trying to heave a deep breath, but was pulled up short each time. That drowning feeling maybe. It does feel bad.

People responded as obediently as children. It seemed as tidy as the hospital corners Mrs Anderson and Stew had contrived around the man's body, at his feet, shoulders, head.

The blood had scabbed over, even on the road, to a crusty brown. It had made a kind of glue that stuck the man to the road. He had to be pulled free and it made a little sound that those close could not help hearing. People's faces twisted at it. They still didn't know his name and yet they were watching this. Till did not want to, but she couldn't help being curious, and it reminded her of that old way he'd made her feel, as if she wanted his attention despite hating him. It disgusted her.

They loaded the body. A stench moved about like bonfire smoke on the breeze. They were all alert as dogs and stayed to witness it as if they wanted to make sure the job was done right to the end, and wanted to be able to recount their presence and the unfolding events for the next forty years at least.

People began to drift about, not ready to leave, though the witnessing was done. Till invited them back to the railway station. She was glad of the waiting room sofas, which Zoe could not help exclaiming over, having offered advice – 'Good job, sweetie!' – and of the platform benches, the woodstove and her camp stove, which she swiftly lit. It helped to be busy. There were some biscuits too. Marian and Ken bustled around helping. Zoe watched and took people cups of tea. Later, she said, 'You made something here.'

Till said, 'I don't know,' which she did not mean at all. She loved it.

Till remembered conversations from that weird morning. One with Bev while they were waiting for the police in which Till had said, 'I brought him here to this town. I'm so sorry. I'm so sorry.' She had squeezed Bev's arm and Bev had pulled her in for a quick side-hug about her shoulders.

Bev looked like she agreed in her heart, but she said, 'You did, but you didn't know. You meant no harm. And we had troubles of our own. My girl Liz. I'm frightened for her. It's not her, it's just not her. She would never leave Isaac. He was everything to her. None of that's on you. And Rod is homegrown trouble. Actually he's from Adelaide. Outsiders . . . Sorry. He's been here for years now. Terrible about Marian.' It was the nicest thing she'd ever said to Till. 'Don't you cry.'

'No, I won't. Not yet.'

'No. Some good too, I'd say. You don't think and you don't know what you're doing, but you don't mean bad by it, and all this' – she waved her hand around expansively at the congregation of people, the sheet-covered body, the black dog, the trickles of blood, the sun lighting it all up like it was an old, old play – 'it's not your fault. It's on him.'

Later, Till went outside for some quiet. Bev was already there. It seemed like she was going to go back inside at the sight of Till, but she patted the bench beside her and Till sat. Bev tilted her head back and shut her eyes for a second or two and opened them and looked at Till.

'I see you in the sun, sitting here now, me too, and I see Liz and Bear sitting just this same way, soaking it in, and each other. Just enjoying it. It's their place to me. I can still see them here. It was the only place I could feel Liz.' She felt around with her hands on the bench's slats and looked about. 'Along here somewhere. I need my glasses. Wait.' She pushed a cushion aside. 'There. "Liz and Bear 4 Eva". They're all over town. Sometimes "Bear loves Liz". They were something.'

Till said, 'I am sorry. I didn't think. I didn't try to see.'

'No,' Bev said.

'I liked it. A lot. It seemed like somewhere I could stop.'

'I see that.'

'I didn't know.'

'Well. That is true. But you didn't listen.'

'No. I didn't.'

'That's what happens. People don't want to hear. They just take.'

'I'm sorry. And you still sent Stew down. I'd never have done it without him.'

'You worked out in the end. You surprised me.' Bev patted Till's knee.

'Yeah?'

'Rod's nose. Service to the community.'

'I've got something for you.' Till handed Bev a key. 'I've been meaning to give it to you. Anytime you want some peace.' Bev felt it, and put it in her pocket. 'Do you mind if I stay here for a while?' Till said.

Bev gave her a tart look. 'I'll think about it.'

Ed rang later, trying to work out what has happening. He'd been out of range and was just catching up. 'So you haven't run away?' he said. 'What was that?'

'No. I'm back. I'm back, but please come. And drive carefully. I'll tell you when I see you. I want to see you.'

He was a couple of days away at least, deep into the Northern Territory, but at least he was coming.

*

When Till later tried to picture the man standing on Main Street holding the rifle and the knife, about to kill her, it was that other man Wilf Batty gloating over the dying thylacine and the destroyed landscape behind that came to mind. He was as certain and as vacant as that. The last wild thylacine, and all he could do was grin. Till was as good as dead to the man standing there. She could have been tied to a fence. It was hard for some people to envision failure, she supposed. And his teeth. He should have teeth that looked like he gnashed them on an iron bar each morning. It must have been the way he smiled. He didn't know how to. He just bared his teeth.

And now it came to her — things she should have mentioned to the police, at least to the younger one. She wouldn't trust Rod with anything on his own. But the man had told her something important, and the police should know.

The house on the westernmost street in Wirowie, where she and Birdy had sensed something, had snagged in her mind. She should have asked the man while she was driving if he'd been there all along, gliding in and out of town in his silent car. It was quiet along there, easy to come in and out at night or at dawn, set himself up in the caryard for the day, or leave for a few days to shop at a bigger town. Whatever plans he had wouldn't have suffered from that. The police might be interested. They should be. She met them there the next morning, leaving Birdy behind at the station with Zoe.

Rod gazed through the doorway down the dark corridor. 'You really think he was here? Why not choose a place with a door?'

'I wonder if he might have been. I didn't say I knew,' Till said. 'I saw something in there one day. Birdy did too. It was something different. There was a feeling.'

'A feeling? Spare me the amateur detectives of this world,' Rod said. 'Could have been a cat, a dog, a fox, a snake, a chicken. Could have been anything.'

'Forget it,' Till said. 'I don't mind going to another police station, or a newspaper, or radio, whatever you think would work better for a person with possible information in a murder case. You should at least look like it might matter. It's like you don't care.'

'I will charge you with—'

'Suggesting a lead for you, providing you with additional information, helping you do your job?'

'Time in the cell. Teach you some respect.'

'Oh, in the cell. My goodness.'

In some way she felt not wholly alive, more half dead, and prepared to say things she would not normally say. This insolence she was speaking with surprised her, for instance. She didn't care about Rod's violence. What was the worst he could do? He knew she could hit back. Scott was almost writhing in discomfort at Till's words.

'Do you think we need someone else here who wants to do their job?' Till asked Scott. 'Come on. I'll go in if you won't.'

Rod shoved her aside.

'So brave,' Till said, and she and Scott followed.

It had been the man. Till knew at once from the books lined up painfully square on a mantelpiece, the blanket folded precisely on an old sofa with a torch on top, exactly centred, a small propane heater, a little suitcase containing neatly folded clothes. On a table below a window were the things anyone might have on a kitchen bench: instant coffee, long life milk, a plastic container of biscuits, a Cherry Ripe chocolate bar, a jar of white sugar. He'd had a sweet tooth – a little comfort there. Looking at the painful tidiness, Till couldn't help wondering about a vengeful carer, an institutional past, misery inflicted for minor transgressions. Maybe nothing like that at all.

'Could be anyone squatting,' Rod said. 'Nothing new in that.'

'See how everything's lined up. That's him. You can keep pretending it's not, but I am right. I will be proved right. But let's find out, shall we?' Till said. 'Let's go about it all the long way.'

'We'll get forensics in,' Scott said.

'Good idea,' Till said encouragingly. 'Tidy it up. Make it airtight. A bit of DNA maybe, something connecting us. And how about that?' She nodded at a small white timber wall cupboard to the right of the window that had drawn her eye. She pulled a tissue from her pocket and with pinched fingers turned the small wooden latch that held the doors closed, and swung them open. They all swayed back, and in again, horror and curiosity moving through them like wind. There was a breath of quiet while they took in the sad little diptych. It was her own face that stared out, her dark hair, her red jumper, and more photos of Till and other girls arranged across the cupboard's two sides. It was like something the man might have seen on TV. Along the cupboard's base lay scraps of cloth and a tiny bracelet and a shell and a hair tie: some kind of aide-mémoire or trophy cabinet or scrapbook or Wunderkammer, or all of these things.

'What a cliché,' Till said, but quietly. (There is something about photographs that does feel like part of yourself. Till felt that then.)

Scott pointed at another picture, tentatively, and not too close. 'That's you here, right?'

It was a profile of Till taken mid stride on Main Street. A few trees were interposed between the picture-taker and Till. She looked at the other images and saw from the framing and the depth of field that he imagined himself a documentarian of artistry. The background, the far side of the street, was blurred, but she knew the white facade. He'd been in the arid gardens on Main Street. At the time the photograph was being taken, Birdy might have pranced and lifted her ears and looked and Till might have ignored her. It would have been something like that. It wasn't enough to have a dog and to know what a dog was capable of. You had to pay attention to what they were telling you. She, Till, was so stupid.

But what would she have done if she had been paying attention? Would she have gone in to explore? If he had nothing but a knife, she backed herself with her own knife and her long bolt and her rage.

'Who are they?' Rod said.

It was hard to look, but they could not look away. 'This one is my friend from kinder,' Till said. 'The one who was taken.'

'And you,' Scott said.

'Yes.' They were under a bush, pulling petals from flowers and dropping them in a bowl, very serious. There were two other small girls she had seen before in newspaper articles. But there were three she did not know at all. 'These ones' – she pointed without touching the photos – 'I don't know them. Wait.' She looked more closely. It was a small girl in a red dress taken through a chain wire fence. 'This one is from here. She catches the bus. Her big sister's a netballer. That's taken from the caryard. He said he used to sit in one of the cars and watch. A light blue Ford Thunderbird? I think that's right. Porthole window.'

'She got lucky,' Rod said.

Scott tapped his notebook with his pencil, and wrote. 'So, yeah, forensics, and for the ruin where, the, uh, third victim was found, the water tank girl.'

Rod turned his head at that, about to speak. But he stopped.

'Woman,' Till said. 'Marian Anderson. Beloved daughter and friend.'

'Right,' Scott said.

'Former wife of local policeman who appears not to care.'

Rod shuffled his feet like a bull considering charging. His fists clenched. 'There won't be anything there anyway. It's what? A week ago that happened. No point.'

Scott put on some gloves and picked up a paper from the mantelpiece. 'Maybe dot the i's? Go and have a look? The tape would be there. He would have touched that. Good prints if we're lucky.'

'The third,' Till said.

'What is it now?' Rod asked. 'And what does it even matter since he's dead.'

Till shook her head. 'No, doesn't matter. It was nothing.'

It wasn't nothing though. It was something.

Chapter 27

It was mild by day, with a golden light in the afternoon, but still cold at night. Later, Till and Zoe sat in the sun like invalids on the deck of a cruise ship, watching the grass billowing in green waves on the lines. Till pottered in and out bringing cups of tea, and later in the afternoon, glasses of cool wine, small snacks of not very exciting sorts – spiced almonds, water biscuits, little soft cheeses from further south – and lulled them along into togetherness. They talked about what happened, moving the pieces of information around to see how they fitted together – how did Birdy get loose when Till had tied her, and how had Till and Zoe not run into each other at the station, which roads had they travelled that they missed each other, and what did they each separately see? It went along like that.

Zoe told Till about her arrival at the silent station, the moment Birdy pulled free, and how she chased Birdy when she ran. There was no calling her back – Till was the only one Birdy listened to.

'I knew she'd slip her collar,' Till said. 'Her head's smaller than her neck – she only has to pull.'

'Who's going to catch her?' Zoe said. 'You should have seen her. She was off.'

Birdy had run up Railway Place towards the WWI monument, the route she knew from their morning run, though Zoe wouldn't know that. The light would have been streaming along the side road, the shadows from trees and buildings and light poles and the monument's soldier rushing ahead across Main Street.

From the corner, Zoe saw figures to the south – Birdy, and could it be Till? and someone of malign intent – dazzling outlines like shadow puppets on walls, as elemental as that. (This is how Till pictured it from Zoe's description.) Then Zoe ran recklessly after Birdy towards them.

'You could have been shot,' Till said.

'I suppose.' Zoe gave a sort of shiver then. 'Oh, I was terrified for you.' She pulled Till in close and they sat like that for a while.

Till couldn't stop thinking of the man who killed E. She began to see that though his death was just – at least deserved and also provoked – it had a weight that transcended this. It existed outside the body that had lain on the road in the middle of its own drifting blood, it couldn't be left on the road, it must be picked up. She could not pretend it away. It was a physical weight, a moral weight and there was also the weight of his now non-existence that they were responsible for. It was all of theirs now. She could tell herself she was sharing it with her mother and Mr Oldham. They all three might look at each other and think the same, that they were each only one third responsible and that he deserved it. But it didn't matter that it was self-defence or protection. It didn't matter that she'd avenged E, and saved herself and perhaps the lives of other girls, including the little girl who she'd watched walking down the side road to the highway to catch the school bus.

Life and death were heavier than justice, retribution, survival, revenge. They were absolutes. They had snuffed out a life and would have to live with that. She could think it but not say it. She wondered if the man had felt any of that, and if he had liked it.

Zoe said, 'You know, I can't understand why I feel like this – I mean, I feel fine, I feel actually fine – when I pushed a man in front of a car. What's wrong with me?'

'Not just any man.'

'No. But he's really dead.'

'Yep.' Till still felt what she felt though. There had been a small report in the media of a pedestrian killed in Wirowie, and that was all. Till wished that was all there was to it.

It really did seem different for Zoe. She was not excited exactly, but she was not weighed down. Zoe sipped some wine and waved her glass around expansively, illustratively. 'I saw this amazing picture of a girl sucking a lollipop a while ago. She's sitting in a shot-out window frame, holding this huge gun. Huge. And a lollipop. She looks about ten. She's got a job – to shoot someone before they can get closer.'

'Photo was staged. She's the photographer's daughter.'

'Oh.' Her face fell. 'But we all believed it. My point is, we might be past the time for tender feelings. Someone staged it and people believed it, the world's falling apart, this is where we are. We just have to get on with it . . . The world's changing, Till.'

Till said, 'Princess days are over?'

'I was thinking more that we didn't disgrace ourselves. We stepped up. Floods on the Murray and people are getting on with it. Things are coming. I feel less pathetic than I did.'

'Found your true calling? Remember when we were talking

about living in a plague-free community somewhere out of the city?'

Zoe made a face of distaste. 'Not really us,' she said, as if survival living was a lifestyle question, which it was really, though perhaps not in the way she meant.

'Good to have a plan though.'

There was another photo Till had seen, also from the war in Ukraine, in which two men look like they are dressed for an afternoon watching football on TV, a beer in hand – they wear trackpants, runners, hoodies – except that they are lifting a dead body from a shelled house using the body's jacket and ankles as handles. (Till knew how that felt. She'd helped move a man from a car crash early in her journey and kept his wife company while he died.) The Ukrainian picture shows two men gripping the body hard so it doesn't slip. There is a blue floral curtain on a stretcher made of scaffolding that they will wrap him in. Behind them are dormant vines in need of pruning (it wouldn't be happening this year) and an untended vegetable garden, also broken tiles, rubble, buckets, bowls. A hook on the house wall has a piece of netting hanging from it – a convenience for gardening. Order and disorder, the everyday and chaos. A body is just an unwieldy weight if you're careful in your thoughts. The men's faces are almost still. If you look carefully, there is an edge of revulsion on one. He is holding it in. It is worse for everyone if it appears. A woman is overcome. She raises her face to the heavens, her back arced, her hands over her face. Beneath the hands is a howl of despair or deepest distress, tears, rage, who knows exactly. It might be her son. Till thought it was.

*

'They were like sleeping people, or children,' Zoe said. 'Not all of them, but mostly they preferred the family stories – the rewards of hard work, triumph over adversity – all that.' One conversation had shifted into another and become itself rather than tangential. She was talking about her oral history project with old pastoralist families in the mid north. It had been complicated – history, geography and climatology together. Rainfall patterns were shifting – as I have already mentioned. A book had come out of it. It had excited her at the time, as far as Till remembered. Her enthusiasm for the subject had disappeared.

'They held to their innocence. They couldn't wake up. They really wanted to believe their families arrived in an empty land. Out of sight . . . *People prefer to believe in a lie or a dream and do not like the people who wake them.* I read that somewhere. But it all happened. If someone tells them different, they sort of look away. They know each other and they're all so nice, so kind, so decent. Well, we all are, as far as we're concerned.' She made a snorting sort of sound. 'I know some of them knew it wasn't right. You could tell from their stories. They'd leave a little piece of bushland for when First Nations people came through; they'd take them pies or a sheep; they'd give them food or clothes so they could feel better about themselves, tell themselves a story about tradition and relationship. And maybe there was some truth in it. Complicated stuff. Guilt, shame.'

Till thought again about the way people mostly turned the angle of the mirror so it showed something or someone else, shut the door on it all. It was like that road she had travelled with the disappearing vistas, the doors shutting behind her. She'd bought an old railway station because she could and because she liked it. She was another one, walking in and taking because she could. 'Ed works with this guy, from around here I think, a First Nations adviser – government, I'm not sure – on land restoration.'

'Oh yeah?'

'Near Yongala, I told you that, didn't I? There's this beautiful wetland – a trough, they call it.'

'A trough,' Zoe said, 'that's right.' She smiled a little.

'It's amazing how it's coming back. Birds and things, insects, reptiles. You should hear it. Things are waiting to grow, Ed says. That's what the adviser says. You need people who can read the land. Traditional owners.'

'Oh, well, that's good.' Then seeming to realise how flat she sounded, Zoe said, 'That really is good. No, it's great.'

'I'll take you over if you want.'

'I would love that,' she said, but her manner said she wasn't sure.

'You could see how things are changing.'

She smiled at that and squeezed Till's arm and rubbed it. 'I don't know. It was mixed up, that time. Too much sadness. You remember the last trip, don't you?'

'No.'

'Everywhere we went there were bones, a lot of death, trees dying.'

'Yeah . . . You can't get away from the bones. But I loved our trips. I used to think about them a lot. Like self-hypnosis.'

'You did?' Zoe stared at her, incredulous.

'I only realised later. I don't need them as much now.'

'What about that last trip through here, further north? Everything was sad.'

'I don't really remember that trip,' Till said. 'I've seen the pictures of course,' she added politely.

'I just meant, you weren't talking, and we couldn't get you to . . . we just had to drive. It was the only thing that—'

'Stop.' Till covered her ears. 'Please. I felt safe in the car. That's what I remember. Just stop.'

'Oh god,' Zoe said. 'I'm sorry. It's—'

'Shut up. Shut up shut up!' Till buried her face in her hands.

Zoe was very still. She put an arm around Till's shoulders and a while later put the kettle on the hotplate. She made a cup of tea, found some sugar on a shelf, put three teaspoons and some milk in and stirred and gave it to Till. 'I thought you were okay about all that.'

'Well I'm not.'

Something crossed Zoe's face then, an old look familiar to Till, but not often seen or recalled, as if someone else was inhabiting her, maybe her mother. Her face became impassive. She folded her arms, then unfolded them. She knew about body language but didn't remember in time. Who knew what she was dragging around from the past.

In Till's mind Marian was a force – furious, and dangerous when furious. She seemed shrunken when Till arrived at the shop in the morning, curled in on herself, listlessly cleaning the windows just to do something, a pointless task since a fine drizzle had settled. She was glad to stop. The seal for The Machine had arrived and it had given Till some hope. It was a task that might be completed and coffee might be drunk, people might smell it and arrive to get some of their own, they might sit on the steps or the kerb or the window box if Birdy budged up, and they might chat and come back in to buy the sweeties or icy poles that the cafe owner so thoughtfully supplied. It was a very small parcel for all those hopes to reside in. She put it on the counter. They hadn't spoken since the man died on Main Street two days ago, and it was less than a week since Marian had been taken and found. Till had left immediately after. Neither knew what the other had been through, not altogether. Till didn't want to talk about it, but maybe she should tell Marian the whole story, and Marian might want to tell hers. It was because of Till. That was part of it. And Till had helped kill a man. The bolt alone would have done it. It was like her hand remembered the moment the bolt struck his skull, the way the shock ran up her forearm. Her mind kept sheering away from that. How could you know how to measure horror and how might it be differentiated? Till felt tired at the thought of teasing it all apart.

Marian picked up Till's hand and patted it listlessly as a drunk. She said, 'We don't have to talk about it. I don't want to.'

'No. Me neither. Maybe later.' But she didn't mean that. 'Another time,' she amended. Maybe they would and maybe they wouldn't. It didn't matter.

'Maybe. It is nice to see you though.' The way Marian felt might not be so different.

'Yeah.' Till felt emptied out. For the first time she stopped feeling she had to be strong, resilient, positive – all those stupid things that would relieve her mother. What was so good about them? It was easier to keep it all inside. Nothing had really changed for her then. 'It's just so nice to sit here, you know, with someone who's . . .'

'Been through shit too?'

'Yes. Sorry.'

'Same.'

It was as if they'd been through something together and

they were still inside it with no knowing if it would end. Best not to think about that, and what point was there in talking about it when things were like this, seeming unfinished and still imperfectly understood.

'But you know what? Fucking hell.' Marian's face suddenly blazed. 'I'd like to raise that guy from the dead just to kill him again. I keep thinking what I could have done different.' Now her eyes were bright with tearful fury. 'But I couldn't at the time.'

'You did everything you could. You're alive. That means you did everything. That's the important thing. Not him. When I was five I thought: If only I screamed. I don't know why I say that as if it will make you feel better. I still think that.' (She should have screamed the kindergarten down. The scream should have rung across the streets. People would have come out to find out what was going on. Marian didn't need to hear all that though.) 'So yeah, I have nothing to make you feel better. No one died because of what you did, including yourself. Hang onto that.'

'You were five.'

'Yeah, but so what. Anyway, my story's old. It's fresh for you, and that's . . . well, it's . . . I don't even know what to say. You can't tidy it away, you just have to find a place in yourself you can bear. Or something.' Till began looking at The Machine and the seal, wiping away any dust. She wasn't really sure how it all went together now. She might ring Mr Finch in a bit, and look up some diagrams. She began laying out the pieces. It was peaceful.

Marian started talking, softly, mostly to herself rather than Till. 'It was so cold at night. I hammered and kicked in the daytime when I heard a car – as if they'd hear from the road.

Maybe someone would stop to take a look. Wrong time of year. Three cars passed the whole time I was there. A shutter kept banging, and like a voice. I don't know what. I was going a bit mad. I was thirsty. I thought I would die. That voice. It made me wonder about religion and other planes of existence, whatever people call it. An angel keeping me company.'

'Marian's angel. A singing voice?'

Marian tipped her head to one side, shut her eyes as if listening for it. 'Actually no, I don't think so. More like calling? I don't know. It's pretty windy there – you can hear it blowing in the roof.'

Till said, 'You know something the man said in the car? This is weird. You know the woman at Yongala, the one who was strung up? That wasn't him. He didn't do it. He came across her and it gave him the idea. It was just having some fun to him. He had a look and left her there.'

'Oh god,' Marian said. 'That poor woman. So there's still someone around who did that?'

'Yeah. I don't know what to think. Something about Rod though. Scott said you were the third person the man attacked, and Rod looked surprised. Why would that surprise him? I have no idea what he's thinking. The other guy, Scott, thinks the man did all three attacks. But he didn't. Now I'm wondering. And there was that woman in Jamestown.'

'Mmmm?'

'When did Liz disappear again?'

'Liz? You think the man did that? Oh my god. Why would you think that?'

'No, no, at least I don't think so. I have no idea.'

'Liz would have gone, I'm not too sure, around when you came? When was that?'

'Beginning of the year.'

'You've been here so long.'

'I know.'

They smiled at each other – almost goofily – then their happiness made them happier. They leaned their shoulders together for a moment. It had been like that with E too.

'Maybe a week or two before that. It was so strange. Just gone. Poor Isaac.'

'The man was in Melbourne then.'

'Right. Yeah, the police took no interest. Just one more disappeared woman. They don't do anything. And she's a single mother, so . . . in their minds, who cares?'

Till looked up from her work on the machine. 'I can't stop thinking about that voice.'

'Are you thinking about Liz?'

'Or what if it's another woman?'

They looked at each other then, for some seconds, thinking things.

'Right,' Marian said.

'We better . . .'

'Yeah.'

'Like, right now,' Till said. 'I'll call Bev and Stew.'

'And get their hopes up?'

'No need to mention Liz.'

'I'll call Mum.'

Mrs Anderson gathered a bottle of water, a thermos of sweet tea, a warm blanket and a thick cardigan. 'Just in case,' she said. Stew took one look at Till's Datsun and offered to drive his capacious ute. It almost had the feeling of an outing. Till gave directions from the back. Bev looked around at them beadily, as if sensing there was something they weren't telling her. We are all just animals. Wayne sat at Bev's feet, sitting up straight to glare at them all, and yelping hoarsely from time to time. 'Now now,' Bev said.

Marian sat in the middle, silent and trembling. Mrs Anderson held her arm and hand, which she patted absently. 'It's okay, it's okay, sweetie.' (What lies people tell. No one knew if it would be. I suppose she meant it kindly. It's how we get along, holding onto the slender threads connecting one moment to the next.)

'A longshot,' Till said.

'You said that,' Marian said.

'Still.'

They were quiet after that. It grew wetter. Way across the plain, the wind turbines on the hills were an armada of ghost ships in the festoons of rain.

The ruins presented a different appearance this day. They were not beautiful, they were ground down, half-submerged. No one moved when the car stopped. Then Till said, 'Wait here. I'm going to call – see if I can hear anything. Quieter with just one person.'

No one disagreed, so she got out. Immediately the chill wrapped around her. She went through the gate and started walking and shouting, waiting before moving forward again. She skirted the front of the house. The pigeons, as before, exploded from the front door. When the noise subsided she shouted again. She beat a plank against a sheet of iron. Still this rain. The water tank was ahead, a short distance from the house. She looked back. Ten or fifteen metres. She stood where Marian had come out, by the ladder, which was still there. She shouted. She shut her eyes, listening with her whole body. Then 'Liz' she shouted with all her might, wildly. It was embarrassing; she was glad she had no witness.

Very faint and distant like the wail of a forgotten child came a thin high sound. It was not a word, just the purest despair, like a needle under your skin. Till wondered, awfully, what cry E might have made. (*Oh E.*) Till could think of no worse sound.

'Liz,' she shouted. There was nothing but the sound of a loose shutter. 'Liz,' she shouted, and again there was the banging, more of it now. She ran back to where she could see the ute and waved and ran back, and she could hear them coming.

They followed the sound, which came from beneath the sodden earth near the back door of the house. The first layer was branches and an old drum of poison, half-full by the slop inside. The second layer was a slab of concrete. The bottom layer was a heavy wooden trapdoor with a fat bolt that exactly matched the bolt Till had found nearby. Before they opened it they knew it was Liz. Bev and Stew tore at things, shouting and bellowing. The ladder was for this, for someone to climb down to Liz in this cellar, and now for her to climb up, and when she arrived near the top, shaking, a strange otherworldly drowned and leached-of-colour creature rising up as bedraggled and distorted as any lost memory, with Bev kneeling at the edge holding her own arm down beckoning her on, touching and tugging at her the minute she could. Stew pulled her the rest of the way and she almost flew into her parents' arms. She held her face into the rain. She said, 'Isaac.' No question, just his name.

No one asked what she had been through and she didn't say then or any time that day. She shook her head and was mute if anyone asked a question about the time she had been gone, nine months. It seemed like she had been in another world for so long she would never again belong to this one, and they could not let her go in case she fell back into that pit. In her face Till saw a shadow of Isaac, as Tundra and Mr Oldham might sometimes see in him a shadow of Bear. Isaac might bring her back and hold her here. Maybe there would be an Annunciata for her. It is true she was in a pitiful condition – terribly thin, distressed, filthy, bruised, but there was some quiet triumph there too: she had outlasted him.

It had been Rod. Not trusting any police person from nearby, Mrs Anderson rang a police station further afield for them to manage the situation. This part, Till did not follow closely. Liz was a private matter, the way everyone suddenly orbited around her was private, only for people she knew. Till understood that. Liz belonged to them and the old world from before Till came. She didn't need anyone new, and wouldn't for a long time. So Till didn't know what was happening, except through visits from people – like diplomatic missions from a foreign country. Rod had not called in a forensics team to go to the ruin. He hadn't visited Liz since before Marian's rescue. (Till remembered how he'd hurried them all away from that house, terrified no doubt.) Liz's supplies were almost finished. She had developed hoarding and rationing ways over the months or she might have died. People speculated that Rod was hoping Liz would die in the end and spare him, since he could neither bring himself to kill her nor release her. It was her freedom or his. And Till had mocked him for his threat of the cell.

'I was still with him when, you know . . .' Marian said when Till visited her.

'When he took Liz?'

She nodded. 'That's my former fucking husband who did that. What am I supposed to do with that? You know what he's saying? That he could have killed her and didn't, that he made sure she was fed, he was going to let her go. Like he's the good guy because he's not a murderer.' Her gaze was blank.

Till wondered what she was seeing, what she might say. But what could she say that might make any difference? She held Marian's hand.

'He could go from her and come home to me. He could leave me and go and do some shopping and drop it in, like literally drop it in, down the hole, to her. He touched me. He had his hands on me, a person who did that.'

'Yes,' Till said. His hands had been on her too. 'What about the woman at Yongala – and the one in Jamestown?'

'Denies knowing anything.'

Chapter 28

THE POLICE RELEASED details of what had happened. It didn't take the media long to reach Wirowie – 'the town that time forgot' – or to realise the story's 'showbiz connection', as they called Till's stuttering singing career. Someone dug further and soon she was 'the little girl left behind' again. Till, Marian, Bev and Liz declined to be interviewed by anyone other than police, which people other than the media understood. They had to make do with police statements. Till was glad of her strong door, which she shut and locked.

Her manager tentatively asked whether she had 'anything new in the pipeline they could potentially release to, er, capitalise on . . .'

'My abduction, and my hand in the death of a man who murdered my childhood friend?' Till said. 'You think we should be making hay in that sunshine?'

'No, no,' her manager said. 'No.'

'No. I don't think so either,' Till said.

It died down after a few days.

*

As if Till and Zoe were truly invalids – their own troubles being so recently past – people came visiting. Ed arrived.

'I can't believe I wasn't here,' he said.

'Really not your fault,' Till said.

'Still.'

Till told him everything she could think of: about Marian's capture, Till's capture and escape, also Zoe's arrival, and the small matter of the death of the man. He had heard about Liz from others.

Then Tundra came by. She was dazed by events – Liz and her survival most of all.

'She can't let Isaac out of her sight. She can't have a single door shut. She keeps washing and washing – herself, everything around her. Hides food. The poor girl. I don't know if we'll find out any more about Bear now Marian's feller—'

'Former feller,' Till said.

'Sorry,' Tundra said. 'Now that he's in so much trouble, someone who knows might speak up now, they might do that. Rod hated Bear, because Liz chose Bear. That should have been enough. People with too much power.'

'And no control.'

'True,' Tundra said. 'Rod picked on them for years. Just made trouble every way he could. He wouldn't let it rest, and Bear wouldn't leave.'

'Save us all from angry men,' Till said. 'Save us all. And fuck them. Maybe it's going to take time. It's eighteen years since E was taken.'

'You know what Roy says? "Killing is quick. Justice is slow." We've waited this long. But oh dear, dear Lizzie. How does she come back from that? How do you move on? When the time is right we'll do something, go out bush maybe.'

Eventually she got talking with Zoe about history and different parts of this old nation, this particular nation, I mean, which might have been a distraction from Liz and Bear and Rod and all that pain. Marian too. And about an area further south, which was on Tundra's mind since it was where her mother was born, and was an important place for other reasons. People were talking about land development, Tundra said. 'Down there's Serpent Country. Develop that and the whole country falls apart. Don't want to mess with that. Don't want to pull that thread.' She said some other things too, which I will not mention here.

'Really?' Zoe said, more than once. 'I wish I'd met you when I was writing my first book.'

Finally, Tundra said dryly, 'Well, I might not have said those things for your book. Why would you want to say all that? What's the point of it?' A flash of distaste crossed her face. 'It doesn't change anything.'

Till watched Zoe adjusting her thinking, trying to see things in a different way – this world as living now with traditional owners, not something past that needed documenting, and in any case not her business, then herself wondering if she had understood it right.

Till went and got a bottle of wine and some glasses, and some almond macaroons, and when she returned Tundra was asking Zoe where she lived, and Zoe spoke of her garden, which she loved and fretted over, and asked Tundra about her home.

'My home?' Tundra said. 'My home? It's not like some little box I need to protect. Walls don't mean anything. It's Country, people, not property.' She looked around at Till's station, dispassionately but not unkindly, which changed before Till's eyes, becoming very small and somewhat pitiful.

'All this' – she spread her arms wide in a huge embrace and swung in an arc towards the horizon that took in everything, oh, everything – 'this is my home.'

'Oh,' Zoe said. The information wouldn't be new to her. Till knew that. It was the realisation that it was life for some, not a concept.

Till observed the agitation in her mother's thinking in the twisting of her hands and the swinging of one leg and the slight set-ness of her expression.

'You've got a good daughter,' Tundra said.

'I do,' Zoe said.

'I have a good son. He talks to me through my heart.' Tundra put her hand to her chest and lifted her fingers and touched her heart three times, soft, light and certain. 'He told me I should speak to Till. He was right. Are you doing something, holding a ceremony for everyone now you have the little girl? For her parents, family, you, for Till – and for your shadow, Till?'

'My shadow?' Till's heart beat hard.

'Something around you needs care.'

Zoe said, 'Oh, well, E's mother is thinking of a memorial garden where she was found. I'm sure they'll want a ceremony.'

Till felt like laughing or crying at her mother protecting her in this moment – as Till could see she was – as if Tundra mentioning Till's shadow was bad manners.

Tundra nodded her approval. 'You should go,' she told Till. 'That's important for you.'

'I don't know.'

'You've got things to do there. Set them at peace. Set her at peace. All of you. We've got things to do here with Liz. Important things. We'll have a look at the place where that house is. Bad things are happening there.'

Later, Zoe said, 'So bossy.'

And Till said, 'She's not really, she just tells you the truth.'

'It was hard with your name,' Zoe said one afternoon.

'For me too,' Till said tartly, which I would not blame her for.

Zoe blinked at Till's firmness and her lack of apology. 'I suppose so.'

Those were the only words on the subject. But for a moment, Till felt the shadow nearby and remembered something about her, the way she, Till, had stepped outside of herself almost as if she was a suit of clothes, how suddenly she could not bear it. What else could she do? She wanted to live. She wanted to live. Sometimes she felt it drawing close. Its touch was soft as feathers, but cold, very cold. It drew some of the life from her and after it was gone, she still felt its chill. Till didn't know who the shadow was exactly, but something more than memory.

They spoke of unimportant things too, their unimportance suggesting all the other things that lay outside the mundane waiting for their moment of attention.

'George is back in his office a couple of days a week.'

'Oh really?'

'Maud doesn't like it. She keeps digging under the fence for company and all they've got next door are chickens.'

'Poor Maudie. She needs some company. She used to have Birdy.'

'I don't know. Two dogs . . .'

'Or a person. Everyone needs company.'

'I suppose. I should get back,' Zoe said, but without conviction. 'Let them stew for a bit – both of them. I might go exploring, I think, travel some of the old routes. Interesting further north.'

Zoe's first book had started with family stories about an ancestor of misty legend, Albert Finch, who had left his family to run a property in the Flinders Ranges and never been seen again. (Till would have to tell Zoe about Mr Finch from around the corner who might be related. He probably was. Not now though. She could not imagine that their shared ancestor, if so he was, had a benign history. He'd probably been a killer.) The book was somewhere in the Melbourne house, in a marginal place where it would not disturb. Some stories had stuck in Till's mind. She couldn't forget them, so she shut a door on them, as best she could, the way people did.

She asked her mother one evening, their feet up on the stove rail, why it was she'd changed her focus to the domestic arts of the colonial era – quilts and embroidery and such.

'Too sad. I was worn out,' Zoe said. 'People lie to themselves, sweetheart. They lie all the time. I got tired of listening to it. But I understand it. Sometimes the truth is too much – you know?'

'Where does that leave us, though?'

Zoe looked at her steadily and Till saw her decide to step around the things she thought and felt. So they didn't say more.

Ed seemed to understand that quiet was necessary, and since Zoe was there and there was no extra bedroom, he couldn't stay. He visited a lot though. He and Till walked up the line a way to where there was a sheltered spot in the sun and scouted around to make sure there were no snakes that might disturb, and made a bed of their two jackets and lay down. Then there was nothing but the look on his face and the touch of his hand and his body.

Afterwards, on the platform, he spoke about Liz, who he'd been to see. Till had been bracing herself for rekindled love in that direction and for him becoming Isaac's official father, but there was nothing there but sympathy and anger. Mostly he was worried about Isaac and was going to try to 'spring him' for an afternoon on the rails.

'I might need to do the grass,' he said.

'Not yet,' Till said. 'Look at it.'

'It is pretty.' He stroked the back of his finger down Till's cheek.

Zoe came out and they sat together. Next morning she put her things in her car and went to find Till. 'Time for me to go, sweetheart,' she said.

'Heading home?'

'We'll see.'

Ed strung fairy lights the length of the station building, and doubled them back and tripled them back. Till couldn't wait for night – what a thought. Now, here at her station, her own place, evening fell and the lights shimmered into existence, swooping along like mad blackbirds' flight. And looping along with the lights a memory of blackbirds in her parents' green garden, hopping about, tipping their heads with darting glances, smashing snails to eat their flesh, their thin shell scattered about, swept and crushed and somehow becoming life again. Every garden was a graveyard, each containing the bones of small creatures, family pets and fallen birds. Till walked to the end of the platform beyond the light and felt the darkness again, remembering walking in darkness with Birdy all those times. It would always be part of her. She looked back at the station, soft light spilling, Ed and Birdy. She went back to join them and sat watching it all, the stars, the deep sky, the stately palms stirring in the first soft northerly, the railway line disappearing into mystery. There was no stopping it. Life kept coming at you. This place.

Ed came out with 'a negroni for the Melbourne girl' and a beer for himself. Birdy lay at their feet, ear twitching. Ed stroked her with his foot.

'Unpretentious guy,' Till murmured.

'Hmmm?'

'Nothing.'

You might suppose this is a happy ending. If vanquishing an enemy and finding love and being likewise found is happy, then it is so. It is happy. But there were so many things E had not experienced and never would. Till would never be free of that small girl, her friend. She knew her name, she would always know her name, things would always remind her of E. She would be a beat through her life, making her own heart skip now and then. *Remember me.* Till knew she would remember, she didn't need reminding. She didn't want to forget.

Everyone had something they carried, perhaps more than one thing, maybe smooth and layered as a pearl, or still rough and uncomfortable. Till was nothing special. She even wondered sometimes whether the child E that she thought of was just her own child self, lost, searching for comfort, for home, for safety. She lost those things along with E. E lost everything.

*

Zoe drove west, carving through steep hill passes and fields of grass trees rising on either side, railway stations marking disappeared towns, and salt flats – Till's old route of flight – and circled in an enormous sweep (north-west, north, north-east, south-east, south, east) until she had her fill of space and began missing home. She drove back slowly, arriving in a vast orange sunset. These things Till deduced from the photos she sent her. In the months to come, Zoe and E's parents, with Adrienne's help and Till's memories, made a garden for E where she had been found. There was a plaque and brightly coloured flowers and berries and things that children could turn into perfume and a place where people could sit.

Till returned to Melbourne for the ceremony. She sang a song in her own voice and a favourite song of E's in hers. Adrienne clapped silently for Till and blew a kiss and clutched her hands to her heart dramatically. Till laughed, despite the occasion. But E had been a laughing girl. Till didn't think she would mind.

> *My pigeons' house I open wide*
> *And set all my pigeons free*
> *They fly all around and up and down*
> *And set in the tallest tree*
>
> *And when they return*
> *From their merry merry flight*
> *They close their eyes*
> *And say goodnight*
>
> *Coo-oo coo-oo coo-oo coo-oo*
> *Coo-oo coo-oo coo-oo*

E had always liked that the pigeons had their own voice in the song.

Afterwards, E's mother said, 'Remember that kaleidoscope E gave you for your fourth birthday?' She spoke E's whole true name. She used it so easily.

Till whispered, 'No.'

'And she loved it so much you gave it back to her?'

'No.' Another whisper.

'Even though you loved it?'

'No . . . I don't remember. I don't think I do.' This was not quite true. It was like driving into that smoke on the Ngarkat Highway more than a year ago. She could see things despite the haze, and they were coming closer and the smoke was falling away behind her.

'I thought you might like it back. You can have it. To remember her. If you would like it.'

Till did remember then. She held the kaleidoscope close and asked E's mother if she was sure and she said she was. 'I will never forget her,' Till said. 'I am so sorry.' (Why hadn't she screamed? Why? She will always wonder this.)

'You were five.'

E's mother turned away then and Till saw that it was too hard for her to be around Till, to imagine E at this age, to feel the completeness of her absence. E's mother had done what she had told herself she would do.

George, watching, came over – 'Okay sweetheart?' – and hugged her.

'Why did I get to live?' Till asked. She was sobbing, but George didn't mind.

'Why not you?'

Till held the kaleidoscope to her eye and turned it and

remembered insects swarming in a wattle tree at dawn, a cloud of butterflies, a dark sky thick with stars. Till wasn't as afraid of dying as she used to be. In the aftermath of a dream years ago she had written: 'The idea of the future holds us together. In it all things will be made perfect.' The future has not disappointed us yet and we have not failed its dream, was her meaning. She watched E's mother walking away. Had finding E's body been her hope for the future, or had she dreamed of her daughter now grown being found, freed, restored to her, and of another future containing what? Hugs, tears, conversation, love, laughter, grandchildren?

I used to wonder if one day we'd all just be swarming and drifting to the horizon like midges on a fading summer evening, feeling land only as a ticklish and uncomfortable thing. On Till's long journey, and afterwards reading of floods and fires and wars, people taking flight had seemed one of the principal arcs of the world. Settling in one place made it easier to find a person, and harder for them to flee. Till felt that. But people have a pull towards shelter despite everything. I suppose we're all looking for somewhere safe to call home.

Maybe Till did feel some peace now. Part of that was the thought of her railway station in the middle of nowhere. (Of course, nowhere is the centre of the world to people who live there. Till felt that too now.) She and Birdy went walking in the lanes. There was a dead blackbird, its feathers still glossy. She stroked its wings and head. Then she covered it with dry leaves, and found flowers along fences – blue salvias, dandelions, heartsease – which she picked and laid on the blackbird grave.

Days of Innocence and Wonder

Birdy watched with interest, and as she did with every once-living thing, touched her nose to it. The loquats had already fallen and the fruit and seeds lay scattered on the bluestone; the wild plums were almost ripe. We hold onto moments of sweetness.

Chapter 29

THINGS A PERSON might wonder in the ongoing ever present, which is to say in the future:

That I – that is, the narrator – am the spirit of E, whose ghost has been haunting or protecting or hovering around, curious, until my body was found and my spirit could be set free.

That I am the man roaming and pacing, studying Till, documenting her movements, her thinking and her conversations, imagined and actual, and considering. People might wonder how I would regard her, Till. With hate, I think. Hate and rage. (What's new?) She is the one who got away.

Or am I the Grand Overseer of Till's world? Come in now, sit in the chair, let me hold you there and tell you what happened.

Or am I the ghost child who went mute, the one before Till, the one who survived, who never went away?

I think you might know, if you think. Still, even after all this, I'm not sure I can tell you my name.

Chapter 30

Sylvie

Addenda on Sundry Other Matters

Notes on the restoration of stone buildings (with thanks to Stew)

Stonework is not like Lego
    Knock out the old lime mortar
    Wheelbarrow – cement, sand from surrounding area, pick hammer
    Order of operations: stone footing, outer wall, inner wall, infilled with dirt, then add a lime mortar
    Fix corners first
    Support wall, carefully excavate corner, clean out the mortar and loose dirt remaining
    A lot of dirt gets washed out; lime mortar is very crumbly
    Lay the rock flat on its bedding plane (horizontal striations remain horizontal, not vertical, which encourages them to split)
    Dustpan and brush to sweep out dirt
    Use diagonal props on exterior to hold wall in place; a collapsing wall can break your legs
    Don't use bore water – don't want it to have too much salt, not good for the mortar
    Mix wetter than normal because everything's so dry
    Build the corner up, backfill inside, any gaps have to be filled, place mortar inside to bond the stones to each other properly

One of the hardest parts is filling in the last gaps. You need the right size stone. Take care with this

Walls built with a batter, leaning back from bottom to top like a hedge – it's more structurally sound

Chinking stone to stop the big stones squashing all the mortar out. Chonk in bigger ones underneath, mortar in. While damp, brush the joins to feature the stone. Brush around the stone in sweeping lines – dustpan brush – sinuous lines. This seals mortar into edge of stone

Trowel – pointed end, clean out loose material around stonework, brush it out to create a clean surface

Mix mortar

Bucket of water, huge brush, wet down the wall by flinging the water from the brush. Wet dust and stone to make mortar stick better

Chip stones to shape them to fit gaps

It's a struggle to find the right size rock for some spots

Holes in base of wall, leaks down the inside of the wall can do this. Water washes out the fill, stones collapse, even the buttresses can collapse. Put in a big stone at the base as a support

Hold palette with mortar on it up to wall, so excess wet mortar falls back onto it

Scrubbing brush to clean mortar off stone, nicer to look at stone than mortar

Backfill the wall (the cavity), it makes the wall more stable

(Stew was Till's hero)

Days of Innocence and Wonder

On the subject of the Cat Stevens song 'Tea for the Tillerman'

If while listening to it you think, *Really? That's it? Questionable taste*, remember that you are judging a traumatised six-year-old. Remember that.

On the subject of the traditional song, 'My Pigeon's House'

Please do not send helpful notes about how the correct original approved traditional version is different, that it is 'pigeon house' not 'pigeons' house' or 'pigeon's house' and 'light' not 'set' or whatever variation you prefer. This is the way E taught it to Till and it is the way they sang it together.

On the subject of the town, Melrose, hunched over the creek on Till's second journey of flight

A website describes the town's history as 'rich and colourful'. The Aboriginal population around here numbered about 900 before Europeans arrived in 1840, but there was 'conflict between Aboriginals and pastoralists from the beginning'. In 1848 the town got a police outpost and four police. By 1880 there were eight Aboriginals (three men and five women). Ten years later there were three men and two women. 'Disease, dispossession and killings' were the cause, the website says, as if these things arrived as randomly as weather systems, unattached to anyone.

It's a story repeated and repeated. There were meetings of thousands of Aboriginal people recorded in Clare and Ororoo in the early years of European occupation. Epidemics of scarlatina, measles and smallpox devastated the Ngadjuri population in the 1850s and the size and frequency of gatherings drastically reduced, though they were still occasionally reported. Many of the animals First Nations people ate are now locally extinct, their habitats having been destroyed by farming practices, and their water sources taken over. Survivors moved north, and after 1868 many of them moved to the Point Pearce Mission, further west, on Narangga land.

The work of reviving and celebrating Ngadjuri people, culture and Language continues.

And the work of documenting sites of massacres and other murders in South Australia is ongoing. (australianfrontierconflicts.com.au)

Till's lists

Edibles to be found in the backyards or hanging over or self-seeding under the laneway fences of Melbourne's inner north
Plums, apricots, cherry, passionfruit, banana passionfruit, almonds, apple, peach, pear, nectarine, persimmon, pomegranate, quince, fig, mandarin, orange, avocado, lemon, grapefruit, lilly pillies, feijoa, olives, chestnuts, walnuts, almonds, loquats, choko, parsley, lettuce, Vietnamese mint, mint, tomatoes

Fruits and nuts/seeds found in Wirowie
Almonds, apricots, prickly pear, olives, wattle seed

There would be more. Take this small list as a sign that Till was an outsider in this world, and that Western farming practices have been devastating.

Dead creatures
Brunswick: rats; birds (blackbirds, wattlebirds, pigeons); possums (ringtails and one brushtail)

South Australia: countless kangaroos and other mammals, sheep, lizards, snakes

Living creatures
Brunswick: countless birds including boobook owls and tawny frogmouths, possums, bats, dogs, cats

Wirowie: an emu, cockatoos, galahs, magpies, poultry, sheep, llama, lizards, snakes, dogs

The turquoise-coloured parrot
Possibly the Australian ringneck or Port Lincoln parrot (*Barnardius zonarius*)

Acknowledgements

I AM INDEBTED to Ngadjuri elder Angelena Rigney for her advice, knowledge and insights, and for generous conversations about culture and Country. The story about the long aftermath of the massacre at Kapunda is Angelena's, as told by her, and is recounted here in this form with her permission, as are other matters related to the character, Tundra. Her work to help revive Ngadjuri culture and language is ongoing.

Ngadjuri Nation and South Australia's Mobile Language Group/Program provided advice and assistance at key moments. Thanks to both. I am also grateful to the State Library of South Australia and the South Australian Museum. Huge thanks, too, to Emma Viskic, a wonderful sounding board throughout.

I count myself very fortunate to be in the safe hands of the amazing team at Pan Macmillan once again; it's been such a pleasure each time. Thanks to the wonderful Cate Blake in particular and to the lovely Danielle Walker, Jane Watkins, Lily Cameron and Clare Keighery. Thanks to Dianne Blacklock, too, for her editing expertise. I am so grateful to Sandy Cull for creating another beautiful cover – I love them all.

Huge thanks to my wonderful agent, Fiona Inglis of Curtis

Brown, for her support and measured advice, and to Mathilda Imlah, who supported *Days of Innocence and Wonder* from the beginning.

And there's my adored family: David, Jack and Tash, Will, Mimi (aka Catherine), and James and Josie. I can't thank them enough. And, because dogs are family too, our darling whippets, Gussie and Nell. I also need to mention Dolly, Jack and Tash's beautiful black greyhound, who moved into their lives after I'd started writing about Birdy. Birdy and Dolly are not the same dog, but they share a great sweetness of disposition and love of their people. Thanks and love to my mother, Aileen (no one could do more to instil a love of reading), sister, Sophie, and brother Andrew.

Special thanks to Marian Anderson, Adrienne Salvaris and Tundra Morschek for their generous contributions to the Authors for Fireys fundraiser held during and following the devastating Black Summer bushfires of 2019–2020. Their names appear in *Days of Innocence and Wonder* in recognition of their generosity.

Thanks to Kate Richards, Clare Strahan, Trish Bolton, Jenny Green, Dana Miltins, Janine Mikosza, Jenny Ackland, Ann Shenfield, Nina Killham, Carrie Tiffany, Sian Prior, Paddy O'Reilly, Angela Savage, Ann Turner, Kelly Gardiner, Toni Jordan, Annie Keely and Lucy Sussex for friendship and much writing talk.

Donations have been made to support Angelena Rigney's ongoing cultural work on Ngadjuri Country in South Australia in recognition of the knowledge she generously shared, and to the Indigenous Literacy Foundation, Free Her, Pay the Rent and the Aboriginal Legal Service in acknowledgement of the incalculable debt still owed.

Days of Innocence and Wonder

Days of Innocence and Wonder was written with the generous support of the Australia Council for the Arts, Creative Victoria and the City of Melbourne. In the early development stages I was fortunate to also have the support of the RTP and David Myers scholarships at La Trobe University. I am so grateful to them all.